an egg
on three sticks

an egg
On three sticks

Jackie Moyer Fischer

Thomas Dunne Books
St. Martin's Griffin ⚌ New York

THOMAS DUNNE BOOKS.
An imprint of St. Martin's Press.

www.stmartins.com

Design by Susan Yang

Library of Congress Cataloging-in-Publication Data

Fischer, Jackie Moyer.
   An egg on three sticks / by Jackie Fischer.—1st ed.
      p. cm.
Summary: In the San Francisco Bay Area in the early 1970s, twelve-year-old Abby watches her mother fall apart and must take on the burden of holding her family together.
   ISBN 0-312-31775-1
   EAN 978-0312-31775-1
   [1. Family problems—Fiction. 2. Mothers and daughters—Fiction. 3. Mental illness—Fiction. 4. Coming of age—Fiction. 5. San Francisco Bay Area (Calif.)—History—20th century—Fiction.] I. Title.
   PZ7.F498775Eg 2003
   [Fic]—dc21

                                                                    2003009126

First Edition: May 2004

10   9   8   7   6   5   4   3   2   1

For Eric, who made it all possible

acknowledgments

Thank you:

To my tireless core reviewers, who read everything: Dawn, Eric, and Stephanie.

To all my other reviewers who gave me great comments: Alison A., Steve A., Wendy A., Cathy B., Julie B., Randy B., Amber C., Joanne F., Mary G., Susan G., Cleone H., Marian I., Ceva K., Donna L., Wendy N., Paul P., Susan P., Becki S., Dana W., and Deb Y.

To Tom Spanbauer, writing teacher extraordinaire, for correcting my course and sending me in the right direction.

To two other great writing teachers: Andrea Carlisle and Fred Pfeil.

To three people who allowed me to ask all the questions I wanted: Hal Dick, Bob Danielson, and Frank Wells.

To a sixth-grade teacher who made a difference: Robert Scarola.

To my dad, Dick Moyer, who taught me consistency and discipline.

To my mom, Gini Van Nortwick, who has always been my number-one cheerleader, and who said practically every day when I was growing up: "What an imagination!"

To my agent, Barb Doyen, who not only sold my book but also grows oleanders in Iowa.

To my editor, Sally Kim, for being always enthusiastic, and always right.

And finally, to Patrick Dennis, who wrote my favorite book in all the world, *Auntie Mame*.

chapter 1

So i'm walking home from school by myself because it's Thursday which is my late day because of Girls' Glee Club after school which most other days I walk home with my best friend Poppy Cordesi who lives across the street and which her mom's divorced and no one knows where her dad is. I get to the top of our street which is a little hill and I look down on the ten houses, eleven if you count the Pierces' but they have their own private driveway which goes right out onto the highway. I look down at all the houses and they look normal as day but when I look at our house there's something different.

Not a big different, just a little different, almost like how toast smells a little different right before it burns.

I look at our dark brown house.

We have the only dark brown house on the street. Every other house is white or beige or pale green but ours is dark brown with red trim, whoever heard of that, plus the red is faded to icky pink and which I have one word for that: *grossamundo.*

Which is this sort of language Poppy and I made up but I'll get to that later.

I look at the dark brown and the icky pink, and something is not right. It's not just that our car is gone, which it is, and which it shouldn't be on a Thursday at four-fifteen. Everything looks weird, the sun and the sky and the clouds and it's too warm for April which by the way is my favorite month because I just had my thirteenth birthday last week so I am now officially a teenager which it's about time.

I walk down the hill and I tell myself I'm just making this up.

There's nothing wrong.

Except there's this thing in my stomach, this thing I get sometimes that I call the big clench only right now it's a little clench and I tell it to shut up, go away, there's nothing wrong.

I walk past the Sullivans' house, then past the five peach trees that belong to the Sullivans but we can pick peaches whenever we want because there's just Mr. and Mrs. Sullivan and they can't eat all those peaches by themselves and there are four of us, Mom and Dad and me and Lisa who's seven, but really it's more like three and a half people because Lisa is such a puny little thing and really more like three because Mom hasn't been eating much lately.

I get to our driveway and I stop and look at our front yard because even *it* looks weird.

The clench in my stomach gets clenchier but I tell it to shut up.

I tell myself it's just our plain old green lawn with the apricot tree and some flowers and six junipers along the fence, which Dad is threatening to take out the whole lawn and put in all junipers because he doesn't want to be a slave to that lawn anymore but then

Mom always has to go lie down when he says that, but then she has to lie down a lot these days.

I get to our front walk and there's someone in our front window who is not Mom.

Which is weirdamundo.

Now I definitely have the big clench.

It's Mrs. Sierra in the window, Mrs. Sierra from next door who lives in a beige house with nothing but gravel for a driveway and who used to be a nurse with Mom in the olden days before Mom married Dad. Mrs. Sierra is this enormous woman with yellow skin who wears these tent dresses but is awfully, awfully nice, I mean you just have to like her because she's just so *nice*, plus you have to feel sorry for her because her son Jimmy is at this very moment over in Vietnam getting shot. I mean shot *at*.

Mrs. Sierra sees me and opens our icky pink front door and her little black eyes look at me all serious and *concerned*, and her forehead goes into a deep **V** and she says, Oh Abby, and her voice is so low and sad that the big clench in my stomach is turning into a *very* big clench.

Because even though I'm pretending to myself that I don't know what's going on, I really do.

No doubt about it.

I know.

I walk in and I say, Where's Mom?

Like I don't know.

Mrs. Sierra puts her big yellow arm around me and squeezes real tight and now I know for sure that something is wrong because it's one of *those* kinds of arm-hugs, the kind where there's something really, really wrong.

So now I know for sure, that thing I knew at the top of the hill.

chapter 2

So this whole *thing*, the thing with Mom, it all starts last summer, when I'm twelve and just a kid.

It's a hot July night and I can't sleep which is nothing new because I always have a hard time getting to sleep.

I get out of bed and tiptoe down the dark hall, past Lisa who's snoring like a jet going overhead and nothing, I mean *nothing*, can wake her up, which she's just like Dad that way.

I get to the top of the dark stairs and I see Mom's light is on in the living room, the light she reads under just about every night. She likes to sit in her green chair and read until real late.

I lie down at the top of the stairs on my stomach and stack my fists on top of each other.

I do this a lot. Lying down at the top of the stairs, I mean. It's what I do when I can't sleep which is a lot. I lay here and I watch Mom read and she can't see me because I'm in the dark but I can see her.

Her black hair looks blue under the tall lamp from Grandma.

There is something so sleepy about Mom sitting so quiet on her green chair with her legs curled up under her, and her black-blue hair under the yellow circle of light, sitting there in her pedal pushers and elbow-sleeve blouse, it's just like looking at sleep.

Some nights when I do this, I fall asleep right there at the top of the stairs but then I always wake up later, like at three in the morning, and I go back to bed.

Tonight it's too hot to fall asleep at the top of the stairs, even with Mom down there reading.

She turns a page and it's a sound like water lapping.

Sometimes I count the pages that Mom turns and that will make me fall asleep, too.

I'm 99 percent sure that Mom doesn't know I do this.

Tonight, nothing is working.

I'm wide awake.

It's so hot up here on the second floor you can hardly breathe.

This is California. It's hot in July.

You'd think my stupid parents would put in an air conditioner up here but Dad doesn't believe in newfangled gadgets because they are invented to make the common man lazy and stupid.

He says.

After about an hour I give up and go back to my room.

It's hot enough where you have to do something more extreme to get to sleep.

I pop out the screen in my window and go out on the roof. I'm not supposed to go out on the roof but it's the only place you can go on a hot summer night like this.

I sit on the roof and lean against the house. The black roof is still warm from the hot day.

It's definitely cooler out here. I have on my Turtle Power T-shirt which is this white T-shirt with a mean-looking yellow turtle and his fist raised up like the Black Panthers and he's shouting *Turtle Power!* One of Dad's students left it in his room which by the way Dad teaches typing at the high school, how boring is that. So he brought the shirt home for me. Mom hates it and won't let me wear it to school. She says it's militant, which I think means it's too much like the Black Panthers which Mom doesn't like them but I think Dad secretly does, just like he secretly likes the Hell's Angels but Mom says they scare the livin' daylights out of her and she always brakes the car real hard when they pass her on the road.

I secretly like the Hell's Angels, too, and when I'm eighteen I'm going to get nine tattoos and buy a Harley and grow my hair out real long and wear nothing but halter tops and Levi's.

The night air is hot and smells like the inside of a tin can.

I look up at the half moon and there's half a face looking back at me.

All you can hear are those bugs that buzz all day and all night, which I call them the twenty-four-hour bugs. You can't see them but they're always there, all summer long, buzzing in the background like a train that keeps going past.

I sit there for a real long time, trying to get sleepy.

You'd think nothing was going to happen because everything is so hot and still and slow, even the twenty-four-hour bugs sound slower than usual. You'd think you could lean back into the warm wood of the house and look at the half moon and get sleepy.

But then a sound.

The front door opening.

I creep around on the roof, fast and silent as a cat, until I'm right above the front door.

I lean back into the shadows and hold my breath.

A head comes out.

Mom's head.

Mom's black hair which looks blue in the moonlight.

She's in her faded red bathrobe, her hands keeping it closed tight in front of her which it's too hot to wear a robe and she must be sweating like crazy.

She walks down the driveway in her bare feet.

Mom goes everywhere in her bare feet, all year long. She says she hates shoes which is funny because she has like nine zillion pairs in her closet.

She walks down the street.

Fast.

Like she's late for something.

I don't think twice, I go over to the oak tree by my window and shimmy down it and follow her, keeping in the shadows so she won't see me.

She goes past the Sierras' house and turns at the Billawallas' house, going down the sidewalk along the side of their house.

I follow.

My heart is beating in my knees and throat.

So my mother is walking around in her faded red robe in the middle of the night, so what.

I'm on the Billawallas' sidewalk when I hear a little slosh of water, so quiet you might miss it unless you're me and you're following your mother around in the middle of the night.

I tiptoe down their sidewalk and peek around the corner, staying in the shadow of their big fig tree.

She's in the Billawallas' pool.

She's naked.

She's doing the breaststroke across the pool the long way.

The Billawallas always leave their pool lights on at night which I guess is to scare away burglars although you'd think you'd want the burglars to fall in the pool in the dark and get caught.

I'm in the shadows under their fig tree and I grab onto a fig branch because my hands are shaking.

I don't know why.

I tell myself so what.

Just a naked swim in the middle of a hot night.

No big deal.

No one will ever know.

It's like something Auntie Mame might do which by the way is my favorite book in the whole world and which Mom got it out of the library once for herself but then she let me read it and now I've read it about thirty times.

I'm sweating in my Turtle Power T-shirt which I never sweat.

Mom goes under the water and I hold my breath because what if she doesn't come back up but then she does and her hair has little shiny diamonds of water all over it.

I tell myself this is a dream.

I pinch my bare thigh so hard it hurts.

I'm definitely awake.

I close my eyes and count to ten and then open them but she's still there and I'm still here.

The smell of pool chlorine makes me want to sneeze so I pinch my nose because no way can I sneeze right now.

I need to think.

Like, is this one of those situations where you're supposed to do something or not.

I can't decide.

I could just leave. I mean Mom knows how to swim, she was even on the swim team in high school so it's not like she's going to drown or anything.

This is not a big deal.

She's just swimming. OK, she *is* naked, but so what.

No one will ever know.

Why don't I just leave.

There's no reason to stay.

Suddenly a light goes on in the Billawallas' house, upstairs.

If I was frozen before, I'm even more frozen now if that's even possible.

This is when the screaming starts in my head.

GET OUT!

GET OUT!

GET OUT!

I'm sending ESP to Mom, who's still swimming and who doesn't even notice that there's a light on in the Billawallas' house. She does the sidestroke, swimming away from me, toward the nine-foot end where the diving board is.

Oh god, why doesn't she see the light.

GET OUT!

I scream at her in my head.

Another light goes on, this time downstairs.

There's a shadow moving around and it can only be Mrs. Billawalla because the shadow is tall and Mr. Billawalla is dead. Unless of course it's Mr. Billawalla's ghost which I don't even want to think about.

Mom gets to the deep end and hangs on the edge of the pool and I can hear her breathing. I imagine her breath floats across the water, across the patio, all the way to me under the fig tree and I can feel it warm on my legs which are ice cold right now even though it's so hot out here you can't even tell if you're breathing or not.

The tall shadow in the house moves into the dining room, where their liquor cabinet is and which I know because sometimes I baby-sit Annie Billawalla who's six like Lisa, sometimes I baby-sit her when Mrs. Billawalla goes to her D.A.R. meetings which Mom goes to, too, but Mom says Mrs. Billawalla is a D.A.R. by marriage which you can't be a D.A.R. by marriage so really Mrs. Billawalla is a fake D.A.R.

Which by the way a D.A.R. is a Daughter of the American Revolution but don't ask me what the heck *that* is.

Mrs. Billawalla's shadow moves across the dining room and toward the family room where there's a big sliding glass door with no curtains on it.

This is the part where I should have been a hero.

Where I should have done something instead of just standing there under the fig tree with my hands glued to the fig tree branches and my tongue glued to the roof of my mouth.

Where a good daughter would have called out something like, *Look out, Mom!*

It's only three words and I can't even make one word come out of my glued-up mouth.

So I stand there.

I watch it all like a movie.

Mrs. Billawalla stands in front of the sliding glass door in her long white bathrobe, the real filmy kind you can almost see through but there's too many folds.

Mom is swimming again and has her back to Mrs. Billawalla.

She pulls her white body through the lighted aqua water in slow motion like it's a lazy summer day and the sun is beating down on your face and turning it red but the rest of you under the water is cool.

Mrs. Billawalla stands there with her drink, her pouffy blond hair flat on one side.

This all happens as slow as when you watch the clouds go by and you have to watch a really long time to make sure that you saw them move at all.

I'm not breathing.

The only movement is Mom.

The only noise is Mom.

Then Mrs. Billawalla opens the sliding glass door and the movie clicks into fast-forward.

Mrs. Billawalla calls out, Henry?

Henry is her dead husband's name.

Mom is in the shadow of the big white patio umbrella and her head turns toward Mrs. Billawalla's voice.

In a split second she leaps out of the pool, grabs her robe, and runs right past me in the fig tree without seeing me, her wet feet slapping the cement.

Mrs. Billawalla walks out onto the patio and says Henry? again.

I unglue myself from the fig tree and tear after Mom on silent feet.

Mom throws her bathrobe back on as she's running.

I run through the shadows, staying way behind her so she doesn't hear me.

She slows to a trot and I can hear her breathing real loud.

She gets to our house and opens the front door real slow and quiet and goes in.

I hear the door lock go click.

Which means I have to get the ladder out of the garage to get back up to my window because you can get *down* the oak tree by my window but not *up* it because the first branch is too high up.

I get the ladder out, real quiet.

I'm breathing kinda hard myself.

I'm so wide awake it might as well be day.

I climb up the ladder onto the roof, then kick the ladder back into the oak tree. I can put it back tomorrow.

I get into bed, still breathing like a steam engine.

I lay there and wonder what Mom was doing, going swimming in the neighbors' pool in the middle of the night.

I tell myself a zillion times it is No Big Deal.

So just stop it.

Stop thinking about it.

She was hot, she couldn't sleep.

That's all.

Over and over.

I don't get to sleep for a long, long time.

It's one of those nights where you wake up the next morning and you're not even sure if you slept at all.

As I'm getting dressed for school I convince myself it was just a dream.

Which I believe it until Mom leans over to spoon a soft-boiled egg onto my plate and her hair smells like chlorine.

chapter 3

So i wasn't going to tell anyone about Mom's night swim but then I told Poppy, which Poppy is my best friend and lives across the street with her mom who's divorced and no one knows where her dad is. Which when they first moved in years ago I wasn't allowed to play with Poppy because her mom was divorced and no one knew where her dad was, but after a while my parents figured out that Mrs. Cordesi was really OK, even if she was divorced and no one knew where Poppy's dad was.

I didn't mean to bring up Mom's swim, it just sort of came up.

OK, it came up because I brought it up.

We're walking to the store to get tomato sauce for Poppy's mom and Poppy has on these new Jesus sandals that go crisscross all over her feet.

All I have is blue rubber thongs.

Poppy is *so* cool.

Way cooler than me.

Sometimes I don't know why she hangs around with me, I mean she could be hanging with a much cooler crowd.

I mean for one thing, she looks way cooler than I do. She has this long blond California-girl hair that's real thick and straight and goes all the way to her waist and she's always flinging it around by flicking her head which I can't do at all.

But then, I don't have flingable hair. At all. I have this near-Afro thing going because my hair is so frizzy.

Curly, Mom says.

Whatever.

Poppy has absolutely no flaws except her teeth, which are real straight but the enamel is all worn off from when she had to take some medicine when she was a baby, so her teeth look like white chalk and aren't shiny or anything.

But it's such a little thing.

I mean there's so many things wrong with my face, starting with zits and freckles and a nose the size of a can of Campbell's soup and boring green eyes that no one will *ever* die for.

But anyway.

Poppy is telling me about something funny that Therin did, which Therin is her mom's boyfriend who rides a Harley and has hair so long that he sometimes winds it around his belt loops. Right in the middle of her story I go, Do you think it's weirdamundo to swim in the Billawallas' pool in the middle of the night?

Poppy stops walking and looks at me like I just turned into a giraffe.

What? she says, her tan face all scrunched up.

I forgot, she also has a great tan, all year round, because her mom is Romanian or something.

I stop walking and look at her.

Do you think it's weirdamundo to swim in the Billawallas' pool in the middle of the night? I say again.

Whyamundo? Poppy says, and her face gets even more scrunched.

Ew, I don't like that one, I say, meaning *whyamundo*.

Like I said, it's this new language Poppy and I invented. We're hoping it catches on at school and then we'll be popular.

Yeah, me neither, she says.

Anyway, I just wondered, I say.

Did you swim in the Billawallas' pool in the middle of the night? she says.

We're standing at the stoplight and the sign changes to *Walk* but we don't walk, we just stand there looking at each other.

No, I say, but I can't look at Poppy so I look down at my bare toes in my blue thongs like they're so interesting. Then I look over at Poppy's toenails which are painted white and mine aren't because I'm not allowed. It's a rule. No nail polish, no makeup, no short skirts, no nylons, no heels, nothing until you're sixteen, that's the rule.

My mom has a *lot* of rules.

Well, maybe, I say to my bare toes.

So why did you swim in the Billawallas' pool in the middle of the night? Poppy says.

Well *I* didn't, my mom did, I say. I look up at the *Walk* sign which is now blinking *Don't Walk*.

OK, why did your mom swim in the Billawallas' pool in the middle of the night? she says.

I can see her looking at me, even though I'm still staring at the *Walk* sign.

This is my way of being cool.

Coolamundo, I mean.

I don't know, I think she was hot, I say. I sneak a look at Poppy's face and she's looking at me with half-closed eyes, like she's thinking real hard about something.

Oh, she says, and pushes the button on the stoplight.

So do you think it's weirdamundo? I say.

The light changes and we walk across the street. I'm kinda behind Poppy and I watch the red heart patch on her cutoffs move back and forth on her butt. I'm allowed to wear cutoffs, but no patches. Mom says patches make you look like a hillbilly.

I guess not, she says. I mean if she was hot.

Yeah, I think she was just hot, I say.

We get to Peterman Avenue and Poppy stops and flings her hair behind her, once on each side.

I try to fling my ball of frizzy brown hair but it just gets bigger. I always have to pat it back down after I fling it.

Mom was just hot, I tell myself.

Just hot.

I have to say it a zillion times to believe it.

chapter 4

September is here.

Which means seventh grade.

Which means junior high.

Which it's about time.

I mean elementary school is *so* dorkamundo.

So this one day I get home from school and Mom's the only one home because Lisa's at her piano lesson and Dad's still at the high school listening to the pounding of thousands of typewriters.

I yell, I'm home!

I get no answer which isn't all that weirdamundo because Mom could be outside hanging laundry although I don't see her out the dining room windows so I guess not.

Which by the way a dryer is another thing Mom wants but Dad says no because it's a newfangled gadget. And we all know that new-fangled gadgets are invented to make the common man lazy and stupid.

I dump my books on the dining room table where they don't belong, it's a rule. One of my books knocks over Mom's little praying angel with the missing wing so I set her up the right way again. I can't remember where Mom got that stupid thing, it's so dorkamundo.

I yell out, Mom?

Still no answer, but maybe she's next door talking to Mrs. Sierra about her son Jimmy who like I said is over in Vietnam getting shot. *At.*

I start down the hall when I see that Mom and Dad's door is closed.

Very weirdamundo. It's always open except at night.

A couple of hairs on my index fingers prickle up.

I keep walking down the hall and I'm passing the bathroom in the hall and that's when I see it.

Something shiny catches my eye.

There in the hall bathroom.

Which this bathroom used to be Mom and Dad's bathroom until they built the new bedroom and bathroom in the back so now the hall bathroom is mostly for guests although Lisa and me use it a lot because we're not supposed to use Mom and Dad's bathroom which I can't remember why but it's a rule.

I turn on the light in the hall bathroom.

There are pieces of broken mirror all over the sink and floor.

My heart starts beating a little faster and more hairs prickle up on my fingers.

Very, *very* weirdamundo.

Mom would never leave a broken mirror lying around like this. I mean she used to be a nurse.

I look at the shiny pieces which some look pink because there's pink tile everywhere in this bathroom and which Mom hates it like poison and wants to rip out all the pink tile and the barfamundo wallpaper which is covered with purple lilacs but Dad says we have to leave the bathroom alone because you have to maintain the integrity of the original design.

This is a *big* rule of Dad's, the integrity-of-the-original-design rule.

Which by the way our house is *really* old, built in 1925.

I mean everyone else has wall-to-wall shag carpeting and we

have these round braided rugs everywhere and you can see the old wood floors around the edges of the rugs which is so dorkamundo.

I walk into the bathroom, carefully stepping around the pieces of mirror. Part of the mirror is still there and part of it is missing so I can only see half my face and it's all jagged and crooked. It looks like someone hit the mirror right in the middle.

I move a piece of mirror with the toe of my shoe. It makes that tinkle of glass on tile.

If you could see into my brain right now you'd see a zillion question marks.

There must be an explanation.

I back out of the bathroom and go down and tap on Mom and Dad's door.

Mom? I say, opening the door.

She's lying on the bed with her arm over her eyes.

Which is very weirdamundo.

Mom never lies down unless it's time for bed. She never takes naps, never gets sick, she's always running around doing eighteen zillion things at once in her bare feet, like cooking dinner and making tomorrow's lunches and sweeping the kitchen floor and writing a letter to Grandma in Ohio and wiping down the old green tile counters in the kitchen which she hates like poison and wants to rip out the green tile and replace it with some nice Formica but Dad always says blah blah blah integrity of the original design.

But here she is, lying down in the middle of the day, with her bare heels together. Her feet are always all white and flaky on the bottoms, with the skin peeling off, which I mean yuckamundo.

She's in a white elbow-sleeve blouse and tan pedal pushers.

This is all she ever wears, elbow-sleeve blouses and pedal pushers. She has about thirty zillion of each, in all colors.

Hi, honey, she says. Her voice is all wavery.

I go over to the bed, put my hands on the bumpy white bedspread, and lean over, my face right above her arm.

Are you sick? I say.

Her arm comes down and her hand rubs her eyes.

I just have a little headache, she says. Would you be a love and go get me a cold washcloth?

Mom never gets headaches.

Something is smelling very fishy in France, as Mom likes to say.

But it could be nothing.

I tell myself.

I mean, why can't Mom get a headache? Lots of people get headaches and anyway Grandma in Ohio gets migraines all the time and so does Mrs. Cordesi.

I walk over to Mom and Dad's bathroom because it's closer, it's just off their room. It was added last summer, along with their bedroom which is also new. Everything still smells like new carpeting and sawdust and paint.

You might be wondering about that integrity of the original design thing.

Which what happened was Mom finally broke down one night and cried about their drafty old bedroom which she said was too small to change your mind in and she wanted a real shower that wasn't so hard to clean as all that awful pink tile and besides she hates pink not to mention that awful wallpaper with the lilacs which she said she'd rather eat than have to look at again.

Which I'd like to see that.

I heard this when I was supposed to be asleep but I was lying at the top of the stairs in my usual spot. They were talking in the living room and after Mom started crying Dad just rubbed her back but didn't say anything, but then a few days later a man in white overalls came and started measuring things and a few months later Mom had a new bathroom with a white shower and an orange Formica counter with a yellow sink and a whole big new bedroom with green shag carpeting and walk-in closets that were almost as big as me and Lisa's rooms.

I get to the doorway of Mom and Dad's new bathroom and what I see makes me grab onto the door frame.

Because this mirror, too.

Just like the other.

Broken in the middle.

Pieces of mirror all over the floor and the orange Formica counter and in the yellow sink.

I look at my broken face in the broken mirror and I can't breathe.

My heart is beating real fast now, as fast as a little bird's heart.

Two mirrors.

Two mirrors in the same day is no accident.

My hands on the door frame are turning white.

Because I mean you come home to your mother with her flaky white feet on the bumpy white bedspread lying down with her arm over her face and two mirrors in two different bathrooms broken on the same day with glass all over the sinks and the floors and no one cleaned it up and someone could get hurt and suddenly you can't stand up because your knees have turned to ice water and . . .

. . . cold washcloth.

Mom needs a cold washcloth.

This is why you're standing here.

I make one foot go forward into the yellow-and-orange bath-room with no integrity. I hear the crunch of my shoe on the glass but it sounds so far away, across the orchard and down Caswell Avenue and all the way into San Jose.

I get an orange washcloth from the towel rack and run cold water over it, then squeeze it in my shaky fingers which aren't working very well.

I make myself take in a big breath and let it out again.

No big deal, I tell myself.

There has to be an explanation.

I walk over to Mom on the bed with her arm over her face again.

Here Mom, I say. I drape the washcloth over her arm. She lifts up her arm and her face looks all saggy and tired and white.

Thanks, honey, she says. Her voice is all saggy, too.

She puts the washcloth across her forehead and closes her eyes. Her arms go down to her sides and I just stand there, next to the bed, watching her with my bird heart beating a zillion beats a second and my hands all slippery and cold and two broken mirrors and Dad will be home soon and then what.

What I'm definitely not thinking about is the third bathroom, me and Lisa's bathroom upstairs.

I could go upstairs and check.

I don't want to.

Mom? I say. It comes out real soft.

What, honey, she says, her mouth almost not moving, her red lipstick faded and sunk into her lips which Mom wears bright-red lipstick every day, no matter what day it is or what she's doing or where she's going and which is *so* embarrassing because no one else's mother wears red lipstick anymore, they all wear things like Raspberry Ice and White Frost.

Did you know the mirrors are broken? I say. The bathroom mirrors?

I say it like it's any old question on any old day.

Yes, honey, I know. I'll clean it up later, she says in her saggy voice.

I wait for more.

I'm waiting for her to say how it was an accident. How she was cleaning the mirror with Windex or something and she scrubbed too hard and it broke.

They broke.

And how she couldn't clean it up right then because the phone rang and it was Mrs. Palmer who always talks Mom's ear off and then she forgot. And then she ate something for lunch that didn't agree with her and now she's lying down.

These are all good explanations.

I'm waiting for one of these to come out of Mom.

I wait some more and nothing comes out except breathing.

Mom? I say.

What, she says with her bottom lip.

Do you want me to clean it up? I say.

I don't really want to clean it up but I can't think of anything else to say that would make Mom keep talking on this subject and maybe still give me an explanation.

Sure, she says with her bottom lip.

I wait some more.

I'm waiting for at least a thank-you.

Mom is very big on thank-yous. We have to write Grandma the exact day after our birthdays and not a second later to thank her for our presents. Same with Christmas.

I wait.

I watch the clock on Dad's side of the bed which is a Big Ben windup clock which ticks on every second. I hate watching clocks but there's nothing else to watch in this room except Mom's chest going up and down.

I've had enough.

I can't stand it anymore.

I tiptoe across the green shag carpeting and go out and close the door behind me, real quiet.

I walk down the hall to the lilac bathroom with integrity to check one more time.

Because maybe I made it all up.

I close my eyes before I get to the doorway and I make a wish.

Guess what it is.

In the doorway I stop and wait for a sec with my eyes closed, waiting for the wishing fairies to grant my wish. Then I open my eyes.

Nope.

Still there. Pieces of broken mirror everywhere.

I walk in and look at that broken mirror one more time.

I don't know why.

I look at the broken girl in the mirror, the girl with the frizzy brown Afro-hair parted down the middle and two frizzy strands forced behind her ears except they never stay there and freckles all over her face and green eyes just like Mom's.

I look at her and I try to lie to her.

It's no big deal.

Just an accident.

Everyone has accidents.

But the girl in the mirror knows it's all a lie. Something has happened. She's not sure what, but something has happened.

chapter 5

So dad comes home.

This is after I've swept up the two broken mirrors and Mom lies on her bed a long time but then she finally gets up and starts fixing dinner.

She didn't get to the mirror upstairs in me and Lisa's bathroom. When I saw it was still a whole mirror, I didn't know whether to feel happy or sad. I stood there and looked at it and thought about the other two broken ones and then I didn't know what to think after that so I swept up the other two and then laid on my bed and read my latest library book the rest of the afternoon.

Dad picks up Lisa on her piano lesson days so they both get home at the same time.

Dad's black Chevy drives up which he always keeps it shiny by going to the ninety-nine-cent car wash over in San Jose every other Saturday. And every fourth Saturday he gets his hair cut by Dominick in the same trip and when I was still a kid I liked to go because Dominick is Italian and he'd call me *signorina* and give me a Tootsie Pop but now I'm too old for that.

You don't have to see Dad's car because you can always hear it. Dad's car has its own sound, different from the station wagons that everyone else on our street drives. Dad's car is also really old, just like our house. It's a 1949 Chevy and Dad painted it black before he met

Mom because black is his favorite color, which how weirdamundo is that.

Dad and Lisa get out of the car, and Lisa slams the car door like always and Dad says, *Lisa!* like always and Lisa says, *What?* like always and Dad says, *Don't slam the door!* like always.

This is the thing with Lisa. You can tell her a zillion times not to slam the car door and she'll keep doing it. Mom says Lisa's brain is like a sieve but I think Lisa does that stuff on purpose just to make everyone *think* her brain is a sieve although I don't know why you'd want people to think that.

Lisa comes running up the sidewalk. Her long white-blond hair goes down to her waist and when she runs it flies up behind her because it's so light and thin and straight. I don't know where she gets that blond hair. No one in our entire family tree, on both sides, has blond hair. Sometimes I think they switched babies at the hospital although Lisa does have Dad's exact eyes, which is this blue that's so light it's almost white, like putting one drop of blue food coloring in a huge pan of water.

Lisa throws open the front door so hard it bounces off the wall and flies back at her.

I'm standing by the front door waiting for Dad, although I don't know why, it's not like I'm going to say, Hi, Dad, how was your day and oh by the way Mom broke all the mirrors in the house.

Lisa frowns at me like I'm the one who pushed the door back in her face.

Mom! Mom! I got four blue stars! Lisa yells, running past me like a little white wind, through the dining room to the kitchen.

Dad's slow steps come onto the front porch. You can always tell Dad's steps, they're always slow and even and measured, each one just like the other, like he's marching somewhere slowly.

He always stomps his shoes twice when he gets to the front porch, which I don't know why he always does that, it's not dirty between here and the car, it's all cement.

Dad clears his throat as he's coming in the door, which is another thing he always does just before he comes in, like he's leaving something outside.

I say, Hi Dad, and I smile and I don't say anything about the mirrors.

He says, Hi Ab, and gives me a one-arm hug and I give him one back.

And then I start waiting again.

I'm waiting for Dad to see the two broken mirrors.

I don't know what he'll do.

No one has ever broken two mirrors in one day in this house, this is a whole new ball game, as Dad likes to say.

I sit down in Mom's green chair in the living room which always smells like her Chanel No. 5 and I pick up the *Reader's Digest* and pretend to read it but really I'm listening.

And waiting.

Nothing happens until Mom calls out that dinner is ready and Dad goes into the lilac bathroom with integrity to wash his hands.

I hear him go in there and I hold my breath and open my ears up all the way.

I go sit down at the dinner table across from Lisa which is where I always sit. I used to sit in Lisa's spot, where you can look out the window to the backyard, but then one day Mom made us switch because I sassed her so now I have to look at the living room which how boring is that.

Which by the way that's another rule, no sass. It's one of the major rules and was made in my honor.

Lisa obviously didn't wash her hands before dinner because if she saw a broken mirror she would've come running and screaming about it.

I hear water running in the lilac bathroom and I'm still holding my breath and listening real hard.

Then Dad's teacher steps come snapping down the hall and into the dining room.

His face is smooth and normal, like he didn't see anything unusual.

He sits in his chair, which Dad has the only dining room chair with arms.

I can't stand this.

Did he miss it?

But how could he?

Mom comes in with a pot of stew and starts dishing up. Her eyes have black circles under them and her face is still all saggy and white and she didn't even put on fresh lipstick.

Dad says all casual, like mirrors get broken every day, How did the mirror in there get broken?

Finally!

Oh, I accidentally hit it with the broom handle when I was in there cleaning, Mom says without looking at Dad or anybody and in fact she's looking at the stew like it's suddenly so interesting.

And she giggles this weirdamundo little giggle that makes goose bumps go up and down my arms because it doesn't sound like her, it sounds like one of those exotic birds you see at the zoo with blue and red and green feathers and some big topknot thingie on their head.

I give her the big eyes because I can't believe she's standing there lying to Dad and all Dad has to do is see the other mirror to know she's lying which how stupid is that.

Mom just stirs the stew and then takes it back in the kitchen.

And then dinner goes on like it's a normal day, only I can't look at Mom and I can't finish my stew and Mom says, Abby, you love stew what's wrong with you, but she doesn't look at me when she says it, she looks at her praying angel with the missing wing.

I don't say anything and Lisa saves me by changing the subject to tether ball and which this is why I don't think Lisa's mind is a sieve because she always seems to know when to save me.

Which sometimes Lisa really is OK for a sister even if she is only six.

that night i'm lying awake in bed and listening.

I'm listening for when Dad comes out of his study to go to bed because that's when he'll see the broken mirror in his and Mom's bathroom.

Dad usually stays up late correcting typing papers in his study but he doesn't stay up as late as Mom.

Finally I hear his study door open and his snapping footsteps.

Dad never wears slippers. He has this old pair of shoes that he calls slippers but they're still just his hard teacher shoes which how dorkamundo is that.

I hear him open the bedroom door and shut it.

I'm waiting.

Then I hear real low voices, which means Mom is not in her green chair reading.

Which is a little weirdamundo but not very. Sometimes she reads in bed.

I'm wondering if Dad will yell, which he hardly ever yells, except when I slide silently off the piano bench when I'm supposed to be practicing the piano because I know no one is listening to me, but which sometimes Dad *is* listening and he yells, Get back to that piano, Abby!

Even though there is no yelling in our house, that's the rule.

Mom says people with class don't yell.

I can't hear anything so I get out of bed and go on quiet feet down the hall and lie down at the top of the stairs.

The living room is dark.

Still all I hear is low murmurs coming from their room.

I sneak downstairs, quiet as night. I can sneak around without making any noise because I do it a lot. It's better than lying in bed wide awake trying to make yourself go to sleep when you're not even tired, and which sneaking around can make you really tired.

I skip the creaky fourth step which Dad has never gotten around to fixing even though Mom bugs him about it all the time. When Mom hears it squeak she says, Some day that stair is gonna give out and someone's gonna get hurt.

Which I don't see how a creaky stair can hurt you but anyway.

I'm in the living room. There's almost no light because there's no lights on our street, the only light is from the lights up on the highway.

I tiptoe down the hall.

The light shines under their door.

I hear their voices but they're so low I can't make out any words even though I'm right on the other side of the door.

I put my ear on the door.

Dad is telling Mom about some kid in one of his classes.

He's real smart, Dad says, but he's so disruptive. There must be trouble at home.

He keeps talking about this kid, how he's a bad influence

on everyone else in the class, how he stirs people up.

I don't care about some high school kid. I just want to know if he's gone in the bathroom yet and seen that mirror. Did I miss it?

I wait, with my ear to the door.

I hate waiting. I want things to happen. Right now I want to throw open the door and point my finger at the broken mirror and yell, Look! Look at what she's done! Explain *that*!

But I wait.

And I wait some more.

I wait for a hundred years.

My feet get so tired of standing there.

After a while there's no talking which probably means Dad is asleep and Mom is just reading.

Finally I give up. I go to bed and I fall right to sleep. Because waiting can make you so awfully tired.

chapter 6

here is what happened with the mirrors, and that is exactly nothing.

Dad never got upset or anything, he never even mentioned them.

Lisa accepted Mom's explanation that they were both accidents while she was cleaning.

Which made me wonder.

Why was I the only one who thought there was something fishy in France?

But then Dad and Lisa didn't know about Mom's little night swim, either.

I had more information.

Which I wish I didn't have.

It made a lot of conversations go on in my head.

Like:

There's something weirdamundo going on here.

No there's not.

Yes there is.

There's nothing wrong with a night swim on a hot night.

Yes there is.

No there isn't.

Well what about the mirrors?

And on and on.

The mirrors stayed broken for a while and then one day I came home from school and they were both whole again.

Which made me wonder if they'd ever been broken in the first place or did I just make it up.

But then Mom started having a lot of headaches and lie-downs, so I knew.

I didn't make it up.

Mom was lying down just about every day when I came home from school now. She still fixed dinner every night and made our lunches and did the laundry and all that, but it felt different. Like dinners were easy dinners like macaroni and cheese or beans and wienies. And she started buying store-bought cookies for our lunches instead of baking them herself. Those store-bought cookies which she used to call "junk."

But she was still staying up late at night reading under the round light that made her hair turn blue, sitting in her green chair with her legs up under her, and I figured as long as she was doing that, everything must be OK.

Boy was I wrong.

Next time I'll know.

Don't believe round lights and blue hair and legs up under.

It looks like it adds up, but it doesn't.

chapter 7

So i had to tell Poppy about the mirrors because we tell each other everything.

We're walking to school and I'm not sure how to bring it up.

I mean you can't just say, My mom broke two mirrors in our house on purpose, do you think that's weird?

I mean weirdamundo.

Poppy has her hair in two braids today. She has the yellowest hair of anyone I ever met but it's real, it's not bleached.

I can't put my hair in braids. I've tried, and all that happens is the braid starts to twist around itself because of all the curl in my hair and I end up looking like Pippi Longstocking.

Poppy's braids lie flat on her chest, which by the way is *not* flat, which by the way mine *is*, so just shut up, it's not my fault I have no boobs. Mom says I'm just a late bloomer which I just want to scream *I'm not a flower!* when she says that.

We're walking through the orchard, down the little path we've made by walking through it so much. You can get to everything by walking through the orchard—the store, the library, the junior high, the elementary school, the public pools, several churches, Holly's Bakery, a bunch of antique shops, and this weirdamundo art gallery called So Be It Gallery that's run by hippies which this one time had human heads in the window that were made out of papier mâché. Anyway it's like the whole world is right there, on the other side of the orchard, only no one ever walks through the orchard except Poppy and me. It's like we're the only ones who know the shortcut to the rest of the world.

Poppy is humming that new Elton John song, I can't remember the name of it.

I never know the names of any songs because I'm not allowed to play rock music in the house which is *another* rule.

Hey Poppy, I say, trying to sound real cool and casual and beatnik.

Poppy flings both braids back with one head swing.

Huh? she says.

Does your mom ever break stuff? I say.

Well, yeah, she says. Doesn't everyone?

She's giving me that giraffe look again.

Is this about your mom again? she says.

Nothing gets by Poppy.

No, I say. Then I don't know what else to say because, duh, of course it's about my mom.

OK, *yes*, I finally say, hugging my denim binder tight across my chest and watching my feet walk like they have all the answers.

What did she break? Poppy says.

Two mirrors, I say. Two bathroom mirrors. I think she did it on purpose, I'm pretty sure.

So? says Poppy. My mom throws stuff when she gets mad.

Poppy takes off her Levi jacket because the sun came out from behind a cloud and now it's actually hot even though it's morning.

I don't have a Levi jacket even though I'd give my teeth to have one. Well, maybe not my teeth, maybe just some of those little wrist bones you don't really need.

But that's the thing, I say. I don't think she was mad, I think she was something else.

Like what? Poppy says.

I don't know, that's what I'm trying to figure out, I say. She was laying down with a headache after she broke them.

Hm, Poppy says, and scrunches her eyebrows way down.

We walk in silence for a while.

It's more like she's sad about something, I say. And she's tired all the time. And her face is all droopy all the time.

Hm, says Poppy. Maybe we should ask my mom.

Poppy's mom, Mrs. Cordesi, knows absolutely everything about everything. I don't know how she knows so much stuff, she never even went to college, but if you ask her a question she always knows the answer.

Always.

I don't know, I say. Maybe my mom doesn't want your mom to know there's something wrong. And anyway maybe there's nothing wrong.

Poppy runs out ahead of me and does this little ballet turn on her toes, her Levi jacket flying out like a wing from her fist and her braids going out straight.

Whatever, she says. She does another little ballet turn. Which I can never do those without falling over.

But then Poppy can do just about anything.

Poppy and her mom. Poppy can do anything and Mrs. Cordesi knows everything.

Just the opposite of me and my mom.

chapter 8

t's a **thursday** night in October, which is choir night for Mom. It's also Dad's night-school night, which he teaches typing once a week at some night school over in San Jose in the bad part of town which he let me go with him once and I got to run the stopwatch while everybody typed but then Mom had a cow about it and I never got to go again.

Like some murderer is going to come into a typing class and murder me.

Right.

It's seven-ten. Mom is supposed to leave before seven because choir starts at seven. Which is weirdamundo because she's hardly ever late.

I've been watching Mom the way she used to watch Lisa when Lisa was little and we'd go into some big store like Macy's. OK, we only went to Macy's once, which was when Mom's cousin Donna got married and Mom had to buy her a wedding gift and we had to get it at Macy's because Donna's family is really rich and Mom bought her this big expensive coffeepot with a zillion buttons and things on it and Mom doesn't even *like* Donna. And Lisa *did* almost get lost and then Mom told me to watch Lisa but I could tell Mom was still watching Lisa anyway.

Just when I'm about to check on Mom, Lisa comes tearing down the hall with her eyes all ga-ga and whispers, Ab, come here! Quick! and runs back down the hall toward Mom's room.

I walk—*walk*—down the hall. This is to calm Lisa down.

I start swallowing a lot because for some reason there's too much saliva in my mouth.

Mom's door is open.

Mom is standing in the middle of the room.

She's in her white slip with the lace on the bottom and the lace is ripped over one knee and hanging down all droopy.

She's standing in a sea of color. All her clothes are on the floor. Her closet is empty except for the gray suit she got married in which is hanging there all sorry and sad and alone. Some of the empty hangers are still swinging.

Mom's hair is too long right now, and it's standing up all over her head in big black pieces like tree trunks that bounce around when she moves. Usually she keeps her hair real short like a boy's. Too short, if you ask me. But right now I'd rather see that too-short hair than these tree trunk things.

She looks up at me and Lisa. We're standing shoulder to shoulder in the doorway. Well really shoulder to elbow because Lisa's a lot shorter than me.

Mom's face is all blank, like she doesn't even see us.

It's the face of a robot.

Goose bumps go down my fingers and up my arms.

For just a sec I think about pushing Lisa out of there and closing the door because no little kid should see her mom's face when it looks like that.

But I can't move.

And besides, we're in this together.

Lisa and me.

Where is it? Mom says, looking at us but not looking at us.

Mom's voice matches her face.

Robot voice.

My stomach goes into the big clench and I close my eyes and send ESP to Dad to get home right now.

Not that ESP ever works for me.

Where's what, Mom? I say. I sound so calm.

Lisa keeps looking from me to Mom to me to Mom, I can see her out the corner of my eye.

Like I'm gonna fix this.

Right.

I'm getting that conversation in my head again.

She's fine.

She's not.

Yes she is.

No she isn't.

Shut up.

Make me.

Mom bends over and scratches through blouses and skirts and dresses, looking like a dog digging at the beach.

Clothes fly all over, landing on the bed and nightstands and lamps and dressers.

My Spanish trees dress, Mom says in the robot voice, what did you do with it?

I don't even know if she means me. Because I'm not sure she knows I'm here. Or Lisa either. I definitely get the creepy feeling that Mom is talking to someone else, someone who's not here.

You know how you know things sometimes? You don't know how, but you just do?

I didn't do anything with it, I say. I say it real slow, like how I talk to Lisa sometimes when I have to explain stuff to her like science.

I'm so calm on the outside.

Lisa goes into the room and starts hunting through the pile of clothes, looking for the Spanish trees dress.

We all know the Spanish trees dress. Mom's favorite. Pale yucka-mundo green with wispy white trees all over which she's had it since forever.

Mom goes over to her dresser and opens the middle drawer. Out come sweaters and vests and I don't know what else, flying through the air, landing on the green shag carpeting.

Lisa is trying to catch the sweaters and vests coming through the air at her. She's making neat piles of things: one pile for dresses, one for skirts, one for blouses. A new pile for sweaters and one for vests.

It's your father, Mom says. He took it. He knew I wanted to wear it and he took it.

I have to swallow several times before I can talk again. I have that feeling like if I open my mouth the only thing that will come out is a scream.

I really, *really* wish Dad was here.

I make words come out of my mouth, quiet and slow and even.

Is it in the hamper? I say. Is it dirty?

No! Mom yells. I just had it, and now it's gone!

There's no yelling at our house. It's a rule. People with class don't yell.

The yelling sort of does it for me.

Something inside me breaks, I feel the snap, just as loud and hard as breaking an Apple Stix, those candy bars that look like green glass.

I have to get out of here.

And I have to get Lisa out of here.

Lisa is trying to hang up Mom's dresses but she's really too short—she can barely reach up to get the hangers, she has to stretch

her little body the whole way up. Lisa's not looking at me, not looking at Mom, she's just concentrating on getting each dress perfectly
on a hanger, her little white-blond eyebrows curled all the way down
like she's concentrating on math.

And then I see it.

The Spanish trees dress.

It's sitting there under several skirts and sweaters that Lisa hasn't
organized yet.

It's enough to make you believe in psychic whatever.

But then something weirdamundo happens.

Which is, I just stand there.

I don't do anything, I just stand there.

I watch Mom open another dresser drawer and start flinging out
socks and bras and underwear.

I watch Lisa trying to catch the socks and bras and underwear
coming through the air.

I look at the Spanish trees dress peeking out there and I just stand
there.

I am a horrible daughter.

I am a child of Satan.

I will definitely go to hell for this.

Mom sits on the bed, breathing in and out real hard, her bare feet
under a pile of clothes.

I tell myself to move.

Go forward.

Now!

No one can hear you yell at yourself inside your own head.

I take one step, then another.

I don't look at Mom or Lisa, I look at all the colors on the floor
and imagine I'm wading through a magical colored river, and I see

the magic stone in the bottom of the river and I'm going to bend and pick it up and then when I rub it the world will go back to right again.

I go over to the Spanish trees dress and pick it up.

Is this it? I say, holding it up.

Knowing very well that it is.

Oh, I am *so* calm.

Lisa stops and stares at the yuckamundo green dress in my hand.

Look, I say, it's not even wrinkled.

Oh, Mom says, her voice all gone out of her.

Mom runs her hand through her standing-up hair, then comes over and takes the dress from me. I try to smile but it's one of those smiles you pull across your face to be polite.

What I want to do is slap her.

You see that in movies, somebody slaps somebody else and the person who got slapped suddenly becomes normal again.

Snap out of it! I yell in my head.

Lisa and I watch as Mom pulls the dress over her head and when her face comes out she looks about a zillion years old, all these lines in her face and everything sagging down and those big black raccoon circles under her eyes.

Mom picks her way carefully through the pile of clothes and goes into the bathroom, looking nothing like Mom and a whole lot like one of those little old ladies at the old people's home where our Girl Scout troop sings every Christmas. You see them, shuffling down the smelly linoleum halls with their backs all bent over, their white heads almost down to their stomachs and their hands rolled up in knots.

Now I *really* have to get out of here.

Come on, I whisper to Lisa. We'll clean this up later.

We get out to the hall but then I have to stop and lean against the wall and make myself breathe in and out because my heart is going too fast and my knees and ankles are full of water.

Lisa leans next to me, real close, our arms touching, and I don't move away.

I could swear she was shaking but maybe I made that up.

The conversation in my head starts again.

No big deal, she just couldn't find her dress. You know how that is, when it's the one you want to wear, you have to find it. It could have happened to me, to anyone.

Yeah, right. What about that stuff where she thought Dad took it, huh? What about that?

Shut up.

You shut up.

No you.

You.

Mom's heels click down the hall behind us and then she's at the front door and opening it and calling out, Make sure Lisa goes to bed at eight-thirty!

And she's out the door and gone.

And there we are.

Lisa and me.

Standing against the cold wall and wondering what just happened.

chapter 9

i decide it's time to have a talk with Dad.

I mean we're up to three things now: the night swim, the mirrors, and the Spanish trees dress.

Not to mention all the headaches and lie-downs and saggy face and raccoon eyes.

I don't even know if Dad has noticed anything about anything yet. It's hard to tell with him. Sometimes he has sharp hawk eyes and sees every little thing, and other times you could march an elephant through his bedroom and it could poop right on him and he wouldn't even notice.

The best time to talk to Dad alone is when he's burning something down by the creek in his beloved incinerator.

Which the next Saturday, that's where he is.

Which is no surprise, it's what he does every Saturday.

You'd think he'd run out of stuff to burn but he never does.

But then we do have a zillion blackberry bushes down by the creek, which always need trimming back, and a whole slope of foxtails which are always overgrowing something.

I see the smoke from my bedroom and I go down there.

Even though it's October, Dad has his shirt off because it's hot by the incinerator.

Which the incinerator is this huge blue metal drum, that's all it is. I don't even know why Dad calls it an incinerator, it's just a big metal drum.

But anyway.

Hey, Dad, I say, all casual, like I'm just bored and need something to do so here I am.

Hey, Ab, he says, and throws a pile of foxtails in the drum which makes all kinds of thick gray smoke go everywhere, including into my eyes.

I step back to get out of the smoke.

For once I'm glad there's a lot of smoke. Because it's hard to look your dad in the eye and tell him his wife is going crazy.

Hey, Dad? I say behind the wall of smoke.

What, honey, he says. At least I think he said it. I can't see him but it sounds like Dad's voice. And I mean who else would be on the other side of the smoke.

Um, do you think Mom's feeling OK? I say.

I'm *so* casual.

Like this is about *nothing*.

La-dee-da, just another day at the Goodmans'.

There's a pause on the other side of the smoke which there shouldn't be. I mean he should've answered immediately if there was nothing wrong but there's this pause and *then* he answers.

What do you mean? he says, and now *he's* all casual but it's a fake casual, you can tell. At least I think so. I could be making this all up.

I don't know, I say to the smoke which just keeps getting thicker because he keeps putting more stuff in the incinerator. At least I *guess* that's what he's doing, I can't see anything over there.

It just seems like she's not really herself or something, I say.

More pausing from Dad.

A little wind comes across and blows some of the smoke away and I can see the orange flames leaping out of the incinerator, going straight up.

Dad is raking his pile of foxtails into a neater pile.

I think she's just been a little under the weather lately, that's all, he says.

But . . . , I say.

But you don't know the half of it, is what I want to say.

I hadn't really rehearsed how to say all this. I should have.

I start playing with my hair. This always helps me think. I grab a piece and twirl it back and forth in my fingers, then try to get it to my mouth to suck on it. It's almost long enough, I can get it with my tongue.

Mom's been doing some other stuff, I say.

Stuff when you're not home, I say.

Dad stops and looks at me, his arm straight out and his hand resting on the rake.

He reaches into his back pocket and pulls out his white handkerchief and wipes his sweaty face with it.

Dad *always* has a white handkerchief in his back pocket. No matter where you are or what you're doing, if you need to blow your nose or cry and Dad's there, *zip!* out comes the white handkerchief.

Like what, Ab? he says. His voice has gone all soft and mushy and you can't look at your dad when his voice is all soft and mushy.

Oh god, there go the eyebrows. Way down over his eyes, all *concerned.*

He leans the rake against a tree and folds the white handkerchief back into a perfect little square, all the edges meeting exactly. He puts it back in his pocket.

I lick my hair and look into the fire.

Take a deep breath.

Well one night she went out in the middle of the night and went swimming naked in the Billawallas' pool and I know because I followed her down there, and then she broke those two mirrors which you don't know but she did it on purpose, and then the other night before choir she couldn't find her Spanish trees dress and took everything out of her closet and threw it on the floor.

I say.

In one breath.

Dad waits, like there should be more.

I look at him and he looks at me.

Anything else? he says.

No, that's it, I say.

He clears his throat.

I think she's just been tired, he says, and goes back to his raking.

He throws another load of foxtails into the incinerator and there's a big wall of smoke again.

I step back even more.

Waiting.

Ab, it's nothing for you to worry about, OK? he says through the smoke.

I'm stunned.

He doesn't get it.

Shit.

You are never, ever, *ever* allowed to say "shit" in our house, but I'm saying it.

To myself anyway.

Shit.

Shitamundo.

I hate words. They never come out right. I wish I could just open up my head, slice it down the middle like a cantaloupe and let dad look inside and *see* all that stuff I saw. The robot face. The robot voice. The talking to someone who's not in the room.

Shit.

Shit shit shit.

chapter 10

Poppy and i are walking to school. It's November and the orchard grass is wet because it rained last night. My legs are getting a little wet even though I'm wearing knee-socks with my miniskirt which is not really a miniskirt because Mom says four inches above the knee and that's it.

Four inches is nothing.

So on the way to school I always roll up the waistband so my skirt *is* actually a miniskirt.

Poppy and me are talking about a zillion things like we always do and Mom is always saying, What do you two have to talk about all the time?

Everything, Mom.

And then Poppy stops and turns to me and her face gets all serious and she flattens her denim binder against her chest and wraps both arms around it and her lips go into a straight line.

Poppy has very big lips. I think it's because her mom's Egyptian or something.

What? I say. What is it?

I shouldn't tell you this, she says.

Of course everyone knows that means, *But I'm going to tell you anyway*, so I wait.

For some reason she looks up at the sky. I look up there, too, but I don't see anything.

Wellllllllll, she says to the sky. The way she drags out the *welllll*, you can see her big white teeth that are like white chalk because the enamel's all worn off.

Her eyes come down and meet my eyes.

I overheard something, she says. About your mom.

I press my denim binder into my chest and wrap my arms around it like hers.

Mom always says, Do you have to do everything the same as Poppy? I always say *No*, but that's a lie. I copy Poppy like crazy.

Something Mrs. Billawalla said, Poppy says.

I raise my eyebrows at her and wait.

Well, Mrs. Billawalla told *my* mom that *your* mom is headed for the big one, Poppy says. She starts nodding like that says it all.

Big what? I say.

You know, Poppy says, still nodding.

Poppy can drive me crazy sometimes.

No, what? I say. I want to yell, *Stop nodding!* But I don't.

Poppy bends her head down because she's a little taller than me. Her lips are right by my ear even though there's no one else within a zillion miles of us.

Nervous breakdown, she whispers.

I roll my eyes.

She is *not*, I say. The words come out real hard, like I know all about nervous breakdowns which I don't even know what one is.

Poppy sucks in her big lips and keeps nodding and looking at me all sorry like my fourteen cats just died. Which I don't have fourteen cats but I wish I did.

You don't even know what you're talking about, I say.

And you know Mrs. Billawalla is full of shit, I say.

I sound mad. I didn't even know I was mad, my voice just came out all mad on its own.

I hardly ever get mad at Poppy.

Poppy's eyebrows go all the way up and she says, I'm just telling you what I heard.

She says it kinda soft but it makes me even madder.

I turn and start walking real fast, the wet grass whapping at my legs and getting my kneesocks all wet. I look straight ahead.

Poppy catches up and walks right next to me.

She doesn't say anything.

I don't say anything.

We walk all the way to school like that.

This is how well Poppy knows me. She knows when to tell me stuff and when to just shut up.

All the way to school, I think about those words, *nervous breakdown*. What it sounds like is not good. What it sounds like is a car breaking down which means it doesn't work anymore and you have to get some strong men to roll it off the road and then it sits there, dead, until the tow truck comes.

chapter 11

Skip ahead to Christmas.

Mom is lying down all the time now and gives us money for school lunches instead of making them herself and doesn't clean the house anymore which Lisa and I have to do it every Saturday, and plus all Mom eats for breakfast is half an egg and all she eats for dinner is white rice which she mostly scoots around on her plate.

You might think, oh, she's just dieting which my mom is always on a diet and never loses any weight, except right now she's *not* on a diet that I know of, but she's melting away. I mean she's almost as skinny as me now and I am just a stick of bamboo according to Grandma who says *bamboo* because she and Grandpa used to live in the Philippines because they were missionaries saving godless souls from the eternal fires of hell, is how Grandpa put it.

It's really weirdamundo having a mom as skinny as you are. I mean most people might think skinny is nice and it makes you look like Twiggy and you can wear tight leather miniskirts with boots and look all fashionable but on Mom it just doesn't look right. Her pedal pushers are all droopy in the butt and she has to tuck sweaters into them to keep them up around her waist and how dumb that looks you can't even imagine.

I mean she just doesn't look like Mom anymore. Her head is the head of a skeleton and her eyes are sunk down deep into her head with those black raccoon circles all the way around them.

But anyway.

It's Christmas morning.

Lisa gets up when there's hardly any light in the windows and she runs into my room and jumps on my legs and whispers, Abby! Get up! It's Christmas!

Only it's not really a whisper, it's more like a trumpet.

I kick her off with my legs and say in a normal voice, Go back to bed, it's too early, creepamundo!

I hate being woken up early.

Lisa gets her lips practically all the way in my ear and whispers real loud, But it's Christmas!

I push her away and say, I know it's Christmas, it's still too early!

Then she does this Lisa thing which is she just stands there.

My eyes are closed but she's still standing there and I know it and she knows I know it.

It drives me crazy and she knows it.

I open one eye and point to the door.

She sticks her tongue out at me and stomps out.

This is the start of Christmas morning.

Fast-forward to opening presents and we're all sitting around the living room.

Me and Lisa are on the floor opening presents, and Mom and Dad are on the couch with their matching coffees and matching sleepy eyes.

Mom's raccoon circles look even darker than usual and there's even more lines all over her face than ever before. I mean they're everywhere. Dad doesn't have any lines at all except for when he gets upset, then he gets these little up-and-down lines between his eyebrows that look like a fence.

Lisa is down to her last present already because she rips everything open like it's on fire.

I still have a neat little pile of presents next to me.

There's Christmas music on the stereo, the Robert Shaw Chorale which sounds kinda churchy but which I kinda like. Right now they're singing "I Saw Three Ships Come Sailing."

There's a big present from Dad to Mom sitting under the tree.

It's wrapped perfectly, all neat and square in this white paper with gold Christmas trees all over it. I know Dad wrapped it himself because every piece of Scotch tape is exactly the same size, and the red bow on top is exactly in the center, and I bet he even measured to see where the exact center was.

I'm thinking maybe it's a hair dryer. The kind with the big blue shower-cap thing and a white hose that goes from your head to the hair dryer part. That's the kind Mrs. Cordesi has.

Although I'm not sure why Mom would want a hair dryer with her short hair, although these days it's pretty long because she doesn't get it cut every month like she used to. Plus Mom doesn't put curlers in her hair like Mrs. Cordesi does.

But the box is just the right size for a hair dryer.

But anyway.

How Christmas morning goes at our house is, first Lisa and me open all our presents while Mom and Dad watch, then Mom and Dad open their presents while Lisa and me watch. Only Lisa never watches because she has the attention span of a water skeeter, she's usually off playing with one of her presents.

I always watch Mom and Dad.

And believe me, I watched this morning because I wanted to see Mom smile a real smile for once.

Mom and Dad open their presents from Lisa and me which I got pot holders for Mom and a tie for Dad and Lisa copied me with a tie for Dad and a stupid vase from the five-and-dime for Mom.

Then I scoot the big present over to Mom, the one from Dad which is maybe a hair dryer.

For a sec I think maybe it's a mink coat but I bet the box is too small. Not that anyone I know ever got a mink coat but Mom always makes these oohing sounds in her throat whenever we watch some old Doris Day movie on TV and Doris is in some slinky fur coat.

Sometimes Mom says, Oh my, will you look at that coat?

Which she always sounds sad when she says it.

Although she sounds the same when she looks at pictures of Mount Rushmore, so who knows.

I put Mom's big present on the banana coffee table which we've always called it the banana coffee table even though it has nothing to do with a banana except it's sort of in the shape of one but not really. Actually, it's shaped like a kidney bean. It's made out of a slab of dark brown wood with yellow streaks and it has three legs and it's always falling over. Dad hates it and sometimes he kicks it after it falls over and then swears under his breath although I could be wrong because there's no swearing at our house, it's a rule.

Mom's cheeks are pink for once and there's this little light in her eyes and her mouth is pretty close to a smile.

I wonder what this could be, she says.

She rips down the white-and-gold wrapping paper and Dad's eyebrows twitch because he likes to save wrapping paper but Mom likes to just tear through things.

We can all see the picture on the box.

The picture is a Crock-Pot.

Mom's face falls all the way to the floor and the light goes out of her eyes.

Oh, she says. Oh, my.

It's not a good oh-my. It's one of those there's-another-car-accident-up-on-the-highway oh-my's.

She opens the box lid and you know she's still hoping that maybe it's a fur coat and not a Crock-Pot, like maybe Dad used an old box.

She looks in the box.

Her face slides down even more.

It's definitely a Crock-Pot.

Mom's hand goes over her nose and mouth and her eyes get all full of tears and she just stares inside that box.

Lisa for once is 100 percent quiet and staring at Mom with her mouth half open.

I don't get what's wrong. It looks like a great Crock-Pot to me. In the picture on the box, the Crock-Pot is full of vegetable soup, which looks pretty good.

Tears fall across Mom's hand.

Dad puts his arm around her and his face is like he just got shot in the stomach like in those old cowboy movies.

What's wrong? he says. Don't you like it?

He's got that fence going between his eyebrows.

What happens next is, I'm pretty sure, nervous-breakdown-ish.

Mom takes the Crock-Pot out of the box.

She holds it up in front of her with tears rolling down her face and slipping under her chin.

She stares at it.

Nineteen years go by.

It feels like the whole room is holding its breath although the Robert Shaw Chorale is still going strong with "Joy to the World."

And then Mom heaves the Crock-Pot into the Christmas tree.

It's a good throw. Real strong and hard. I didn't know she could throw like that.

It knocks the Christmas tree over and then smashes into the shelves by the fireplace.

It breaks into about six pieces and lies there on the floor looking a lot like a nervous breakdown even though I don't know what one is.

The Christmas tree lights keep blinking even though the Christmas tree is lying on its side. The water from the Christmas tree stand is leaking out and it's getting the white sheet under the tree all wet.

Lisa and I catch eyes and her eyes are big fish eyes, busting out of her head.

No one moves.

No one says anything.

This goes on for years.

My heart is beating so fast, in little bird beats.

In my brain are ninety zillion thoughts going ninety zillion miles an hour.

Thoughts like, *So this is what Mrs. Billawalla meant by the big one.*

Mom just sits there looking dumbly at the tree and tears running down everywhere.

Dad has his orange coffee cup halfway to his mouth which is hanging open and dark and he's frozen into a Polaroid snapshot.

Ladies and gentlemen, my family on Christmas morning.

If only I had a camera.

The Robert Shaw Chorale switches to "O Tannenbaum" which is actually pretty funny when you're looking at a Christmas tree that's lying on the floor on its side and the lights are still blinking like nothing's wrong.

Only I'm not laughing.

Finally Dad puts down his coffee cup and gets up real slow, like the air is glass and he might break it. He goes over to the Christmas tree and stands it up straight. Then he starts mopping up the water with the white sheet and he forgets that the nativity set is sitting on the sheet and baby Jesus and Joseph and Mary and the three wise men and two shepherds and the cow and the camel go rolling onto the wood floor, making all kinds of breaking sounds and I squeeze my eyes shut because I don't want baby Jesus to break.

I don't know why, it just doesn't seem right, especially on Christmas.

I open my eyes but nothing is broken.

Well, except for the Crock-Pot which we already covered that.

Mom gets up as slow as Dad did and goes out of the room and I hear her bare feet slapping down the hall to her room. The door shuts real quiet.

Dad picks up the pieces of Crock-Pot and stacks them in one of his big hands.

You wouldn't think he could type with such big hands, but he can type really fast, lots faster than Mom.

Dad's face is a blank wall.

What happens next is nothing.

Christmas is ruined, there's nothing more to tell.

Me and Lisa and Dad have a silent breakfast together.

I can hardly swallow my bear claw which is my favorite thing in the world to eat for breakfast.

Lisa doesn't look at me because there's nothing to say, even with our eyes. Dad doesn't look at either of us.

But here's the thing.

A new thing.

Which is I'm so mad at Mom I could spit a big spitball right in her eye.

Because you don't fuck with Christmas.

I know I'm not supposed to say *fuck*, but who's gonna hear me here in my head.

I'm so mad I need to say *fuck*.

Nothing else fits.

Because up until now I was feeling sorry for Mom but now I hate her.

You don't fuck with Christmas.

It's a rule.

It's not Mom's rule, it's my rule.

chapter 12

i **'m pretty sure** Mom is having a nervous breakdown.

Which I tried to look it up and it's not in the dictionary but I think I know what it is. It's when your mom has to lie down all the time and has raccoon circles around her eyes and when she walks her feet are as heavy as the whole world and her face isn't her face anymore and when she looks at you she doesn't see you and when you look into her eyes, you can't find her.

It's when you can't tell her anything except happy things, so you have to make up a lot of stuff.

You have to exaggerate.

OK, lie.

You say you got a hundred on a test when you didn't.

You do it because then Mom's frozen lips, which are frozen into an upside-down U, crack for a second and you can pretend it's a smile.

And she might say something like, Good for you, honey. Only sometimes she forgets the honey.

But then she forgets a lot of stuff. Which is the other thing.

Like she's supposed to pick me up after Girl Scouts so there I am, standing in the school driveway where the buses go, and I'm standing there in my green Girl Scout uniform all by myself and then Mrs. O'Leary the Girl Scout leader comes out and I have to make up some excuse for why my mom isn't there and then Mrs. O'Leary has to take me home but the whole time she's giving me this look like, Oh poor little Abby, which makes me want to punch her right in her crooked front teeth.

Sometimes Mom forgets she's supposed to cook dinner so then Dad heats up some TV dinners, and some nights Mom doesn't even come out of her room and there's the three of us at the table having another silent meal except for our forks scraping the metal TV dinner trays. And then one night Dad turns on the TV during dinner which was a big rule, no TV during dinner, but he turns on the news and after that we always have the TV on at dinner because all the Vietnam stuff is better than the icky silence.

Sometimes when I go into Mom's room to talk to her, she isn't awake.

I go in and even if her eyes are closed, I whisper, Hey Mom?

And sometimes she doesn't answer.

Maybe she's asleep.

Maybe she's faking it.

Or maybe she just forgot that when someone says Hey Mom you're supposed to at least open your eyes and look at the person.

After a while I don't go into her room anymore.

After a while you can get used to anything.

You can get used to someone being gone even if she's sitting there at the dinner table pushing her rice around with her fork, making Japanese art.

You can get used to Dad trying to make conversation.

You can get used to Mom looking out the window, ignoring the three of us.

When Mom sits there like a ghost, Lisa and me look at each other and we hold each other's eyes real tight for a long time.

Because we both know that I'm all she has and she's all I have, even if she is only six and pretty dorkamundo sometimes.

chapter 13

t's a rainy February morning. It's raining so hard the drops bounce back up when they hit.

It's a school morning and I come downstairs with my denim binder balanced just so on my hip and in the crook of my elbow which is how you're supposed to carry your binder if you're a girl and you go to Sequoia Junior High.

Lisa is practicing the piano and Mom is in her faded red bathrobe bending over Lisa. Lisa plays another wrong note and Mom stands up and puts her hand the whole way across her forehead like she's holding something in.

No, Lisa, Mom says, her voice all worn out. F-sharp, not F-natural, can't you hear it?

It sounds right to me, Lisa says.

Try it again, Mom says.

I get to the front door and open it and yell, Bye!

I almost get out but Mom is too quick for me, even with her hand all the way across her forehead.

Her eyes are on my feet, on my brown suede shoes which I've worn so much the toes are scuffed white.

Where are your galoshes? Mom says.

Crap.

I knew it.

Mom was having one of her better mornings if she was noticing things like feet.

My mouth starts moving even though I hadn't thought about what to say yet.

I'm not wearing those stupid galoshes, my mouth says.

I look Mom right in her raccoon eyes.

I can't believe I'm doing this because possibly the biggest rule at our house is no backtalk.

No sass.

No lip.

Young lady.

Lisa stops playing the piano and turns to look at me, her eyes and mouth open all fish-face.

Mom takes her hand off her forehead and puts it on her hip.

What did you say? she says. The words hit me like sleety rain which we sometimes get even in the Bay Area. It even freezes here in the winter, with ice on the puddles and everything.

I'm not wearing them, I say, they're stupid.

This is *huge* backtalk and I am in so much trouble.

But I don't even care.

I have no idea why I'm doing this and I don't even care.

I hold Mom's raccoon eyes with my eyes. I'm not scared because I'm not really here, this is not me doing this. The real me is sitting on the highest shelf beside the fireplace, up there by the ceiling where the white paint is cracking, watching the girl with the frizzy hair talk back to her mom in the faded red bathrobe.

Showing no respect.

Breaking the fifth commandment.

Honor thy father and thy mother.

Mom stares at me without blinking for like a year and I don't blink either so we're both standing there with our eyes drying out and my body in two different places at once and I feel the whole world stop just for a few seconds. The rain outside stops and the cars on the highway stop and the only movement I can see from my perch near the ceiling is Lisa's one leg going back and forth at the knee because she's too short for the piano bench.

Mom raises one faded red arm and points to the garage.

The garage is where we keep the galoshes.

Where my yellow galoshes are.

Which no one calls them galoshes except my stupid parents, everyone else says rain boots.

For a sec I consider running. Running out the door and running all the way to school.

Running through every puddle on the way to make sure my feet get soaking wet.

Running would be *enormous* backtalk.

I would be in the most trouble I've ever been in in my whole life.

I don't even know what the punishment would be.

I stand there. I mean, the girl with the frizzy hair, she stands there, frozen.

Mom's arm is still up there and pointing, her index finger looking very white and bony and long and it seems to be getting longer, the longer I stare at it.

And then, it's over.

Because I don't have a lot of choices here.

My brown suede shoes with the white toes take one step and then another and another and then I'm in the garage picking up my yellow galoshes.

But something happens while I'm in the garage.

Something explodes inside me.

Something like a glass balloon and I have little pieces of glass stuck all over inside me now and they hurt like crazy.

I come back out and Mom is bent over Lisa again who is playing again and hits the wrong note *again* and Mom goes, Ah! Lisa! She says it like someone just shot her in the back.

Mom's hand goes over her forehead again.

I divide into two me's again.

One me is on the top shelf by the fireplace, and the other me, the me full of glass, is holding the yellow galoshes.

I toss the yellow galoshes at Mom's feet. They hit her bare white feet and sit there looking like stupid yellow galoshes.

Here, you wear 'em, I say.

There's a siren going off in my head.

I have just crossed a line I've never crossed before.

Lisa stops playing.

Mom looks at the yellow galoshes.

This is all in slow motion, one Polaroid at a time.

At this speed I can see stuff I didn't notice before.

Like there's a big rip under the arm of Mom's faded red bathrobe and you can see her filmy blue nightgown underneath.

Like Lisa's leg is still going back and forth at the knee, like a really fast grandfather clock.

Like there's a lot of gray in the roots of Mom's black hair, at the part.

Like Mom's hands are all dried out and flaky and her cuticles are all grown up on her fingernails and you can't see the half-moons anymore.

Like Mom's lips are all dry and cracked and faded red.

And then the world starts up again in regular motion.

Mom picks up the yellow galoshes.

She looks at the yellow galoshes like she's never seen them before.

She turns toward the fireplace.

Her hand with the yellow galoshes swings back and then forward.

She tosses my yellow galoshes into the fireplace.

They land in a pouf of ashes and bathroom trash, which is sitting there waiting for Mom or Dad to burn it. Rolled-up Kleenexes and brown toilet paper tubes and big balls of my frizzy brown hair from my hairbrush and long stripes of Lisa's white-blond hair from her hairbrush.

Mom walks right up to the fireplace and just for a sec I think she's going to jump in.

I don't know why I think that.

That siren is still going off in my head.

Getting louder and louder.

Mom gets the matches from the mantle and everything gets all slow again and suddenly I'm so tired of slow, I'm so tired of every-thing. I'm tired of Mom being tired and dried out and faded and lying down and swimming in the neighbors' pool at night and throwing Crock-Pots into Christmas trees and forgetting to pick up her own daughter at Girl Scouts and I'm tired of this whole mess that our whole family has become and it's all her fault and I am really, really, *really* starting to hate her.

Some days I hate her so much it makes my stomach hurt.

Like today.

Oh, if she only knew.

And if she only knew that Lisa hits that F-natural on purpose and that I talk back to her on purpose, and the purpose is to shake her good, slap her on both cheeks, wake her up out of this half-sleep she's in all the time.

Mom lights a match and throws it in the fireplace with the bathroom trash and my yellow galoshes.

The Kleenexes catch fire immediately.

There's little orange flames all around the yellow galoshes.

Then more flames and more flames and pretty soon the yellow galoshes have orange flames all over them and the room fills up with this grossamundo smell of burning hair and burning rubber.

Mom just stands there, watching the fire.

It's what we're all doing, like we're hypnotized.

No one moves, not even Lisa.

Lisa's hands are gripping the edge of the piano bench so hard her knuckles are sticking out all bony and white.

One of the yellow galoshes starts to melt, a little yellow river runs down the side of it and into the orange flame.

No one's breathing.

There's no air in this room.

Mom stares into the fire.

Me and Lisa stare at Mom.

The clock in the hall ticks.

I don't have to look at it to see that it's so late that Poppy already left for school.

Mom drops one hand from the mantle and puts it in her bathrobe pocket.

There, Mom says to the fire.

Her voice is real hard and flat.

Now nobody has to wear them, she says.

I slide over real slow and quiet to Lisa on the piano bench and I stand real close to her. The back of her shoulder touches my arm and she leans back into me, her shoulder making a little indent on my arm. That indent has my heartbeat in it, it's beating a zillion miles a second, even faster than a hummingbird heart.

Mom dips her head down like she's praying.

You two, she says to the melting yellow galoshes.

For a sec I think she means the two yellow galoshes.

She shakes her head real slow.

You two make me so tired, she says.

I don't think she means the two yellow galoshes.

Without looking at Lisa or me, Mom turns and walks out of the room, her bare feet making no sound on the carpet but the floor creaking like crazy, like she suddenly weighs nine hundred pounds.

Mom's bathrobe comes open as she goes into the hall and it hangs in tired folds behind her and for a sec it looks like a faded red bathrobe walking all by itself, with no one in it.

Mom's door closes and I hear her bedsprings squeak.

Lisa and I don't move.

We watch the fire, which has almost burned itself out.

I don't know what we're waiting for.

I wait until the fire is all the way out.

Then I say, We better get to school.

My voice sounds like I'm six years old.

Lisa gets up and puts on her raincoat and we walk out to the front porch and get our umbrellas. Lisa's is blue and mine is pink and they have the same flower pattern because they're from Grandma and which they're real parasols from Japan.

Which by the way Lisa gets *everything* blue even though it's *my* favorite color. It's her favorite color, too, but she just copied me. But everyone always remembers it's Lisa's favorite color because it matches her blue eyes.

No one ever remembers what my favorite color is.

It's still raining really hard.

I point to Lisa's feet.

Go get your galoshes on, I say.

Lisa looks out at the rain and then looks at me with such big sad eyes I almost want to hug her.

No, she says in a little quavery voice.

I roll my eyes at her.

I run into the garage and get Lisa's blue galoshes.

She doesn't say anything as I put them on over her shoes.

For just a sec I feel like I'm six and she's three.

We go out into the hard rain which hammers on our umbrellas so hard I can hardly hear all the crazy thoughts in my head.

We don't talk all the way to Lisa's school, which is on the way to my school.

I want to say stuff like, *Lisa, it's OK*, or *Don't worry, it'll be all right*, but my mouth is glued shut. Instead, I bump my pink umbrella against Lisa's blue umbrella about fifty times until she gets mad and goes, Quit it!

And then I smile at her and she kinda smiles back.

We get to her school and she says, Will you pick me up after school and we can walk home together?

And I say, Yeah, sure, I'll see you at three-fifteen.

Which might seem like nothing except that Lisa and I *never* walk home from school together.

chapter 14

When lisa and me get home from school the melted yellow galoshes are still in the fireplace.

Lisa takes one look at them and runs upstairs.

I stand there and look at them, yellow shoe-shaped things with black smudges and yellow bubbles all over. It's really only the tops that got melted, the shoe part is still OK. I mean you could still wear them.

I can't decide what to do with them. Leave them right there for Dad to see or put them in the garage with the other galoshes or throw them in the big garbage can out back or maybe even into Dad's beloved incinerator down by the creek.

Different scenes go through my mind.

Like, Dad comes home and sees the melted galoshes in the fireplace.

What's this? he says.

Mom burned my galoshes, I say.

It's Abby's fault, Mom says, she talked back to me.

Then I point at Mom and yell, It's all *her* fault for getting so faded and tired and laying down all the time and forgetting to make dinner and why can't she just wake up and be normal again?

And then I burst into tears and run out of the room.

Of course that scene will never happen.

Another scene is I put the melted yellow galoshes in the garage and the next time it rains Dad goes out to get his galoshes and he sees the melted yellow things.

This is weeks later, maybe months.

And maybe Mom is better by that time.

And maybe we can all laugh.

Oh, *Mom!* We all laugh and hiccup and slap our knees. Remember when you went crazy that time and burned up my galoshes in the fireplace?

And we all hold our stomachs from laughing so hard, all four of us, even Mom.

Sometimes you can lie to yourself and it works.

Other times the truth is already inside you before you have time to swallow the lie.

I hate that.

I leave the melted yellow galoshes in the fireplace.

Let Dad see them, I don't care.

Let Mom blame me, I don't care.

I figure, the worst that could happen is they'll send me to reform school. When Dad gets mad he threatens to ship us off to the Navy but I don't think the Navy takes twelve-year-old girls. But Roberta Downing's parents sent her to reform school and reform school *definitely* takes twelve-year-old girls.

I don't even know what reform school is.

In my mind, it's like an orphanage.

You have to wear rags and scrub wood floors with buckets of dirty cold water and heavy brushes. They feed you watery oatmeal three times a day and you're not allowed to talk to the other girls and if you do you get whipped thirty-eight times and locked in a rat-filled dungeon.

Just like in *Oliver!*

I take off my raincoat and hang it in the hallway. My brown suede shoes are soaking wet so I take them off and put them on the heat register. Then I stand on it so my socks will dry right on my feet.

Mom's door is closed.

Which means we'll be having TV dinners tonight.

Mom buys stacks of TV dinners now.

TV dinners used to be a special treat, we only got to have them on January 25, my parents' wedding anniversary. Mom and Dad would go out to the Villa Felice for a fancy dinner and Lisa and me would get to stay home with Kim the baby-sitter and eat TV dinners and watch *The Monkees* or *My Three Sons*. Kim had long red hair and she let us brush it and braid it, only Lisa never learned how to braid a real braid, even though I showed her like eight zillion times, and hers would come out all bumpy and stupid. Of course this was when I was a little kid, before I could baby-sit Lisa myself.

From where I'm standing on the heat register I can see the melted yellow galoshes and they make me feel so tired, like I'm a hundred and ninety years old.

I'm tired of TV dinners with those peas that are just little grease-balls and me and Lisa creeping into each other's bed at night, whoever can't sleep walking across the hall to get in with the other one.

OK, usually it's me who can't sleep, usually it's me crawling into Lisa's bed at night.

I'm so tired and I can't wait anymore and I just want something to happen.

Which is one of those things you should never say, even silently to yourself.

chapter 15

So dad comes home.

On the day of the burning of the yellow galoshes.

Dad comes in the door and he sees the yellow galoshes in the fireplace *immediately*.

I mean it's like he has ESP or something.

I'm sitting in Mom's green chair, pretending to read *Reader's Digest*.

Dad doesn't even say hi, he just gets that fence between his eyebrows and goes, What are your galoshes doing in the fireplace, Abby?

He doesn't sound mad, just *concerned*.

God, I wish someone would get *mad* around here.

Mom threw 'em in there, I say. I look right in his eyes without blinking so he'll know I'm telling the truth.

Dad puts his briefcase down and goes over to the fireplace. He gets out his white handkerchief and covers his hand with it, then picks up the yellow galoshes.

He shakes the ashes off of them and turns to me.

Why? he asks, his voice kinda quiet.

This is when I notice the new lines. Horizontal lines going across his forehead like the stripes in a flag.

I keep staring at him with my face all serious and my voice all serious so he knows, this is serious and it wasn't my fault.

I don't know, I say.

OK, that's kind of a lie.

But something tells me I can get away with it.

Maybe because somewhere deep down I know: Even if your daughter talks back to you, you don't throw her yellow galoshes into the fireplace and burn them up.

Dad stands there staring at the melted yellow galoshes in his hand.

He stands there a long time.

He stands so still that I have to keep checking his chest to see if he's even breathing.

Like he was zapped by a lightning bolt and paralyzed all over.

It goes on too long and it's spooky.

Dad, I say real quiet and looking at his eyes which are frozen onto the galoshes, I didn't do anything to her, I swear.

I know, he says, like almost to himself, and starts nodding.

He nods and nods, looking at those yellow galoshes.

Which is even spookier than standing there frozen.

Finally he bends down and places the galoshes oh so carefully on the hearth, like they're something fragile and precious.

He snaps his white handkerchief twice in the air to get the ashes off and folds it into a perfect little square.

Then he wipes his forehead with it.

Which his forehead wasn't even sweaty.

He pulls in his lips and turns and goes down the hall.

His steps are weirdamundo.

They're not snapping down the hall.

They're almost shuffling.

And even slower than usual.

Dad goes into his and Mom's room and shuts the door and after a few minutes he comes out and calls Dr. Whitmore. I don't know what he says to Dr. Whitmore because when he saw me there in the living room where I could hear everything, he took the phone into his study and closed the door.

For once I feel good.

Hopeful.

Like maybe *something* is going to happen now that Dr. Whitmore is in on it.

Dr. Whitmore will fix Mom right up and next thing you know, Mom and I will be going to the fabric store to get some green corduroy for those pants she keeps promising to make me. Dark green corduroy pants with two scoop pockets in the front and the biggest bell bottoms you can imagine.

Dad stays in his study a real long time, talking to Dr. Whitmore.

later the three of us have TV dinners with the TV on and nothing feels different and I'm dying to ask Dad what the doctor said but something is not letting me ask.

I don't know what it is.

It's just, sometimes you know when to shut up.

Maybe it's that Dad's eyes are all bloodshot and you can tell he's not even hearing the TV.

Which I really should have just appreciated that TV dinner moment because things were about to get worse.

chapter 16

So finally april gets here which means finally my thirteenth birthday gets here.

Which I've been waiting to be a teenager since forever.

I mean I feel like I've been one for a long time, I just didn't have the actual age to go with it.

My birthday is on a Tuesday this year, which means no big sleepover or party, but actually I'm relieved because I really don't think Mom could handle a big party.

So I just have Poppy over for dinner.

We have hot dogs that Dad roasts out on the grill on the patio, just like it's summer.

I told Mom I wanted a summer picnic for my birthday.

She even made potato salad and a Jell-O mold in red Jell-O, my favorite.

We're all sitting on the floor in the living room, on the picnic blanket which is not red-and-white checks like a picnic blanket is supposed to be. It's tan and navy blue–striped. But oh well.

Mom even has a hot dog on her plate instead of just rice.

In fact, there's no rice anywhere.

We're all gobbling down our hot dogs and beans and potato salad and Jell-O and I'm watching Mom out of the corner of my eye.

She's poking at her potato salad with her fork, moving the potato salad all around on her plate.

Just like with the rice.

She hasn't touched her hot dog.

All she does is stare at her plate.

I decide not to watch her anymore.

She's not going to ruin my first teenage birthday.

I haven't seen my cake yet, but that's because at our house the birthday cake is supposed to be a surprise. You're not supposed to see it until the big moment with the candles lit and everyone singing.

Although my cake is never that big a surprise because I have the same thing every year: angel food. It's my favorite.

So we're all done eating and it's cake time.

Lisa and Poppy take away all the paper plates and plastic silverware.

Mom's plate looks like she didn't even touch it.

But I don't care.

This is *my* day.

The singing starts.

Out in the kitchen, Mom and Poppy and Lisa start singing "Happy Birthday."

Dad joins in.

Out they come with the cake and the candles all lit.

It's not angel food.

Is the first thing I notice.

And the second thing is, it's a bakery cake.

We do not have bakery cakes around here.

Mom always bakes the birthday cakes from a Betty Crocker box.

They keep singing as I stare at the white rectangle covered in pink and yellow flowers.

Mom puts it down in front of me.

I don't know what to think.

I mean I love bakery cakes, but.

But this is a Goodman birthday.

Mom is supposed to make the cake.

From a box.

It's a rule.

The candles are melting down in front of me.

They all stop singing.

I'm supposed to make a wish.

But I can't think of anything to wish for.

They're all staring at me.

The candles are burning down.

I lean over with my blank mind and I just start blowing, with no wish in mind.

Which I learned you should always wish *something*, even if you can't think of anything.

Because right then my hair catches on fire.

I'm sitting there Indian-style on the tan-and-navy picnic blanket with my bakery birthday cake in front of me and I guess I leaned over wrong.

Lisa screams, Abby! Your hair!

I look up, because I don't know it's on fire yet.

Then I see it out of the corner of my eye.

On the right side.

The tiniest little flame, too close to my head, I don't know what it means.

I mean, it's not every day your hair catches on fire.

You don't know what it looks like.

There is also smoke, right next to my head.

And then that smell.

Worse than Dad's beloved incinerator.

This is all happening in real slow motion until Poppy does the smartest thing ever.

She throws her whole glass of red Hi-C on my head.

It puts the fire right out.

What's even funnier is Dad thought of the same thing only he wasn't as quick as Poppy, so I got *his* whole glass of ice water just a split second after Poppy's.

I'm real wet now.

That awful burned-hair smell is all over, it's all you can smell.

Part of the birthday cake is covered in red Hi-C and ice water.

During all this, I've forgotten all about Mom.

I look over at her.

She's looking out the living room window.

Looking out the living room window.

Her face is as blank as nothing.

Looking out the window.

Like her oldest teenage daughter wasn't just on fire.

Stuff is dripping down my neck.

Everyone is staring at me.

Finally Dad says, You OK, Ab?

I guess, I say. My voice all slip-slidey.

I feel up to where my hair just burned. It didn't go all the way to my scalp, thank god. Just a few inches burned off on one side in front.

I think I'll go change, I say to no one.

I get up and go upstairs and Dad and Lisa and Poppy start mopping up the mess.

Mom is still looking out the window.

Like something more important is happening out there.

chapter 17

this is when things get worse.

Which it all starts with me piercing my ears.

Which involves Poppy, who's had pierced ears since two years ago, which her mom took her and paid for it and everything. Poppy might not have a dad, but she has the coolest mom of anyone I know. The other moms on our street don't like Mrs. Cordesi because she wears hot pants with bikini tops and boots with real high heels and she goes out on dates with pony-tailed guys who ride Harleys and which my mom says are young enough to be Mrs. Cordesi's sons but I don't think so. And anyway, it's only *one* pony-tailed guy, it's the same guy she's been dating since forever, only my mom made it into about five guys.

So anyway it's Saturday and it's the end of April and the sun is out and Mom is actually doing the laundry for once and she yells at me up in my room to come hang out the wash on the line. Which I hate that job like poison but what are you going to do. The last time I sassed Mom certain things melted in the fireplace.

So I go down there. I do a little minor backtalk by stomping down the stairs and jumping from the fourth stair to the living room floor which is a total rule but Mom's in the laundry room and probably doesn't even hear it.

I drag my flip-flops all the way to the laundry room, which is also kind of backtalk but she doesn't hear that, either.

Mom is loading dark colors into the washing machine and she's actually humming to herself, which I haven't heard her hum since like the Dark Ages and I think, wow, maybe this is it. Maybe she woke up this morning and it's over, maybe she's all better now.

The wet load of whites is sitting there waiting for me in the laundry cart.

Oh joy.

They smell like bleach.

Which is a smell I secretly like.

And maybe it's the bleach up my nose or maybe it's the sun coming through the dirty laundry room window or maybe it's Mom's humming, but this thought comes crashing into my brain like a tidal wave.

Which is this: Now's a good time to ask Mom about getting my ears pierced.

It's perfect. She's in a good mood and I'm in a good mood and I'm about to do her this huge favor of hanging out the wash without backtalk and the sun is out. Perfect.

Mom's back is to me, she's taking a white handkerchief out of Dad's pants pocket.

I lean on the laundry cart and make it inch back and forth on its squeaky wheels.

This is it. I'm going to ask her.

I take in a big breath.

OK, there's one thing I forgot to mention.

And that is that I've already asked Mom about seventy zillion times to get my ears pierced.

And seventy zillion times she has said no.

It's the same scene, every time.

Mom, can I get my ears pierced?

No.

Mom, can I get my ears pierced, please?

No.

Mom, can I please please please with sugar on top get my ears pierced?

No.

Mom, if I save up all my baby-sitting money can I get my ears pierced?

No.

Mom, if I clean the bathrooms for the next sixteen Saturdays without having to be asked and if I promise to be nice to Lisa from now on and practice piano for an hour every day after school and never bug you again about anything ever ever ever *ever* again, can I get my ears pierced?

No.

So, OK, sure, there was this history about asking this question.

But sometimes I think you just know things. You just know things like, today is the day.

The day Mom would say yes.

So I take in that breath. I hold it.

Mom? I say really *really* nice.

What, honey, she says.

Ah ha! I knew it! It's the good Mom voice! Today's the day!

Mom pours some Amway stuff in the washing machine with one of those little red plastic measuring cups.

Can I get my ears pierced? I say. It comes out so sweet it practically sticks to my teeth.

She pours the rest of the soap in the machine and then stands up straight and looks out the dirty window.

I stop pushing the squeaky laundry cart.

I can smell the Amway soap even though I'm a few feet away. It has that old-lady smell, like roses or lilacs.

Mom puts the little red cup on the edge of the washing machine. Real careful.

Like she's setting it down on eggs.

She watches herself do it.

I'm still holding in that big breath and I let it out because I can't hold it anymore.

Mom stands there so long looking out the dirty window which you can barely see anything out of it and even if you could it's just the Sullivans' peach trees next door.

I move the laundry cart a little, just one squeak. Just to remind her I'm still here and there is an unanswered question hanging in the air between us waiting for an answer.

Mom turns and looks at me with her tired red eyes with the raccoon circles and her droopy white cheeks with lines in them and she shakes her head back and forth real slow, and right then I would have done anything to start this day over from the top.

Jesus Christ, Abby, she says.

Her voice is like how cowboys sound in those old movies when they're shot but they have to say something right before they die, like, *Tell Marie I love her*, and then they keel.

Jesus Christ. My mother just said Jesus Christ and not in a church way.

There is no swearing at our house. This is a huge rule. No one, I mean *no one* at our house ever says Jesus Christ in that way. I mean even if Dad swears he just says goddamn it and that's under his breath and you're not supposed to hear him.

My mother never, ever swears.

I mean she was raised Presbyterian.

I mean no one in my whole *family tree* has ever said Jesus Christ the way Mom just said it.

It's making my mind not work right.

None of my thoughts are making sense, it's just a gush of nonsense, like Niagara Falls in my head.

I swallow even though I don't mean to but it seems to wake up my brain.

I blink and that wakes me up, too.

I think, I can still save this. I can make this OK.

Just go hang out the wash and never, ever bring up pierced ears again.

And all that stuff about being nice to Lisa and practicing an hour a day and cleaning the bathrooms, I'll do that, too.

But just when I take in a breath and tell myself everything is fine, I can fix this, that's when Mom closes her eyes and slides down the smooth front of the washing machine, slides down making a terrible screeching sound of skin against metal that I heard somewhere so deep inside me that I didn't even know that place was there. She slides all the way down to the floor, her knees bending in her blue pedal pushers and her flaky white feet going straight out in front of her and then she sits there and bends her head down and puts her hands on her face and you have never heard such terrible sounds come from a human being, much less your own mother.

Animal sounds. Like an animal being hurt bad.

I stand there.

My mother is a ball of animal cries and I just stand there.

And all I can think is, I guess I'm not getting my ears pierced.

This is the kind of terrible daughter I am.

I don't bend over, I don't put a hand on her shoulder.

I don't say something comforting, like, it's OK, Mom.

I don't call someone, call Dad, call the doctor, call Mrs. Sierra who used to be a nurse.

I don't say, forget it, Mom, I don't need pierced ears.

I don't say, sorry, I didn't mean to upset you.

I'm the worst daughter that God ever made.

And then I get worse.

I run.

I leave my sobbing mother on the floor of the laundry room making sounds that would make you pee your bed if you heard them in the middle of the night.

I run out the back door and into the bright sunlight and down the white sidewalk past Mom's flower bed where she grows sunflowers in the summer and out into the street, across the street, across Poppy's front lawn and up Poppy's front steps.

On Poppy's front porch I stop and listen to myself breathe in huge gulping breaths and I still can't get enough air.

I'm dizzy.

My head is floating.

I sit down on the cold brick steps.

I'm breathing so fast and I can't control it, it's like the air is controlling me, forcing itself in and out of my body, it's pressing against my chest, like two hands, one on my back and one on my chest, squeezing in and out.

I open my hands and I can see my fast heartbeat in my fingertips.

Jesus Christ, Abby.

Jesus Christ, Abby.

Jesus Christ, Abby.

I put my hands over my ears and shut my eyes hard, trying to squeeze it out of me.

More bad thoughts come crowding in there.

I hate my mother.

I could kill my mother.

I hate God.

I hate everyone.

I hate Dad, Lisa, Mom, Poppy, Grandma, Mrs. Cordesi, Mrs. Sierra, Aunt Katie, Fred MacMurray, Donny Osmond.

Heck, *all* the Osmonds, the whole Osmond family.

And the Jackson Five, too.

I could kill them all.

I'll kill the whole world.

Anything that can make noise, I'll kill it.

I'll kill everything until the world is silent and it's just me and the clouds.

Boiling-hot tears come out of my squeezed-shut eyes.

I don't even know why I'm crying.

I've never had this much hate in me before.

Everything inside me is boiling hot, I can feel the bubbles in my blood, I can feel them in my head.

My head feels like it's going to blow up.

I lie back on Poppy's brick porch and the cold bricks are hard under my head but I don't care. The cold feels good on my back.

I start breathing more like a human again.

My heart goes back to human beats.

For the first time since I got here, I wonder where Poppy and her mom are. Then I remember: Saturday morning, grocery shopping.

I put both my hands on my heart and feel it. I figure if it's beating then I must still be alive.

God didn't kill me.

He should have.

I deserve it.

Oh, the long list of sins that have my name on them.

God must be shaking his head. Wondering what to do with me.

This is when the Cordesis' station wagon drives up.

I sit up. Wave and smile at Poppy and Mrs. Cordesi like I'm just enjoying the sunlight on their front porch.

Poppy runs up with her yellow hair looking gold in the sunlight and her skin all tanned real dark and she looks just like the girl in the Coppertone ad.

I never look like anyone in any ad, even the people with dandruff.

What are you doing here? Poppy says.

Waiting for you, I say. I want you to pierce my ears.

I didn't know I was going to say that.

Liquid fire shoots through my veins and makes my eyes burn but I don't take it back.

Right now? she says.

Right now, I say.

chapter 18

fast forward to me walking home with swollen red ears that remind me with every heartbeat what I've done.

Walking across the street, combing my hair with my hands, combing it down over my ears. With enough oils from your hand, any hair will lie down flat, even mine.

Thank god I've been growing my hair out. Thank god it's long enough. As long as I don't toss my head or turn it fast or lean back or anything like that, my ears won't show.

My earlobes are on fire.

They're giving me a giant throbbing headache which I just bet it's a migraine because Mrs. Cordesi gets migraines and she says it's the worst headache you ever had, times a thousand.

Poppy iced my poor earlobes all afternoon, trying to get the swelling to go down.

I get inside the house and Lisa is setting the table for dinner and I wonder if it was my night to set the table.

Lisa gives me the skinny eyes and sticks her tongue out which means it *was* my night to set and I try to smile but it hurts my ears so I raise my eyebrows instead.

Isn't it my night to set? I say, real sweet like she's the dearest, sweetest, kindest sister in the whole wide world even though just hours ago I wanted to kill her.

Even talking hurts my ears.

Yes, but you weren't around so Dad made me do it so you owe me, she says. You owe me *two* nights.

OK, I say. I smile even though it hurts so bad I want to bend over and puke all over the tweedy green rug in the dining room which is made out of this ropey stuff all knotted together like macramé.

I sit in my chair and Mom comes in with a pot of hot steamy something that smells awful which means it's goulash. Goulash is what we have when there's lots of leftovers. Mom puts all the leftovers in one pot and stirs it all together and calls it goulash or sometimes slumgullion. I don't know where she gets these words. They don't make anything taste better.

Well, at least she cooked dinner.

Which makes me feel better.

Like, I guess I didn't kill her by asking about getting my ears pierced.

I comb my hair down with my hand.

I tell myself to stop combing my hair down or someone will notice.

I comb my hair down on the other side and then I tell myself that's it, no more touching your hair until dinner is over.

This is dinner.

Mom uses her nice voice to talk to Lisa and Dad, but her voice goes all flat when she talks to me and all she says is, Will you pass the salt, please.

I don't talk to anyone or look at anyone, I just choke down my goulash which is meat loaf plus chicken cacciatore plus three-bean salad plus beef-noodle casserole plus some other things you don't want to know.

It's *so* grossamundo.

And my ears hurt so bad I can hardly chew.

chapter 19

mom doesn't find out about my pierced ears.

At least I don't *think* she does.

But five days after I get my ears pierced Mom tries to kill herself.

Which makes you wonder.

chapter 20

they save her at the hospital.

Mom, I mean.

I'm not there when it happens. I'm at Girls' Glee Club which is after school on Thursdays and it happened on a Thursday.

I was also born on a Thursday.

I'm walking home by myself that day, Thursday. Poppy doesn't walk home with me on Thursdays because of Glee Club. I'm feeling my pierced ears with my fingers which they don't hurt as much as they did five days ago, they don't throb anymore, they only hurt if I touch them and I'm always touching them, mostly to remind myself that I really did it.

I have pierced ears.

It's even better than getting your period because it's something you did all on your own.

I decided to pierce my ears and I did it.

I'm thirteen, I can do whatever I want to my body.

I get to the top of our street and this is where I get that funny feeling, where I'm looking down at the ten houses on our street and something is different and Dad's black Chevy is gone.

OK, we've been here before, blah blah blah. You already know I walk into my house and Mrs. Sierra is there and she says *Oh Abby* and her big fat arm hugs me in one of *those* kinds of arm-hugs.

You never know the worst that can happen. You think you do, but you don't. You imagine the worst possible thing, but then what really happens is so much worse.

Where's Mom? I say to Mrs. Sierra. I already know the answer is bad because I can feel it all over my skin like creepy crawlers and anyway why else would Mrs. Sierra be in our house on a Thursday afternoon with no one else around and Dad's black Chevy gone.

Before Mrs. Sierra can say anything, I zip through all the answers in my head, trying to think of the worst possible thing.

Dead.

Hit by a car.

Hung herself in the garage.

Dead.

We don't know.

Dead.

Murdered.

Strangled.

We don't know, she's just gone.

Dead.

Shot.

Hacked in half by a crazed lunatic axe murderer.

Dead.

Carried off to the funny farm.

Ran away with the milkman.

Dead.

Dead.

Dead.

Dead.

Dead.

Mrs. Sierra starts rubbing the back of my head but I back away from her because she's freaking me out. Then she grabs my hand and holds it in both of her hands which are all hot and slimy and I really want to pull my hand out of there but I have to leave it to be polite.

Your mom's in the hospital, says Mrs. Sierra, and a little tear plops out of one eye and turns black with mascara and makes a black skidmark down her cheek. She brushes it away and makes even more skidmarks on her cheek.

I can't figure out why she's crying.

I mean it's not *her* mother.

But then her son Jimmy *is* over in Vietnam getting shot, so maybe that's it, maybe it's all related.

My mouth is full of that dry kind of saliva.

But she's going to be fine, Mrs. Sierra says. She just had a little accident.

She stops and her big pink lips go together into something sort of like a smile but not really.

I pull my hand away from her hot hands and I say, What kind of accident?

My heart stops beating so I can hear the answer.

She moves toward me and puts one hand on my shoulder and I want to scream, Will you *please* stop touching me!

But I don't say it, that would be rude.

Well, she took some pills, honey, says Mrs. Sierra. I think she accidentally took the wrong kind.

Her hand pinches my shoulder and her thumb goes around like a little massage only it's not, it's just her being nervous or something.

Don't get me wrong, I like Mrs. Sierra. Really.

It's just, I don't know.

I just don't want anyone touching me right now.

Because my skin hurts all over.

Because I know the truth.

And the truth is, there are no accidents when your mother slides down the washing machine and animal cries come out of her that make you want to pee your pants.

You saw it.

You were there.

Every time.

The night swim and the broken mirrors and the Spanish trees dress and the Christmas Crock-Pot and the melted galoshes.

You were there.

Lisa was only there some of the time.

Dad was only there some of the time.

You were there every time.

Me, I'm it.

Mrs. Sierra wipes her eyes and cheeks with a balled-up pink Kleenex that she drug out of somewhere on her big self.

Oh Abby, she says. I'm so sorry.

Sorry for what?

I don't say.

All I can hear in my head is, *Jesus Christ, Abby.*

Jesus Christ, Abby.

Jesus Christ, Abby.

the rest of the afternoon my brain doesn't work right.

I'm floating around in these clouds.

Mrs. Sierra gets on the phone to Mrs. Billawalla and tells her it's

OK to send Lisa home. Which is I guess where Dad sent Lisa after he found Mom.

I mean I guess that's what happened.

I don't really know.

And I'm not asking.

Dad is still at the hospital.

Lisa comes home and I'm on the couch pretending to read and Mrs. Sierra is in the kitchen doing the dishes which I guess Mom forgot to do before she killed herself.

I mean, *tried* to kill herself.

Lisa comes and sits right next to me on the couch, her leg touching my leg, but I don't move like I normally would.

I don't know why.

They took Mom to the hospital in an ambulance, Lisa says, her voice all hushy like it's some big secret.

I look at her over my book which I'm not reading.

I know, I say in a normal voice. But she's going to be all right.

I think she was bleeding, Lisa says, hooking her leg all the way over my leg like we used to do when I was a kid. Which I'm a teenager now but I let her do it anyway. I mean, she's still a kid.

I put down my book.

Lisa has information.

Really? You saw her? I say.

Well, no, not really, she says, her leg going back and forth and bumping mine. I saw part of her on the floor in their bedroom and then Dad ran out and grabbed me and we went running down to Annie's house.

Lisa knows nothing.

Her leg starts going harder and harder into my leg.

Abby? she says, her blue eyes looking all watery.

I shake my head and hand Lisa her library book from the banana coffee table.

No questions, I say. We have to wait until Dad gets home. Let's just not worry about anything till Dad gets home, OK?

Lisa takes her book and nods and scoots back on the couch.

Mrs. Sierra cooks dinner but Lisa and I don't hardly eat anything even though it's home-fried chicken with mashed potatoes and corn and which is better than anything Mom ever made.

OK, that's not fair, but anyway.

Just after dinner, Dad comes home.

Dad and Mrs. Sierra talk in low voices out on the front porch.

Me and Lisa are sitting in the living room and we're both on the couch with our feet flat against each other like me and Mom used to do and we're both pretending to read.

But really we're straining our ears to hear what Dad and Mrs. Sierra are saying.

Did you hear that? Lisa hisses at me.

No, what? I hiss back.

Dad just said *a couple months*, she hisses.

A couple months for what? I hiss back.

Shhh! she says.

Her ears are way better than mine.

I can't hear a thing.

But I can see them out the windows.

Mrs. Sierra keeps patting Dad's arm.

Now she's rubbing it.

I don't know why she needs to be so touchy with everybody.

But maybe it's because her son Jimmy is over in Vietnam getting shot. *At.*

Dad is standing there in his usual teacher pose, one arm crossed in front of him and the other one bent at the elbow with his hand cupped under his chin like he needs to hold up his head or it'll roll off.

He nods a lot.

Mrs. Sierra wipes her nose a lot with her pink Kleenex.

Lisa hisses, Dad just said *I think she'll be in there for quite a while.*

In where? I hiss.

Shhh! she says.

Finally Dad comes in.

This part gets all dreamy and cloudy. Everything in slow motion like under water and me not really here.

Like I'm still at the top of the street looking down at the ten houses, nine light-colored houses and our dark brown one.

Wanting to start over.

From the top of the street.

Dad sits down in Mom's green chair and it squeaks as usual.

I have to blink a couple of times to convince myself that it's not Mom sitting there.

It's Dad.

His face is all flat and sagging and grayish and for just a sec he doesn't look like Dad at all, like how clouds can sometimes change so fast.

He clears his throat.

Me and Lisa look at him.

We wait like we're waiting for some kind of answer.

Whatever the question was.

Your mother is going to be away for a little while, Dad says. His voice is all light and soft and it doesn't sound like Dad at all and he is totally creeping me out.

His hands are in a tight knot in front of him, so tight that his wedding ring is sticking up off his ring finger.

How long? Lisa says.

Good old Lisa. Sometimes she has so much more guts than I do.

I don't know yet, Dad says. At least a few weeks.

His hands are knotted together so tight but his face is so flat, even his forehead is all flat.

Things are going to be different around here, he says.

I don't want to hear the rest.

This is all too weirdamundo for me.

I'm checking out.

Dad's voice is saying something else and I can't hear it.

I'm gone.

I don't mean to stop listening, it's just that someone flipped the switch in my brain to OFF.

Dad's lips are moving and his eyes look at me, then Lisa, then me, back and forth like those thingies on a typewriter.

My brain is off and my ears are blocked and all I can hear is a loud hum like a pool motor in the middle of the night.

i'm lying in bed that night.

The moon shines through my window, onto my pink bedspread from Grandma. Of course, Grandma gave Lisa the *blue* bedspread.

The moonlight makes my bedspread look white instead of pink.

I'm waiting for Mom to come home.

Because I don't think she's really gone.

My ear is tuned into the driveway, waiting for a car to drive up with Mom in it.

She's coming.

She has to come.

There are four of us in this family.

One of us can't just go. It's a rule.

I spread out my fingers on my white bedspread in the white moonlight.

My fingers are long and white, just like Mom's.

I start playing an old Bach piece, number fourteen. I had to memorize it for a recital once and I can still play it by heart.

I hear it in my head.

Mom came to that recital and afterwards she said she was so proud of me because I played that Bach like I wrote it myself.

I played it really, really fast.

It's my only talent. I can play everything really, really fast.

I watch my fingers on the bedspread in the moonlight.

They're going so fast and I'm not missing a note.

I get to the repeat and I go back. Play it all again.

I doubt even old Bach could play it this fast.

I play my Bach in the moonlight and I wait for Mom.

chapter 21

om overdosed on Seconal.

That's what Dad said when I asked him what kind of pills they were.

He said, Why do you want to know?

I said, I just want to, that's all.

He stopped raking the grass clippings into a pile and said, It was Seconal.

I just said, Oh.

I mean what else do you say after that.

I was kind of disappointed that he told me. I mean part of me wanted to know, but part of me wanted him to say, You don't need to know that.

Seconal.

I tried to look it up in the dictionary, but it's not there.

Seconal.

It's a hard word with edges like a knife, it can cut up your mouth when you say it. It's like when you first learn the word *fuck*. You carry it around with you like a weapon. Watch out or I'll whip this thing out.

I asked Mrs. Cordesi if she knew what Seconal was and she looked at me funny, like how you look at Mrs. Hutz when she tells you the reason her roses look so good is because she goes out there and pees on them once a week.

Mrs. Cordesi is so cool.

I mean after the funny look, she was very cool.

She said, It's a sleeping pill, honey.

Seconal.

It sounds dirty.

chapter 22

dad hasn't had to cook anything yet because the neighbors keep bringing casseroles.

I'm wondering what's going to happen when the casseroles stop coming because as I far I know, Dad can't cook.

So one night it finally happens.

The freezer is empty and there's no casserole sitting on the stove covered in foil.

Dad opens the fridge, then the freezer, then all the cupboard doors in the kitchen.

There aren't even any TV dinners.

So he takes us to the steak house and Lisa has a hamburger and Dad has a steak and I have a grilled ham sandwich with extra mustard.

The next time there's no casserole Dad opens the freezer and it's full of TV dinners which he must have bought.

He smiles into that freezer like ninety-eight TV dinners just made him the happiest man alive.

I see those ninety-eight TV dinners and I feel like fainting because of what Mom would say, which is that TV dinners aren't good for you and you can't eat TV dinners every night.

I mean TV dinners are supposed to be a *treat*, not a way of life.

So one night we're eating our TV dinners.

Lisa is having the beans and wienies and I'm having my favorite, salisbury steak, which Mom used to say it's just a hamburger and I'd always say nah-uh.

Hey, Dad, I say.

Hm? he says and looks up at me from his turkey dinner, and that's when I see all the lines in his face that weren't there before. Lots of them. Like those blow-up maps of San Francisco. Little crooked lines going everywhere and if you follow them you eventually get to the edge of the map and then where are you.

I know how to cook, I say. I can cook lots of things.

Which is mostly true. I used to help Mom in the kitchen sometimes, I've watched her make casseroles and stuff. I know where her recipes are, in the pink metal recipe box.

Lisa goes, You do not!

I kick her under the table, hard.

Do too, I say.

Ow! she yells, and looks at Dad for sympathy but Dad totally ignores her for once.

Lisa kicks me back but I don't even look at her and I don't kick her back, I just look at Dad who is still chewing his turkey.

Sometimes I can be really mature when I feel like it.

Dad chews and looks at me for a sec and then nods.

OK, he says, talking with his mouth full, which by the way is another rule.

You can cook tomorrow night, he says.

So it's tomorrow night only it's today and I'm in the kitchen going through Mom's recipes and Dad has bought two pounds of ground round because that's what I told him to get because that's what Mom always said to Mr. Marino, the butcher.

Two pounds of ground round, please.

I don't know what ground round is, I just know it's some kind of meat that Mom uses a lot.

I'm looking at this round doughnut of red meat, sitting there on the kitchen counter in the white butcher's paper. The meat looks just like a crown and I wonder how they get it into that shape.

So ground round must be hamburger.

Which is a big shock. I was expecting something more like chicken.

I get out Mom's hamburger recipes. There's a big stack, all written in her bad screamy handwriting which no one can read except her.

I thumb through them, looking for an easy one, one with not too many ingredients and not too many directions.

The meat loaf one looks easy except there's no directions. Just a list of ingredients and then 375 degrees for one hour.

Like you're supposed to know what to do with all those ingredients.

I mean, do you cook the egg first?

Do you cook the hamburger first?

Where do you get bread crumbs?

That kind of thing.

Hamburger-noodle casserole.

No directions.

I'm starting to get a little clench in my stomach.

I tell myself, you know how to do this, you helped Mom a zillion
times.

I'm thumbing through the recipes.

My ears are starting to throb.

Hamburger gravy.

Hamburger gravy!

It has directions.

Brown and drain two pounds hamburger.

I can brown and drain.

Stir in remaining ingredients and heat well.

The other ingredients are flour, paprika, thyme, salt, dried onion,
beef boullion.

Oh yeah.

I know where everything is.

Easy as pumpkin pie.

Not that I know how to make that.

we're sitting down to my first real cooked dinner.

Dad and Lisa sit at their places.

I moved to Mom's chair so I can look out the window now.

I come out with the frying pan full of brown gunk which I hope tastes like hamburger gravy but which I haven't tasted it yet because I was too scared to.

Dad smiles a big wide smile and all those lines on his face get even deeper.

Looks good, Ab! he says.

Lisa looks in the pan and wrinkles up her whole face and says, Grossamundo, what is it?

I knock her silverware onto the floor and smile at her.

Oops, I say.

I spoon some brown gunk onto Lisa's plate.

I'm not eating this, she says, and pushes her plate out into the middle of the table which is when I notice that Mom's little wooden angel with the missing wing is gone and I wonder where it went and I wonder if she took it with her.

No, wait, how could that work? Mom was out cold when they took her away.

I mean I'm guessing she was out cold.

Yes you are too eating this, Dad says to Lisa, and moves her plate back.

I spoon the brown gunk onto Dad's plate, then onto my plate.

We sit down and we all try it together, all three of us at the same time almost like we planned it which we didn't.

It's really, really salty.

It's so salty you can hardly eat it but Dad smiles at me in that way like when he has to listen to Grandpa go on and on about the war.

Good job, Dad says in this real high voice like how he says *How interesting* to Grandpa about the war.

It's too salty, says Lisa. She wrinkles up her nose so hard it's practically in her forehead.

I kick her under the table and she kicks me back.

I keep eating my hamburger gravy which I made all by myself which is so salty I have to drink milk between every bite.

It starts again.

Her voice in my head.

Jesus Christ, Abby.

Jesus Christ, Abby.

Jesus Christ, Abby.

I hum real low to myself to get the voice to stop but maybe I'm humming too loud because Dad gets up and turns on the TV which for once was off I guess in honor of the first dinner I ever made.

Lisa says, Can I be excused? and she pushes her plate away and it's full of the brown gunk which she's hardly eaten any of it and Dad says, Yes you can be excused, but his face is watching the TV.

He's spooning the brown gunk into his mouth and chewing but you can tell he's not thinking about what he's eating, he's watching David Brinkley.

I'm getting the big clench now.

It's the biggest clench I've ever had.

It's turning into something, like maybe diarrhea or maybe vomit, I can't tell which.

I run to the lilac bathroom in the hall, the one with integrity, and shut the door and lock it.

I sit on the toilet while my body decides, diarrhea or vomit.

I sit there a long time and listen to that voice in my head and wait while my stomach and intestines and whatever else churn around like sixteen merry-go-rounds going really fast.

My ears are throbbing like you wouldn't believe.

Jesus Christ, Abby.

Jesus Christ, Abby.

Jesus Christ, Abby.

It's diarrhea.

I wonder if I'm really sick or if it's the hamburger gravy or what.

Dad knocks on the door.

You OK in there? he says. God, he sounds so *concerned.*

I'm OK, I say. I try to sound normal even though my insides feel like a tornado.

For some reason I start wondering how Dad's voice sounded that day, the day he found Mom lying almost dead on the green shag.

I mean I'm guessing he found her lying on the green shag.

I don't really know.

But just how did it all go?

Like this, maybe—

The door to their bedroom is closed but Dad goes in anyway, into the room with the green shag and there's Mom lying on the green shag, not on the bed where a person would normally be lying, and her arms are all spread out on the green shag and her head is all crooked and her eyes are closed and her knees are pointing the wrong way and what is the first thing he does?

I can't think of what it would be, so I stop there and go back to the beginning.

Him walking in.

There she is.

The green shag.

Her eyes closed.

There's something wrong, he knows it immediately, who wouldn't.

I play this little scene over and over while I'm sitting there poop-ing out my entire insides. Just when I think it's over, more poop comes out and I'm afraid next it'll be my intestines and then my liver and stomach and kidneys and lungs and heart.

I close my eyes and make the little scene start again.

Mom lying there on the green shag.

She's cold.

Her eyes are closed.

Her mouth is open.

I make it keep going.

There's an open bottle on her nightstand, a pill bottle. It's open and lying on its side. The white cap is on the floor. There's a glass half full of water on the nightstand and Mom's red lipstick is on it, a perfect print of her lower lip. Mom is lying on the green shag with her flaky white feet sticking out where they shouldn't stick out and maybe that's what you see first when you go into the room, her flaky white feet on the green shag.

You see those white feet which are so still and your fingers go all icy because you already know.

Then you see the rest of her lying there with elbows and knees and hands and feet sticking out all over the green shag looking like she is not supposed to look, not like a person just laid down but like they fell from somewhere and every bone in their body is broken.

You stand there, looking.

Your brain turns to liquid and drains down to your feet.

Maybe your own mouth is open, just like hers, only hers is open crooked and her tongue is coming out of her mouth just a little and it looks thick and heavy and maybe it's the wrong color, blue or green or white.

You stand there.

You can't do anything.

You stand there looking down at her flaky white feet and her closed eyes and her open mouth and you don't remember to check whether she's breathing or not.

You stand there.

You stand there for a zillion years and you don't move and you don't even scream because your brain is no longer in your head.

You know you should move.

You know if you don't move she could die.

Your tongue swells up and sticks to the roof of your mouth.

You stare at her closed eyes.

You stare at her knees which are all wrong, knees don't go like that.

All you can think is, *Close your mouth before you get flies in there.*

Which is what she used to say.

Finally you shake yourself and run to the phone, you call the operator but your tongue is too thick to make words and your throat is closing up and the operator sounds like she's in Laos and they will never get here in time.

And then you wait.

You kneel beside the body on the green shag and only now do you think to check her breathing, check her heartbeat. Your hand between her breasts. You think you feel something but maybe it's your own heartbeat in your own hand.

Maybe by now you are screaming.

Shirley, Shirley, oh my god, Shirley!

chapter 23

it's june and Mom has been gone for two months. We haven't gotten to see her yet. We can't even talk to her on the phone because she's not strong enough which makes no sense to me, I mean how strong do you have to be to pick up a phone.

It's Saturday and Dad took Lisa with him to get the car washed and get a haircut over in San Jose and he said, Do you want to go too and I said no.

So here I am alone.

I wander into Mom and Dad's bedroom because I'm just bored and I haven't been in here alone since it happened.

I look on Mom's nightstand but there's no empty pill bottle, no half-full glass of water. I check the carpet, but there's no indent of a body in the green shag. Someone has vacuumed in here, there are vacuum stripes all over. Probably Mrs. Lee, the Chinese lady Dad hired to clean the house on Wednesdays when we're at school.

I wander into Mom and Dad's bathroom.

I know why I'm in here and it's crazy and I don't care.

I open the medicine cabinet.

There are lots of bottles of pills. They all have Mom's name on them.

Shirley Goodman, take one at night.

Shirley Goodman, take one every four hours.

Shirley Goodman, take as needed.

There are lots of those, take as needed.

Of course I'm looking for Seconal.

There's no Seconal in the cabinet so I open a drawer.

Bobby pins and makeup and hand lotion and that stinky pink stuff Mom puts on her hair after she washes it, which it comes in a toothpaste tube and I certainly wouldn't put anything on *my* hair that comes in a toothpaste tube.

I try the other drawer. More pill bottles.

The drawer won't open all the way so I cram my hand all the way to the back.

Bring up three more bottles.

One says Seconal.

I look at myself in the mirror.

I see a thirteen-year-old girl with very frizzy brown hair wearing gold hoop earrings and a dark yellow poor-boy shirt.

The bottle says, Shirley Goodman, take as needed.

The frizzy-haired girl opens the bottle.

There are three red pills at the bottom of the bottle. They are touching each other like ring-around-the-rosy which if you don't know is a song about the plague.

My little sparrow heart starts beating fast.

I pour the three red pills into my hand.

I mean the frizzy-haired girl in the mirror does.

She looks at them in her hand and they seem so small.

The bottle says there were thirty pills so I wonder if Mom took twenty-seven pills that day.

Twenty-seven seems like a lot.

Enough to kill somebody.

I look at the frizzy-haired girl in the mirror. Her hair is parted down the middle and her hair goes out around her head in a frizzy ball, except for the two front pieces tucked behind her ears.

The three pills are really, really red.

It never occurred to me they'd be red. I figured white, white like aspirin. White like maybe, just maybe, it could have been a mistake, Mom thought she was taking aspirin.

But red.

Red and there's no mistake.

When you have red pills in your hand, you know it.

And *twenty-seven* red pills, well.

This was no accident.

No fucking way.

You put twenty-seven red Seconals in your hand and there's only one word for it.

Suicide.

That's what those pills scream.

Suicide, suicide, suicide.

I look at the frizzy-haired girl in the mirror and I see Mom's green eyes looking back at me.

People are always saying, Oh you must be Shirley's daughter, you look just like her.

Which I used to like that when I was little.

Now I hate it.

I look at my face and I see Mom's face.

Same bumpy nose, same big lips, same big straight teeth that never need braces, same giant forehead that goes up forever, same frizzy hair only Mom's is black and short. The same face except I have freckles and brown hair.

The frizzy-haired girl drops the red pills back into the brown pill bottle.

All except one.

One in the middle of my palm, one red, red Seconal like a drop of blood.

The frizzy-haired girl fills the yellow glass with water.

I watch in the mirror as one hand goes up to her mouth.

My mouth.

The red pill goes in.

And she drinks.

Swallows.

I feel the red monster sliding down my throat.

It feels huge, like I'm swallowing a tennis ball.

I feel it in my stomach.

I wonder if it's too late to throw up.

But I could never make myself throw up on purpose. That whole finger-down-the-throat thing never worked for me.

I wonder what next.

Do I lie on the floor or what.

I look in the mirror and I see Mom's green eyes.

Scared.

Jesus Christ, Abby.

Jesus fucking Christ.

You are out of your fucking mind.

chapter 24

So what happens with Seconal is you just sleep.

I stand there awhile in Mom and Dad's bathroom and watch myself in the mirror but nothing happens so I go upstairs and lie on my bed. That's the last thing I remember until I open my eyes and all my windows are dark but someone has turned on the lamp on my dresser and there's Lisa standing at the foot of my bed looking like some little junior angel with her white-blond hair all lit up by the lamp.

Get out of here, I say.

Or try to.

My tongue feels three feet wide and I wonder if any real words came out.

I kick at her with my bare foot but I don't make contact, she's too far away.

How come you're asleep? she says. Dad said not to wake you up, he said to let you sleep.

What Seconal does to your brain is it makes it into hamburger gravy.

Get out! I yell and kick at her again.

My kicking foot feels like it's in Cambodia, like it's not even connected to my body.

Lisa backs toward the door and stares at me hard with her little thumbtack eyes.

Like she knows.

I swear Lisa has ESP, you wouldn't believe how many times she has actually read my mind and been right.

Lisa plants herself right outside my doorway like she's not going to leave so I get up and shut the door.

OK, maybe I slam it.

Which is a huge rule but anyway.

I look at myself in the mirror over my dresser and I look the same except my hair is flat on one side.

Shirley Goodman's daughter.

The drug addict.

My eyes have raccoon circles around them but maybe it's the weirdamundo angle of the light.

So this is what Mom felt like when she woke up in the hospital.

Well, twenty-seven times this.

A head full of hamburger gravy and a tongue like a water balloon.

I stick out my tongue but it looks the same, it's not bigger or anything.

I lie on my bed again and I try to remember what it felt like.

But there was nothing to feel.

You just go to sleep.

There has to be more.

All I can figure is, twenty-seven Seconals must be a whole lot different from one Seconal.

You take twenty-seven Seconals and you lie down on your bumpy white bedspread to die.

You lie down and you close your eyes and where are you.

That's the thing I can't get, where are you.

And what made her take twenty-seven Seconals in the first place is what I really don't get.

I mean how do you even get there.

What makes you go into the bathroom and take twenty-seven Seconals.

Do you plan it or does it just happen or what.

This is what I don't get.

chapter 25

t's july and Mom's been gone for three months and we still haven't been allowed to visit her or even talk to her on the phone.

She's not strong enough.

I imagine Mom as one of those heroines in a romance novel, dying of some mysterious disease which always just sounds like the flu to me but then they die of it.

She lies there in an enormous fluffy white bed with gold pillows and filmy pink curtains all around and her face is white and her lips are red and her black hair flows down in two wavy rivers over her breasts and she is too weak to talk or even lift an arm and she has to say everything to the nurses and doctors with her eyes.

Her green eyes.

the weirdamundo thing is, I'm already used to her being gone. I mean it feels like she's been gone years and years.

And here's the really bad part.

I'm starting to think, if she doesn't come back, that's OK.

Which makes me totally awful and sinful but I don't care.

I am the evil daughter of Satan.

But I mean we're fine, the three of us.

I've learned how to make five dinners and Dad remembered that he knows how to cook an omelet so we're fine.

And we can both make hamburgers.

And Dad knows how to broil steak in the broiler.

And Mrs. Sierra showed Dad how to roast a roast.

So we're fine.

About the only thing I miss is Mom's sweet-and-sour chicken which has about eighty zillion ingredients, and maybe her Mexican chef salad with the tortilla chips and thousand-island dressing and which I tried to make it once but the chips got all soggy. And, OK, maybe her chicken 'n' cornflakes which is way too complicated for me to make plus we never have cornflakes in the house anymore and which I'm pretty sure it wouldn't taste the same if I used Sugar Pops.

But that's it.

The list of what I miss is a lot shorter than the list of what I don't miss.

Which makes me feel really weirdamundo because I mean you're *supposed* to miss your own mother.

I mean what is *wrong* with me.

I've even tried to miss her and it doesn't work.

I try to think of the good times, like going to the boardwalk in Santa Cruz to ride the roller coaster or camping in Big Basin or walking along Sunset Beach looking for periwinkles and agates, but nothing happens.

I don't get sad or anything.

I just feel like nothing, like I'm just a plain brown paper bag with nothing inside it.

chapter 26

One day dad says we can write to Mom if we want. He says she'll write back.

So I guess she's strong enough to pick up a pen.

It's Saturday and I'm sitting at my homemade desk which Dad made which looks really crummy but it has a zillion shelves and drawers and places to put things and which I have a *lot* of stuff so it's a good desk for me, I just wish it didn't look so crummy.

I get out my Snoopy stationery and I start with *Dear Mom.*

Comma.

I suck on my Bic pen and look out the window above my desk which would look down on the Sierras' house except our roof is in the way but you can see across the creek where all the blackberries are and there's a few date palms behind the blackberries which the sun always comes up right behind those date palms and turns them pink in the morning and which a date palm is different from a regular palm, they're a lot shorter. The date palms I mean.

Dear Mom, school is finally over and summer is here.

It's like I'm writing to Grandma.

I have a stack of books from the library and I'm now reading Blue Tomatoes on Mars. *It's pretty funny.*

The part I don't say is when I went to the library by myself it felt funny. I was over in the young adult section and I kept waiting for Mom to come over with her arm full of plastic-covered books and tell me it was time to go.

Come on, honey, we don't have all day. Just pick a few and let's go.

Sometimes she'd have a few books from the adult section that were for both of us to read.

I also don't say that Mrs. Kenney, the librarian, looked at me with big sad eyes when I was checking out and she put her wrinkled gray hand on top of my hand and said, I'm so sorry to hear about your mother, Abby. How's she doing?

Fine, I said with a fake smile that stretched from here to Kansas.

She's coming home soon, I said. Which was a total lie.

I also don't say that when Mrs. Kenney was done clicking the book cards into the clicker to check them out, she put her skinny fingers all the way around my wrist and said, If you need anything, honey, you call me here at the library, OK?

Like I'm gonna call that gnarly-faced old hag.

I also don't say that when I finished reading two of those books and had to return them, I just dropped them into the outside return slot instead of going inside like I always used to. And I didn't look in the windows when I did it, I just shoved the books through the slot and ran.

I also don't say that now I only go to the library on Tuesdays, which is the only day Mrs. Kenney isn't there.

I ball up the piece of Snoopy stationery and throw it at my wastebasket but I miss.

I think about what I really want to write.

Dear Mom,

I don't really miss you. I thought I would but I don't. Lisa misses you and Dad misses you but I don't. I am the most terrible daughter in the universe but I don't care. I'm just glad I don't have to come home to you lying down anymore. I'm glad I don't have to remind you to get up and make dinner. I'm glad I don't have to get cold washcloths for you and tiptoe around after school and clean up broken mirrors and scare you out of pools in the middle of the night. We don't have any rules anymore and I like it a lot better this way. I don't have to wear my galoshes anymore and I don't have to brush my teeth and I can leave my dirty clothes all over my room and never make my bed and hit Lisa and call her names like she deserves when she is being a creepamundo and I don't have to practice the piano if I don't want to and I can stay up as late as I want reading and I don't have to eat goulash or that terrible thing you call Cheese Bake Surprise.

I am not going to write Mom a letter.

Let Lisa write her.

chapter 27

t's a hot Saturday afternoon in August and I'm taking up the whole couch and reading yet another Grace Livingston Hill romance which I've read like fifty of them so far. Mom reads them too, and we always flip a coin to see who gets to read the new one first.

Of course now I always get to read the new one first.

Some Saturdays Mom and me would sit on the couch and read all afternoon. I'd be at one end and she'd be at the other and sometimes I'd stack my legs on top of hers.

So this Saturday Dad comes in and he's holding his old faded blue shorts by the elastic which is coming out.

Do you know where your mother keeps the thread? he says.

There is something about his shoulders, how they follow the same line as the shorts drooping from his finger and which the shorts are all frayed at the bottom and I don't know why he doesn't just get a new pair.

His eyes are the same faded blue as the shorts and the skin on his face is all stretched out like the elastic.

My dad used to look so good.

I sit up and take the shorts from him. The fabric is real thin from being washed too many times.

I'll fix 'em, Dad, I say.

He smiles all the way around himself.

Will you, Ab? Thanks, honey! he says.

He walks out of the room straighter than he's been in a long time.

Geez, and all because of some lousy old shorts.

What I should really do is run down to Whitlow's and buy him a new pair, but I know how Dad is about spending money, especially when you already have an old, thin, falling-apart pair you could wear.

Mom's sewing machine is in the corner of their big bedroom.

Which is another reason why they added on the new big bedroom, Mom said she needed a dedicated sewing space and how much money we could save if she had a place to sew.

She moved her sewing machine to the corner of their big new bedroom and there it sat.

No fine new clothes came out of it, ever.

I sit in Mom's sewing chair and uncover the sewing machine.

Yes, I can sew. I had Home Ec. All seventh-grade girls know how to sew an A-line skirt and make banana muffins.

The boys take wood shop from Mr. Grimes who is missing two fingers, one on each hand, and you just have to wonder.

I know how to work Mom's sewing machine, she showed me.

I haven't done elastic before, but how hard could it be.

I tuck the elastic into the waistband, put the edge of the waistband under the needle, let the presser foot down, roll the needle down into the material, pull everything out tight.

Wait a minute.

I need three hands. Two for pulling, one for feeding.

If I let go on one place, it will all go crooked.

I try it anyway.

Yep, crooked.

I hold the front part of the shorts in my teeth and press on the foot pedal.

Still crooked.

I'm getting a little clench in my stomach.

I put the heavy thread holder on the back part of the shorts to keep it tight and try again.

Still crooked.

The clench gets tighter and my earlobes are starting to throb.

I want you to run down to the end of the street and back, Mom would say right now. That's what she'd say whenever I got frustrated at something.

I'd be mad but she'd make me go and it always worked.

I tell myself to run down to the end of the street and back, but I don't obey.

I hit the foot pedal hard, press it all the way to the floor.

The needle bobs up and down a zillion miles an hour and the thread sews itself all over the blue shorts in a crooked white line.

I rip the shorts out from under the needle and the needle breaks and half of it stays in the shorts and I throw those stupid shorts into the wall as hard as I can. They hit the wall and slide to the green shag in a little faded blue heap.

This is the part where I *really* should have run down to the end of the street and back.

Red-hot tears are sliding out my eyes and down my cheeks in red-hot stripes.

I pick up the thread holder full of thread and heave it into the wall.

It makes a black mark on the wall, not to mention a really loud *thunk* which I wonder if Dad heard it but he's outside probably burning something in his beloved incinerator which is where he should have thrown his fucking old shorts in the first place.

Some of the spools of thread come off their nails and land in little spots of color all over the green shag.

There's a hot-coal glow you could roast marshmallows on right behind my eyes and I pick up the pile of clothes to be mended from behind the sewing machine and I heave the whole pile into the wall.

If you were there you would've heard this gagging crying coming from the frizzy-haired girl.

You would've seen tears all over her red screwed-up face and snot running from her nose and drool coming out her mouth and what a mess.

I pick up the metal can with the needles and hooks and eyes and snaps and buttons and I heave it into the wall where it makes another black mark and now I just have all kinds of black marks to my name, Abby Goodman, a zillion black marks you go to hell.

If I could throw the sewing machine I would but it's bolted to the table.

I throw the box of patterns and the pincushion and the pile of fabric scraps and the half-glasses Mom uses to thread needles and the little clock and the plastic box of pins which opens up and sprays silver pins everywhere and pretty soon everything that's not bolted to the table I've thrown into the wall and there are little black marks all over the green wall not to mention little white spots where the green paint has come off and a heap of everything that is Mom's sewing stuff is there on the floor.

And two seared rivers down my two cheeks and the big clench in my stomach.

Mom would say you go to your room right now, young lady.

Oh but first she'd say you clean up that mess right now, young lady.

I listen for her hard steps pounding through the kitchen which means you're in trouble, I listen for Dad's hard steps, anybody's hard steps, anyone coming in here to say something-something in a loud voice, young lady, pointing a finger at me, at the pile, at my room, right now, young lady.

This house is so quiet, so stuffed with cotton, stuffed with daughters who aren't daughters anymore, sisters who aren't sisters, dads who aren't dads, husbands who aren't husbands.

This is the worst house anyone could possibly live in.

The quiet in this house will eat you alive.

I sit in the sewing chair and I lay my head on my arms and I choke on my own tears and just let everything come out of me, drool and tears and snot, I don't care.

Inside my head two voices are screaming, Mom's voice and my voice, it's all your fault, no it's yours, no it's yours, you fat toad face, you dirty slimy goat face, you rotten maggot booger butt face.

I call my mother all these things, I scream them, I'm screaming the worst I can scream, big bloody screams in my head that come right from the big clench in my stomach.

If you were there you'd only hear sobbing that sounds like choking that sounds like sobbing.

But there's no one to hear any of this.

Dad's outside, Lisa is, I don't know, I don't care.

I'm all alone in this house of cotton stuffing and for the first time in four months I think, *there is someone missing.*

I scream in my head, *There is someone missing!*

I'm all alone in the wall-to-wall cotton and I'm screaming and there is no one to hear because the someone who is supposed to hear it is missing.

That someone is in some white hospital bed somewhere eating yellow chicken broth and yellow Jell-O and yellow apple juice, which is what they gave me when I had my tonsils out, the yellow dinner.

She's there and I have to be here.

In this goddamn silent house.

I lift my head and look outside and it looks hot outside already even though it's morning which you can always tell by how bright the sunlight is on our white patio and what color of blue the sky is and how nothing moves anywhere at all and how the leaves on the pyracantha are already curled down, away from the hot sun.

It's gonna be a scorcher, Mom would say on a morning like this.

I can barely see Dad's head over the back fence and sure enough he's burning something in his beloved incinerator. Light gray smoke rises above his head, above the fence, goes up into the big leaning oak tree, goes up into the even taller pine trees, the tallest thing around, our three pine trees which there used to be four, but one got the red spider so they had to cut it down.

Something about Dad and his stupid incinerator and all that stupid gray smoke makes me feel better.

It's just a normal Saturday.

Dad is burning as usual, probably a pile of foxtails he raked off the slope.

I don't have to do this.

I can go back to my long-necked heroine with the evil boss and the dying mother and the no-good rotter of a brother.

I clear my throat and blow my nose on a scrap of fabric on the floor.

It's a piece from one of Mom's old dresses, red with black ballerinas all over it.

I put it over my nose and breathe in real deep and I swear I can smell her Chanel No. 5.

chapter 28

finally, school has started.

Finally, things are back to normal.

Well, Mom's not back, but normal without her I mean.

It's a new normal. It's the normal that would've happened if, like, Mom had never been born but everyone else had, including me and Lisa.

Poppy and I are walking to school and I don't even care if she brings up Mom.

So she does.

It's enough to make you believe in ESP, which I totally do.

I know why your mom tried to kill herself, Poppy says.

She flings her hair back once on each side. Her hair swings and her new fringed purse swings and the fringe on her leather jacket swings.

I stop and look at her. She stops, too, swinging all over.

Huh? I say.

Like I didn't hear her which I totally did, I just can't believe she said that.

I know why your mom tried to kill herself, says Poppy. She flings her hair again, once on each side.

Why? I say because I don't know what else to say. It's so weirda-mundo to hear someone say the words *kill herself* out loud like they're real words. Those words that no one else will say out loud and you don't even say them to yourself.

Accident, everyone says.

I look down at my shoes because I can't look at Poppy, I don't know why. The bottoms of Poppy's bell-bottom jeans are all frayed from dragging on the ground. Mom hemmed all my bell bottoms so short I have to slide them way down on my hips so they'll drag on the ground like they're supposed to.

Because of the muse, Poppy says.

The *what*? I say. I look at her all crazy because what she just said was crazy.

The muse, she says. It's the same reason Jimi Hendrix and Janis Joplin killed themselves. The muse was too strong in them.

Poppy stands there looking at me, like she's waiting for something like applause.

All these holes have opened up inside me.

All the holes are bleeding.

I give Poppy a fuck-you look and I grab my binder real tight in front of me and I start walking real fast, leaving her behind me.

Hey! she yells, running to catch up.

I didn't mean anything by it, she says.

I keep my head down, I pretend she's not there. Which never works with Poppy. She's one of those people which you can't pretend she's not there.

Ab, it's a *good* thing, Poppy says.

The muse, she says, it's the thing that makes people do music and art and stuff like that.

I look straight ahead and I grab my binder even tighter and walk even faster. My feet are starting to ache but I don't care.

Because the thing is, there is nothing good about suicide.

I mean attempted suicide.

I mean accident.

Poppy puts her hand on my arm and I shrug it off.

Sorry, Ab, Poppy says. I was just trying to make you feel better.

I look straight ahead and I keep walking real fast.

I have to bite my teeth down hard to keep from crying.

I don't even know why I want to cry.

Poppy's walking just as fast beside me, and I can see her looking at me out the corner of my eye. All *concerned*.

You can't make this into a good thing, I mumble at her through my tight teeth, still looking straight ahead.

What? says Poppy.

I stop suddenly and look right at her and my eyes go all skinny, all by themselves.

Poppy stops too, everything on her still swinging like crazy.

You can't make this into a good thing! I yell right in her face.

Poppy just stands there, blinking and swinging.

I wasn't trying to, Ab, she says real quiet.

We stand there and stare at each other.

There's a big clench in my throat but I refuse to cry. I swallow over and over to make it go away.

A little breeze starts up, which blows Poppy's hair into her face but she doesn't fling it back.

I don't even know why I'm so mad.

It's just, there's so many things I want to tell Poppy but I don't know how to say them.

I hate that you can feel things but there's no words for them. There should be a rule about that, that you can only have feelings if there's words to match.

All I know is, I say real low, there's nothing good about your mother taking twenty-seven Seconals, OK? If it was your mother, you'd get it, but it's not, so you can't. And anyway, there's no such thing as a muse, you just made that up.

I start walking again, fast.

Poppy doesn't catch up with me.

I don't know where she is because I can't look back.

chapter 29

One night dad comes into my room when I'm reading in bed and he stands at the foot of my bed with all those map lines all over his face. I put my book on my chest and I try to smile at him but it feels crooked on my face and it reminds me that maybe I haven't been smiling too much lately but so what. I mean you don't have to smile all the time to be happy.

Dad looks at me, all *concerned*, with that fence between his eyebrows, and grabs my foot through the blankets like he used to do all the time when I was little, he'd grab my foot and tickle it through the blankets. Only he's not tickling it, he's just holding on to it for some dumb reason.

Ab, he says, pinching my foot, are you OK? You've been kind of quiet lately.

Pinch pinch pinch.

I bet he doesn't even know he's doing it.

I try harder with the smile, I stretch it way out, it's sixty-eight miles long.

I'm fine, Dad, I say in this real perky cheerleader voice which I don't know where *that* came from.

He gives me that parent stare, the one where they're trying to psych you into confessing something. Mom does it, too. She's really good at it.

I roll my eyes at him.

Dad, I say. I'm *fine*.

I give him the big I'm-not-lying eyes.

Even though it probably is a lie.

But maybe not.

I don't know.

I just don't know anything anymore.

I mean the weirdamundo thing is, it's like everyone wants me to be *not* fine. It's like they want me to be all sad and crying and sorry and looking all the time like my dog just got flattened by a big Buick up on Highway 9.

Dad stands there still gripping my foot through the blankets and he's gripping so hard now that my toenails are digging into my toes, and he's still staring at me with the fence going between his eyebrows and the map lines all deep in his cheeks and chin and forehead and if he doesn't stop soon I'm going to scream and strangle him and run away to Kansas.

I don't know why Kansas, but it's far away from California.

God, all this *concern*. Which is so wasted on me. I mean, why isn't he concerned about Lisa? Why doesn't he go pinch *her* foot through *her* blankets?

I'm biting the inside of my cheek so I don't explode.

That fence between Dad's eyebrows goes deeper.

OK, Dad says. He smiles this tight, sideways smile at me and all the map lines on his face go even deeper which reminds me that Dad hasn't been smiling too much lately, either.

But so what.

We're all *very fine*.

Dad lets go of my foot and heads toward the door but then he turns around.

Ab, he says, you'd tell me if something was bothering you, right?

He says this with the most pitiful look on his face, like he gets sometimes when I've picked on Lisa one too many times and he can't deal with me anymore and he's just tired of the whole thing.

Which I hate that look. It makes me feel like I crossed some line which I didn't even know it was there.

Yeah, Dad, I say. I would.

It's a total lie but who's gonna know.

Just then something makes me sneeze. It's just a normal, every-day sneeze.

Dad's beside me in two steps and whips out his white handker-chief from his back pocket. I wave it away. It was just an air sneeze, not a snot sneeze.

Dad's looking so concerned his eyebrows are almost covering his eyes.

Are you catching a cold? he says.

I roll my eyes at him.

Here's a big difference between moms and dads: moms know the difference between an everyday sneeze and a getting-a-cold sneeze.

No, I say. Just got something up my nose.

He stands there with his white handkerchief dangling from his hand. His bloodshot blue eyes are going all over my face like he lost something in there.

Dad, I say, and for just a sec my voice sounds like Mom's no-nonsense-young-lady voice.

I'm *reading*, I say in Mom's voice.

I lift up my book.

This conversation is over.

Dad folds his handkerchief into a perfect little square and tucks it into his back pocket and heads once again to the door.

Good night, honey, he says.

He sounds so sad it makes my heart lurch, but just for a sec.

'Night, Dad, I say.

And I kiss the air in front of me, in Dad's direction.

Which I've never done that before.

Weirdamundo.

chapter 30

One day everything changes because Dad says we can call Mom this weekend if we want.

If we want.

Like we wouldn't want.

He says this over Thursday night beef stroganoff.

We have beef stroganoff every Thursday.

Dad knows how to make it now. Mrs. Sierra showed him.

This week it's over rice.

Last week it was over noodles.

Dad switches back and forth, every other week. Rice, noodles, rice, noodles. I keep waiting for him to make a mistake but he never does.

Lisa says, Can we go see her?

Lisa doesn't get the whole thing about steps, how you have to take things in steps.

Dad says, Not quite yet, but pretty soon we'll go for a visit.

He says this and I swear his face looks like he hopes that day will never come.

His eyes now have the map lines, too—in red.

so we call Mom.

It's a cold Saturday morning in October and there are red and orange leaves from the liquid amber tree all over the patio.

It's raining, which it's not true that it never rains in California even though I love that song.

Lisa stands by the hallway door which we never close and she plays with the door handle, turning it one way and then the other, making a jingly sound which is driving me crazy and if she doesn't stop in about four seconds I'm going to kick her even if Dad is standing right there.

I'm sitting on the phone stool and wrapping the curly black phone cord around my fingers, so tight it makes my fingertips turn white.

Dad puts on his big black glasses and dials the number of the hospital which is written in his perfect teacher handwriting on a little piece of paper. Dad's handwriting is just like how he walks, every letter neat and perfect and in a straight line with the other letters. And, like, the total opposite of Mom's itchy-scratchy handwriting that looks like someone writing with long dirty fingernails in their own blood, like a letter from a Vietnam POW or something.

Dad finishes dialing and clears his throat about seven times which is what he does when he's nervous and which Mom does too but I think Dad started doing it first and which anyway Mom does it different, with her mouth open. Dad holds the bottom of the phone receiver way out from his mouth but the ear part pressed tight into his ear. He knows he has a real loud voice, he can't help it, it's because he's a teacher and has to yell at kids all day.

Dad asks for Shirley Goodman.

Yes, a patient, he says.

We all wait.

Lisa jingles the door knob and I wrap the phone cord around my fingers and Dad stares at the calendar that Mom pinned up above the phone which has all the presidents on it including President Nixon which Dad says President Nixon is a class-A rat.

Dad voted for Hubert Humphrey in '68. Mom voted for Nixon. We wait.

Shirley Goodman, please come to the phone.

We're waiting, Shirley Goodman.

My stomach is beating with my heartbeat.

I unwrap the phone cord from my hands and there are red stripes all up and down my white fingers, they look like straight candy canes.

I rehearse in my head.

Hi Mom, I'm fine, we're all fine, we miss you, come home soon, we love you.

I've been practicing lying all week.

I've never been a very good liar. Mom can always hear that I'm lying after I say about two words.

Dad's voice explodes into the room.

Hi, honey, he says.

His voice is about sixteen octaves too high and loud as a train.

Like Mom is deaf, not crazy.

Lisa and I look at each other and those sister things that aren't words zing back and forth between us.

Yes, we're all here, Dad says, Abby and Lisa are here, too.

His high voice is scaring the blood right out of me.

I feel like I might fall off the stool so I hold on with both hands.

Dad clears his throat again and stares at the calendar of presidents like he's reading it which maybe he is.

Uh-huh, he says. Well sure, that sounds great, honey.

What sounds great? That they had the chicken and Jell-O dinner again last night at the crazy hospital?

We're not supposed to say crazy hospital. We're supposed to say mental hospital or psychiatric hospital or else just hospital.

And we're not supposed to say Mom is crazy.

This is what Dad said the last time we had spaghetti which is one of the five dinners I know how to make, the other four of which are chicken-and-rice casserole, bean bake, porcupine meatballs, and sloppy joes, and which you'll notice hamburger gravy is not on the list because I'm too scared to ever try it again.

She's not crazy, she's sick, Dad said over spaghetti.

All I could think was, if twenty-seven Seconals isn't crazy, what is?

Yes, Dad says into the phone. Yes, uh-huh, OK.

I can't stand this waiting and I need to pee bad but I can't leave.

Lisa is wrapping the curly phone cord around her neck. Dad tries to twist it away from her but she holds on to it and keeps twisting.

I rehearse some more.

Hi Mom, I've been practicing piano like crazy and Mrs. Lincoln said I'm ready to move up a level.

OK, Mrs. Lincoln said *maybe* I could move up a level *next year*, but technically it's not a lie.

And, OK, *practicing like crazy* is kind of a lie. OK, a huge, enormous lie, I've hardly been practicing at all.

And, oh yeah, maybe I shouldn't say *crazy*.

This is too hard.

Well here's Abby, Dad says.

And here comes the black phone receiver, looking huge and heavy and like it might just swallow me which at this moment doesn't sound so bad.

I'm not ready for this.

I stop breathing and my back does this twisty thing and I almost fall off the stool.

I take the receiver and it's hot and slimy from Dad's hand. I hold it between my thumb and finger and screw up my face at Dad and whisper, Ewwww. He immediately whips out his white handkerchief from his back pocket and wipes the sweat off the receiver. Then he hands it back to me and gives me this kind of fake-o smile and starts nodding up and down like crazy.

This all happens in like two seconds.

Oh god.

Yesterday I was looking forward to this.

The big clench is going crazy in my stomach.

Hi Mom, I say. My voice is about ninety octaves too high.

Hi honey, she says.

It's her.

It's Mom.

But there's something wrong with her voice.

It's too tight, like a rubber band stretched all the way out.

How have you been, honey? she says.

I have to remind myself: that's Mom there, on the other end. My mom.

I look at the calendar of presidents and I start reading it but not out loud. Grover Cleveland, 1885 to 1889.

Fine, I say into the phone.

My voice is this little squeak.

How have you been? I squeak out. I don't know where these words are coming from because my head is totally empty except for Grover Cleveland, 1885 to 1889.

This is all real dreamy, like maybe I'm asleep.

Dad unwraps the cord from Lisa's neck and she lets him. Then she leans over the phone dial and puts her finger in each hole and then out again, all the way around.

Mom is saying things to me and I can't make out a word, it's like she's talking Vietnamese or something.

There's this hum going in my ears.

Dad goes over and sits down at the dining room table in his chair and crosses his legs like a lady and knits his fingers around his knee like he always does when he's nervous.

Abby? Mom says. Are you there?

She's talking English again.

I'm here, I say.

Oh, thought I'd lost the connection, she says, these phones these days.

When are you coming home? I say. Which makes Dad spring up from his chair and charge toward me in about two steps, shaking his head all wildly, no no no!

Oops, I forgot. That question's off-limits.

I don't know, Mom says. Pretty soon, I hope.

Her voice didn't even change, still rubber-band tight.

How's school? she says.

I was prepared for this question.

I rattle on for like an hour, going on and on about every school thing I can think of.

Mom just goes uh-huh and oh how nice.

I keep talking because I don't want her to talk.

I don't want to hear that rubber-band voice, it makes my stomach clench even more.

And I don't want her to ask me something I can't answer, something like Do you miss me or Do you love me.

Finally I'm out of breath and out of things to say so I hand the phone to Lisa, who has been drawing with a pencil around every president's picture, outlining each one in silvery lead and Dad didn't even yell at her to stop.

He probably didn't even notice but when Mom comes back I bet that's the first thing she notices and she'll know who did it, too.

That night I dream I'm in deep water and I'm treading water just fine but then my arms come off and start floating away from me and I have to kick real hard to keep my head above water. Then my legs get tired and I can't kick hard enough and my head goes underwater and I try to use my arms, but I can't because they're gone. When I finally get my head above water again, there are my arms, floating farther and farther away from me.

chapter 31

We call mom every week now. Every Saturday morning.

Dad's voice gets lower every week and so does mine.

Mom's voice still sounds like a pulled-out rubber band, but I'm getting used to it. I tell myself, it's the new Mom. I tell myself, things are bound to change after you swallow twenty-seven Seconals. I tell myself, change can be a good thing.

But really, way down deep in my real inner genuine Abby soul, I hate change.

Lisa can change with a snap of your fingers, she doesn't care, she's like the wind. This way, then that way.

But not me. I mean I've had the same hairstyle since forever, parted down the middle and always trying to grow it out which I've been growing it out for like a zillion years but it always stays the same length because it's so frizzy. And I've had the same room since forever even though Lisa and Mom keep begging me to trade rooms with Lisa, just for a change.

No way.

Mom's always moving Lisa's furniture around in Lisa's room, like, every month, and Lisa loves it.

My bed and dresser and desk are still in the same spots since forever.

Mom also likes to rearrange the furniture in the living room which she does all the time and you can tell Dad hates it even though he never says anything except, Well, look at this—a new arrangement! And then Mom says, Do you like it? And then Dad looks around at it and nods real slow and says, Well, it's different all right. And then he always has to go out in the backyard and smoke his pipe by the pyracantha to get over it.

But anyway.

This one Saturday, I'm talking to Mom on the phone.

I say it and I don't even know why.

I say, I miss you.

It's a total lie and I don't mean to say it and I didn't even know I was thinking it but there it is.

Hanging out there in the phone lines between us.

I hate it when things just come charging out of my mouth and I don't even know they're there till they come out.

There's this big long silence at Mom's end.

Which makes me wonder if my words got stuck in the phone lines somewhere and didn't make it to her end yet or what.

I imagine my little lie out there in the phone line, maybe it's making a knot or something.

More silence from Mom, it's been like a year.

Then she clears her throat with her mouth open like she always does.

I miss you, too, honey, she says.

Her voice is different.

The words are coming from way back in her throat and I know she's trying not to cry.

I bite the inside of my cheek but it's not to keep from crying, it's to keep from throwing the phone to the floor and running out of there.

I've got the big clench in my stomach and I can't breathe.

I can't believe how stupid I am.

I don't know what made me say that.

Oh god, she's crying.

I dig the heel of my shoe into my calf really hard, then start pounding it, making sure it hurts, making sure it'll be a big black bruise later.

To remind myself.

Stupid, stupid, stupid.

She's crying. Little sucky sobs like she's trying to stop.

Quick.

Change the subject.

I say, Cindy Hardaway broke her leg skiing and so did her brother Mitch, they both broke their legs on the same day at Squaw Valley and now they're both on crutches only Mitch has to keep his cast on longer because he broke his leg in two places but Cindy only broke hers in one place and we were all signing Cindy's cast in Algebra but then Mr. Armfar took all our pens away and made Cindy sit in the very front of the room which it was hard for her to move and it was so unfair.

I can't believe how fast I'm talking.

Go, Speed Racer.

There's a sniffle on the other end.

Oh my, Mom says. When did this happen?

Her voice is all saggy and she sniffs on every other word.

I say, It was last Saturday but they didn't come back to school till Thursday or maybe it was Wednesday no it had to be Thursday because it was Glee Club day because I finished signing Cindy's cast in Glee Club and which Mr. Goldberg didn't mind at all but that's because he's so cool and Mr. Armfar is a total square.

I'm trying to slow down. Really I am.

I make myself take in a deep breath and let it out again but I swing the receiver up so Mom doesn't hear me.

I close my eyes and I can hear Mom's old voice in my head: Honey, slow down! Where's the fire?

Which is what she always says when I start talking too fast and which Mom always says she doesn't know where I get that from because she doesn't talk fast and neither does Dad, which Dad talks just like he walks and just like he writes which is all slow and even and measured and perfect and sometimes you just want to scream at him to speed up.

Well, that's quite a story, Mom says.

Her voice is so soft and weak I can just see those tired words swimming a slow breaststroke down the phone line and into my ear, some of them too tired to make it and dying right there on the line.

Then there's more silence at Mom's end.

I don't know what else to say.

My heel is still knocking against my calf and only now do I realize that it hurts.

Well, I guess I better go, I say. I'll yell to Lisa to come down and talk.

OK, honey, Mom says.

I love you, she says.

Me, too, I say.

LISA!! I yell.

Lisa comes whipping down the stairs two at a time which I taught her how to do it and not fall and her white hair whips behind her like a little wind and I hold out the phone to her.

I go upstairs with my calf throbbing and I can't remember what Mom puts on bruises to make them feel better.

I chant to myself in my head: Never, never, never, never again.

Never say, I miss you.

Never never *ever*.

chapter 32

Christmas without mom.

This is the Christmas after the Crock-Pot Christmas.

Dad puts the lights on the tree, which used to be Mom's job. Dad makes sure all the lights are perfectly spaced, with just as many at the top as at the bottom, which Mom could never get them to come out even, the way she did them there was always this traffic jam of lights at the top of the tree and then hardly any on the bottom.

I tell Dad the lights look nice.

But really I miss Mom's traffic-jam lights.

Mom always puts on *The Nutcracker* while Lisa and me put the ornaments on the tree, then Mom arranges the white sheet under the tree and puts the nativity scene down there. Mom likes to put the three wise men on the other side of the tree, away from Mary and Joseph and the manger because she says the wise men didn't really make it to Bethlehem by December 25 because they were far away, like in Scandinavia or something, and they didn't get there till sometime in January but which she always puts the camels right next to the baby Jesus and I always figured the camels came *with* the wise men but whatever.

Last Christmas Mom spent the whole tree-decorating time lying down. There was no *Nutcracker* because Dad put on some stupid symphony thing with some big stupid choir that sounded like ten zillion old ladies singing Shakespeare. And then Dad practically decorated the whole tree himself because Lisa stuck the treetop star up her nose and then walked around the room that way until Dad came in and saw her and I have to say I never laughed so hard at anything Lisa did. But then Dad sent her to her room and then it was just me and Dad, and Dad has this thing about spacing the ornaments just right and he kept moving mine around after I put them on the tree, so after a while I just threw down the whole box and screamed, Do it yourself, then! And ran out of there.

And then there was the Crock-Pot incident.

That was last Christmas.

You can see why maybe I'm not excited about this Christmas.

I think I'm not in the mood but then I put on *The Nutcracker* and Lisa starts dancing around the tree doing little spins and pretending she's the Sugar Plum Fairy and I think of all the Christmases when Mom and Lisa would dance around the room together to *The Nutcracker* and how the house smelled like the spritz cookies Mom was baking in the oven and Mom would paint the front windows with a scene of snowy hills and little snowbound houses with white smoke out their chimneys and little snowy trees and suddenly I feel this invisible hand going around my neck and squeezing so tight and I can't swallow and one of my eyes goes out of focus and I sit down hard on the piano bench and Lisa stops spinning and says, Are you OK?

I'm fine, I say maybe too loud but who cares it's just Lisa.

I bend into the big box of Christmas stuff and maybe some tears fall out of my eyes and onto the boxes of ornaments, I don't know, that water could be from something else.

I hand Lisa a box of red balls without standing all the way up, I keep my head in the box.

No reason.

I just don't feel like standing up.

And anyway I'm digging for more ornaments.

I find the box of little porcelain bells and I go to the other side of the tree, away from Lisa, and start hanging the twelve bells, one for each of the twelve days of Christmas.

Every time one of those bells rings I get that hand clamped around my neck again.

I try to hang the bells without making a sound.

There's no smell of spritz cookies baking and no one has painted the windows, but it's beginning to feel just a little like Christmas with the smell of the fresh Christmas tree and *The Nutcracker* going and Lisa humming along with it.

Not that I'm into it.

I'm doing this for Lisa.

Lisa needs Christmas.

I can take it or leave it.

The music gets bigger and louder and Lisa starts spinning faster, so fast that her white hair goes out from her head straight and some of it wraps around a Christmas tree branch and she just about pulls the whole tree over and I yell, Lisa! Cut it out! Which then she drops the box of red balls and of course two of them break.

God, you're such a klutzamundo! I say.

Lisa wrinkles her nose at me, like that's supposed to be some great comeback.

Dad yells from his study, What's going on out there?

Nothing! Lisa and I yell at the same time.

Which makes us both do a laugh-snort at the same time even though it's not *that* funny and then I say to Lisa real nice, Just watch what you're doing, OK?

Then I give her a box of nonbreakable ornaments which is a better idea anyway because she put all the red balls in one place so there's this giant red-ball cluster near the bottom of the tree, right in front, like a big bleeding sore, and at first I was going to move them but then I just said to myself, What the heck, it's Christmas.

And Dad will probably move them later anyway.

chapter 33

Christmas morning at exactly six-ten Lisa comes in and jumps on my legs.

Get up! she whispers, it's Christmas!

I kick her off with both legs and say in a normal voice, Go back to bed! It's too early!

I don't care, I'm going downstairs, she whispers.

I hear her run down the stairs, not even bothering to tiptoe. I have no idea what she's going to do when she gets down there. The rule is, no present-opening until everyone is up.

I try to go back to sleep but of course I can't so I get up and go downstairs to see what Lisa is up to. I mean, somebody has to make sure she doesn't open any presents before Dad gets up.

Lisa has turned on the tree lights and is crawling around the tree, looking at all the presents.

She turns to me and her eyes are huge, like she just saw a rattlesnake.

Ab, she says, there's presents under here from *Mom*.

She holds one out to me.

Here, this one's for you, she says.

It's a flat square box, not very big. The wrapping paper is this ultra-modern red-and-green print that maybe looks like wreaths but it's hard to tell because it's all straight lines and squares.

It hardly weighs anything, like maybe there's nothing in it.

The tag is in Mom's itchy-scratchy handwriting you can barely read: To Abby, Love Mom.

Lisa is holding one with the same wrapping paper, the same size as mine.

What do you think it is? Lisa says. She puts her ear on the box and shakes it.

I don't know but we have to wait for Dad, I say.

I sit on the couch with Mom's present on my lap and I look at it and the whole thing makes me very nervous because I'm adding it all up. I'm adding up Mom's rubber-band voice and her crying on the phone and the twenty-seven Seconals and the weirdamundo wrapping paper and a box that's too light and a mom that's been away from her kids for eight months and we can't even visit her, you add it all up and you just know that whatever is in this box is not good.

It gives me a little clench in my stomach, just looking at it.

There's no ribbon or bow on it, which I can only think of one reason for that which is they don't let the crazy people have ribbons because they might hang themselves.

Lisa is picking at the tape on her present from Mom.

Hey, Lisa, let's open our stockings, I say. I put Mom's present back under the tree.

We're allowed to open stockings even if Mom and Dad aren't up yet. It's supposed to keep us quiet and entertained.

Lisa gets the stockings down. They don't look as full as they're supposed to.

Usually Mom stuffs them full of tangerines and walnuts and candy canes and those jellied orange candies that come in the clear wrappers, and then she'll throw in a toy or two, or a little game like car bingo, and maybe some Hershey's kisses, and some homemade fudge or divinity, and then some little wrapped presents like socks or underwear or like last year we got clackers and of course Lisa got blue ones and mine were snot-yellow. Anyway nothing big or expensive, just stuff to keep us busy until Mom and Dad get up.

I dump out my stocking and there are a few candy canes, a little box of See's chocolates, a little stuffed white bear which is actually pretty cute, some dark pink nail polish which I'm not even allowed to wear nail polish, a paperback romance novel by someone I never heard of, and a tiny square box wrapped in dark blue paper with a fancy silver bow and the whole thing looks very expensive. I look over at Lisa's pile and she has the same as me, with the same box only hers is wrapped in gold paper with a fancy red bow.

We hold our little fancy boxes and look at each other.

What do you think it is? Lisa says.

I don't know, but it looks expensive, I say.

Can we open them? she says.

I don't see why not, I say. They're in the stockings, so I guess it's OK.

I take off the silver bow on mine, real careful so I don't mess it up and we can use it again.

I take off the dark blue paper real slow without ripping it. It has this strange shine when the light catches it.

Under the paper is a little black velvet box, the kind you get from a real jeweler's. Mom has one from when Dad gave her a pearl ring on their anniversary one year.

I peek over at Lisa and for once she's going as slow as I am.

She has a little black velvet box, too.

We both open up the hinged lid at the same time.

Mine's a ring.

A sapphire ring. At least I think it's a sapphire. It's the same dark blue as the wrapping paper and it looks real.

The ring part is gold.

The little sapphire sits there and winks at me.

I can't believe this.

I've always wanted a sapphire ring, but I don't think I ever told anyone.

My heart is beating fast but for once it's the good kind of fast.

It's the most beautiful ring I've ever seen, even better than Mom's pearl ring or Poppy's opal ring.

Gol! Lisa says. Ab, look!

She shows me her box.

It's the same ring as mine, only with a red stone, like a ruby or a garnet.

I show her mine and she says, Gol!

I slide the sapphire ring onto my finger, then hold my hand all the way out to look at it. It even fits. Perfectly.

I feel like the queen of something.

This is by far the best present I ever got, almost as good as getting your period.

Lisa and I hold up our hands for each other, showing off our new sparkly fingers.

Do you think they're real? Lisa says, turning her hand back and forth so her stone sparkles in the Christmas tree lights.

I put my sapphire right up to my eye and look into it and I see about eight Christmas trees with lights going on and off.

They look real to me, I say.

Gol! says Lisa. Are they from Dad?

Well *duh*, I say. Who else would they be from?

Lisa gives me the wrinkled nose like that's some great comeback.

They could be from *Mom*, she says.

I roll my eyes at her.

I don't think so, I say.

Just then Dad's bedroom door opens and his teacher steps come clipping down the hall real loud because he wears hard shoes even when he's wearing his PJs and bathrobe and even though Mom buys him slippers every year but he hardly ever wears them.

He stands in the doorway in his hard black teacher shoes and his blue flannel PJs and his blue corduroy bathrobe which Mom made him and he says, Hey, girls!

And for just a sec I forget and I look behind him to see if Mom's there, in her faded red bathrobe and bare feet.

Which of course she isn't.

And I get a little clench in my stomach.

Dad says, Merry Christmas!

He even sounds like the old happy Dad, but his face is still full of lines and there's even a new one going right through the middle of one cheek, but maybe it's from his pillow.

Lisa goes running over with her hand backward to him, showing him her ring, and she yells, Look! Look!

Lisa's wearing a bathrobe Mom made, too. It's a blue background with little yellow sunflowers all over it and the material is like a quilt. Only hers isn't worn out like Dad's because she just got it last Christmas.

I'm wearing my Turtle Power T-shirt and a pair of old gray sweats which were Dad's.

The last time Mom made me a bathrobe was in fourth grade and it was lime green and fluorescent orange and I refused to wear it because it was so ugly. Plus it had a zipper up the front instead of a sash to tie around your waist and you had to step into it to put it on which how dumb is that.

Are these from you, Dad? says Lisa, shoving her hand into Dad's face.

I think those are from Santa, says Dad. His eyebrows go up and he smiles like he's trying to be all mysterious.

Oh, *Dad*, Lisa says. Cut it out, you know there's no Santa.

And she rolls her eyes at him which I wonder where she learned *that* from.

Dad says he needs some coffee and then we can open presents and he goes off to the kitchen and Lisa follows him doing some kind of weirdamundo dance and singing "Ding Dong Merrily on High" in absolutely no key you ever heard of.

That's when I look down and see Mom's present for me, sitting there under the tree looking very weirdamundo and out of place.

I get a clench in my throat.

I pick up the present and move it way in the back of the tree, behind all the other presents. I get Lisa's and put hers back there, too.

For a sec I think about hiding them in my closet but Lisa would notice in a wink.

I sit on the couch and show myself my new ring.

And then it hits me, which I don't know why it didn't hit me before.

It's blue.

I got the blue one.

Lisa got the *red* one, I got the blue one.

I wonder if Dad got them mixed up. I mean they didn't have any tags on them or anything.

But mine fits my finger and Lisa's fits her finger and which Lisa's fingers are a lot smaller than mine.

It has to be mine.

Now I'm *really* wondering who these are from. I mean who else besides me knows that Lisa gets everything blue even though it's *my* favorite color?

Mom.

Can only be Mom.

Everything on me goes into one big clench.

I was so sure the rings were from Dad.

I wanted them to come from Dad.

I don't even know why.

there's not much else to tell about Christmas Day except what was in Mom's presents which was embroidered white handkerchiefs, yellow stitching for Lisa, purple for me.

I would never use anything as old-ladyish as a white hankie, but the embroidery was pretty. I'm sure Mom did it herself which she does embroidery really good. She even embroidered her own wedding dress but which you can't hardly see it in the pictures because it's white on white but I've seen her wedding dress in the cedar chest and you can see it up close. Which she didn't even get married in that dress, she got married in a gray suit because she and Dad eloped and now I can't remember why she even has a wedding dress but anyway.

Oh and we also call Mom on Christmas Day.

We sing "We Three Kings" to her over the phone because it's her favorite carol and she doesn't even cry or get sad, she joins in and sings with us.

And something weirdamundo happens to me while we're singing.

For some reason I think, It's "We *Three* Kings," Mom. You don't get to sing. There's no fourth king.

But then I just tell myself to shut up and be nice, it's Christmas.

chapter 34

finally we get to visit Mom.

It's February and she's been gone since last April.

Dad tells us over Tuesday night spaghetti, which I made myself. The first time I made it, Dad said it was so good let's have it every week. So now we have Tuesday night spaghetti. Mrs. Sierra next door showed me how to make it and she said the secret was oregano and garlic powder.

I also put in dried onions, that's my own invention.

Dad is twisting his spaghetti on his fork and he looks at his fork and he says, How would you girls like to visit your mother on Sunday?

Of course Lisa drops her fork, full of spaghetti, onto the floor.

Good one, dorkamundo, I say, and I laugh.

But I'm thinking wow.

Visiting Mom.

I mean, wow.

It's one of those things that jolts through you like electricity and you're left there with your hair smoking and wondering if it really happened or did you just make it up.

Lisa gets her fork off the floor and says, Really, Dad? Do we really get to visit Mom?

Her blue eyes are as big as her forkful of spaghetti.

Yes, we really do, Dad says. The doctor says it's OK.

You could just swear there's something in Dad's voice that's like he doesn't want to go see Mom.

I'm smiling one of those smiles you paste across your face when you don't know what else to do but you have to be polite or someone will think you're sick or something.

I'm nodding my head up and down with my pasty smile because if I open my mouth I'm afraid of what will come out.

I'm chewing on the inside of my cheek to keep my mouth shut tight.

Because the thing is, I don't know if I want to see Mom.

I am the worst daughter ever born.

I feel like that girl Regan in *The Exorcist*.

Not that I got to read that book which of course Mom wouldn't even let it in the house but Poppy got to read it of course because her mom's so cool and she told me all about it, how this girl Regan gets possessed by the devil and this priest has to come and exorcise the devil out of her but first a lot of other stuff happens like she sticks a crucifix up her you-know-what and yells *Fuck me Jesus* and I bet Mom doesn't even know about that part.

chapter 35

So sunday comes and we're going to visit Mom and I make a plan which is to smile a lot and keep biting the inside of my cheek and speak only when spoken to and answer all questions with just yes or no or maybe one sentence.

Because I know my mouth.

If I let it stay open, certain things will come out.

Like, why did you take twenty-seven Seconals.

Like, why did you want to leave us.

Like, what kind of mother are you anyway.

Like, I hate you and I wish you weren't my mother.

OK, I don't really hate my mother, but sometimes you just have to let the worst thoughts fly around in your head like you believe them or else one day the pressure builds up so bad they come bursting out of your mouth when you don't want them to.

So anyway it's Sunday and we drive to the crazy hospital.

Psychiatric hospital.

All the buildings are brick and there's one main building that's real tall. There's California oaks all around, and eucalyptus trees, and some daffodils blooming, and lots of grass everywhere, like a park.

It's almost pretty, except for the bars on the windows which they're all painted white like that's supposed to make it cheerful or something.

And except for that sign, MERIDIAN PSYCHIATRIC HOSPITAL.

There's a big flagpole in the middle of the cement walk leading up to the front doors and there's two flags on the pole, one the

American flag and one something else I can't tell because there's no wind and they're drooping around the pole.

I wonder if it's some special flag for the crazy hospital, you know, the international flag for crazy or something.

It's probably the California flag but you never know.

We walk up to the flagpole and I grab the white cord that goes all the way up to the flags. I jiggle it, hoping the flags will move and I can see that other flag but nothing happens.

I look at all the windows with bars and I wonder which bars are Mom's.

We go in and there's a woman behind the counter with yellow skin and yellow hair and her face all wrinkled up like a dill pickle. Her yellow hair is piled up real high and she has on *way* too much makeup, I mean if you scraped all the blue eye shadow off her eyelids you'd have a ball of blue Play-Doh.

May I help you? she says to Dad. She kinda smiles. If you call *that* a smile.

Dad says, We're here to see Shirley Goodman.

A patient? she says.

Yes, Dad says.

She squints real hard at Dad and I just bet she's supposed to wear glasses but she's too vain like my aunt Mitzi who wrecked her brand-new black MG because she won't wear her glasses, even to drive, because she says they make her look like Ethel Merman.

Whoever *that* is.

I look around the lobby which is completely uninteresting except for a big fish tank by the window which Lisa is over there watching the fish swim around.

Something about Lisa and the fish tank suddenly gives me the big clench in my stomach.

Lisa looks so small next to that big tank, and she's so skinny and you look around at this big place full of crazy people and then you look at skinny little white-haired Lisa, all lit up by the fish tank, and I just want to grab Lisa by the hand and run out the front doors, I don't know why.

I have to hold on to the counter to make myself not do it.

Already this is worse than I thought.

Dad says, Come on, girls.

He's heading for the elevators.

Oh crap, we have to go up.

I was hoping Mom would come down. I wanted to be close to those front doors.

Lisa goes running over to Dad and I take my own sweet draggy time, like maybe if I'm slow enough Mom will come down.

The three of us get into the elevator and we start going up which if you think about it is much better than going the other way.

In the elevator I take out the blue barrette in Lisa's hair and put it back in because it was sliding down. She lets me do it, which is very weirdamundo because usually she doesn't let anyone touch her hair. She stands there, stiff as a broom, like she doesn't even feel me touching her.

There's a fuzzy reflection of the three of us in the silver elevator doors.

Dad watches the numbers light up as we go up.

I've got that dizzy elevator feeling in my head.

There's a ding and the door opens and I have to take a deep breath before I can make myself get out of the elevator because my feet don't want to move.

The hallway is white linoleum and pale green walls. It stretches out really long, into forever, into how much I don't want to be here.

We follow Dad like two little ducklings.

It's so quiet, except for Dad's hard snapping footsteps. You can hardly hear Lisa and me walking.

I thought there'd be screaming and moaning and crazy wild faces peering out from behind bars, but it's solid quiet and all the doors are closed.

All except one.

At the end of the long green hall.

On the right-hand side.

Which is where Dad is heading.

Bright light spills out from the room where the door is open, like God is in there or something.

Dad's steps get faster and Lisa and I have to almost jog to keep up.

And here we are.

In the doorway of Mom's room.

The first thing you think is, yellow. Everything in that room is yellow, except Mom. She's sitting on a yellow bed and at first you think she's the same old mom, with her too-short black hair and her black pedal pushers and her white elbow-sleeve blouse with black and red chickens all over it which I never liked that blouse and her red lipstick going all the way around her smile.

Which is fake.

It's the fakiest fake-o smile you ever saw.

It's not Mom's smile.

And you look at her face and it's hardly even Mom's face, it's like a bad drawing from a fuzzy photo.

I mean her eyes are green and her teeth are the right teeth and her archy black eyebrows are there, but the whole thing together isn't Mom, I don't know why, I just know it's different and this gives me the big clench in my stomach.

I paste a smile on my face that feels like those wax lips we used to buy at Halloween which Poppy used to eat hers but I never did.

Dad goes in and kisses Mom with his stiff body almost not bending at all, and then he says, Here we are! and his voice is two thousand octaves too high.

This room is *really* yellow. Yellow shag carpet, yellow walls, yellow bedspread, yellow pouffy chair, yellow drawers built into the yellow wall, yellow stool in front of a yellow table with a yellow-rimmed mirror above it. The only thing not yellow is two avocado-green pillows on the bed.

And the bars on the window which are white.

Mom's favorite color is red but I doubt they'd let a crazy person have a red room.

I'd hate living here.

I hate yellow.

Lisa is hugging Mom and my ears have suddenly gone deaf, I can't hear a thing.

I bite the inside of my cheek.

Lisa backs up, giving me room to hug Mom.

I look at Mom and she's smiling too wide, all the way to her gold teeth in back which she never smiles like that.

Mom's arms go up to me real wide and I bend down and my arms go under hers and she pulls me into her real tight.

She smells different, like too many flowers in one room.

I can feel her bones through her chicken blouse which I couldn't before.

She squeezes but I don't squeeze back.

Already this hug has gone on too long.

I pat her a couple times on the back, which everyone knows is code for *the hug is over now.*

She won't let go.

I jerk backwards out of her arms and back up to where Lisa is, standing by the door playing with the door handle, making it jingle, which is the only noise I can hear and for once I don't want her to stop.

Mom's lips move and she's looking right at me but I can't hear a thing.

I nod and smile which seems to work because then Mom looks at Dad and her lips move again and I'm off the hook.

Lisa leans into the door and I lean into it next to her. Our arms and legs touch on one side. I'm so close to Lisa's hair I can smell it and it smells so good that I bend down closer, until my cheek is touching her white hair which is so very soft, the opposite of mine. I breathe in deep, my nose right in her hair, because I need to smell something besides this icky hospital smell of too many flowers, I need to smell something that came with me, and something I can take home.

Mom and Dad are talking, or at least their mouths are moving, just a few steps from me and Lisa, but it feels like they're twenty zillion miles away.

Then Mom's head turns to me and Lisa. Mom's mouth says something and Lisa grabs my hand.

I don't pull away even though we haven't held hands since I was like six.

Moms says something to Lisa and Lisa grips my hand so tight it hurts but I don't pull away.

Mom holds out her arm to Lisa and smiles that gold teeth smile.

Lisa moves toward Mom but she doesn't let go of my hand so I go over, too.

We're not about to let go, either one of us.

chapter 36

the scariest thing about seeing Mom is, if she's strong enough to see us, she's probably strong enough to come home pretty soon.

And I don't want her to come home.

This is the evil daughter speaking. The one who's going straight to hell in about nine minutes.

It's funny how you think you can't possibly live without someone, and then she leaves and you can.

I mean I miss the old Mom, the one before all the lying down and the broken mirrors and the yellow galoshes, but that Mom was so long ago that sometimes I think I made her up.

So mostly I ignore the fact that Mom is coming home soon even though Dad said those very words last Wednesday night over lasagna which Mrs. Sierra brought over which usually on Wednesday nights we have TV dinners but for once I was glad to see that lasagna coming through the door even though I don't even like lasagna. But I've had every TV dinner they make and I'm so sick of TV dinners I could puke right into the empty ice cube trays in the freezer which no one ever remembers to fill.

Mostly I pretend Mom is never coming back and mostly I believe it and this mostly makes me happy and I can breathe with both lungs.

Only one day I'm over at Poppy's and Mrs. Cordesi totally ruins it for me.

Poppy is handing me a can of Coke from the fridge and in walks

Mrs. Cordesi, wearing this real tight jumpsuit in bright purple, with red shoes and red lipstick and huge red beads around her neck.

She's on her way to work. She just got this new job where she's a secretary at some kind of mill, like maybe a steel mill or a paper mill, I can never remember because she just says *the mill*. It's all the way out in Mountain View but now she makes twice as much as she did at the insurance place where she used to work which of course means Poppy gets even *more* cool clothes and jewelry and stuff now.

Mrs. Cordesi says, Hey Ab, I hear your mom's coming home in a couple weeks.

I drop the can of Coke. It lands on the floor between me and Poppy and rolls over to Mrs. Cordesi's red shoes and stops.

Mrs. Cordesi's red shoes are even redder than the can of Coke.

A couple weeks? I say.

I must have looked like someone just shot me in the head because Mrs. Cordesi whaps her hand over her mouth and goes, Oops! and her eyes get really big.

My heart starts doing this squishy double-time thing, like there's too much blood in it, and at the same time all the blood leaves my head and I'm getting really dizzy so I put my arm out what I hope is nonchalantly and hang on to the kitchen counter which theirs is Formica of course.

Mrs. Cordesi takes her hand away and says, You didn't know?

Poppy picks up the can of Coke and goes to the sink to open it.

No, I say. I didn't know.

I mean I know she's coming home soon, I say, I just didn't know it's in a couple weeks.

Which I wish I hadn't said *a couple weeks*, because now it's tap dancing all over my head.

A couple weeks, a couple weeks, a couple weeks.

Oh Christ, says Mrs. Cordesi, and she shakes her head which makes her teeny black curls quiver.

I'm sorry, Abby, she says.

Poppy opens the Coke in the sink and it squirts all over the sink, the fridge, the wall, and all over Poppy, which makes her giggle and then I start giggling and then Mrs. Cordesi starts giggling and the whole conversation is over, thank god.

Except that now I have to carry around the fact that my mother is coming home.

In two weeks.

Right in time for my fourteenth birthday.

chapter 37

mom's coming home in one week.

It's time to take inventory.

To see what's changed since Mom left and will any of the changes make her run crying from the room.

Because I really don't need any of those scenes.

I mean I don't want even *one* of those scenes to happen.

So I start checking around, starting with my room which the only things different are all the clothes on the floor and my new poster which Poppy gave me for Christmas which is a Siamese kitten hanging by one paw from a rope and it says *Hang in there, baby!*

I decide to leave the poster up.

I can clean up the clothes later.

I go into Lisa's room and it's the same. She hasn't moved her furniture around since Mom left.

I wander around the rest of the house.

It's hard to remember how things looked a year ago.

The kitchen is the same except Dad leaves the clean pans right on the stove so he can get to them easily because sometimes his back bugs him and he doesn't like to bend over.

The living room is the same except Dad moved the banana coffee table over to the corner where no one can use it but where it won't tip over and then he doesn't have to kick it and swear at it which he says he doesn't swear but I heard him.

I'm about to check Mom and Dad's room when I hear this big motor drive into our driveway. It can't be our car because it's too loud.

I run to look out the living room windows and it's a big white truck from Farrell's Appliances and it's backing into our driveway.

Dad's black Chevy pulls up on the street and parks next to the apricot tree.

Which is weirdamundo because Dad said he was going into San Jose for a ninety-nine-cent car wash and a haircut from Dominick and Lisa went with him. He didn't say anything about going to Farrell's Appliances.

I go outside and Lisa comes running up to me with her white hair flying and she yells, We got a dishwasher! We got a dishwasher! It's for Mom!

She's running so fast she forgets to stop and just about knocks me over on the cement porch.

Watch it, creepamundo! I yell and slap her on the arm.

Ow! she yells and tries to slap me back but I'm too fast and I jump out of the way.

Two men get out of the truck and roll up the back door of the truck and inside is all kinds of big white things like dishwashers and refrigerators and washing machines and dryers. They pull out a ramp that goes into our garage. Dad goes over there with a bunch of pink papers in his hand and he stands with his hands on his hips looking into the truck and acting like he's in charge of the whole operation.

I can't believe this.

Dad buying a dishwasher.

Dad hates newfangled gadgets and is always saying they're a waste of money and they're invented to make the common man lazy and stupid.

The two men are dressed all in tan with their names sewn over their shirt pockets.

It's John and Gaylord. I didn't even know Gaylord was a name.

I go over to Dad and jam my hands into my back jeans pockets, hoping I look very cool. I'm watching Gaylord, who is *extremely* cute. He looks like that guy who played Lancelot in the movie *Camelot*, which Mom took us to. Real big blue eyes, even bluer than Lisa's.

Are we really getting a dishwasher, Dad? I say.

It's for your mother, he says, his eyes watching John and Gaylord wheel the white dishwasher real slow down the ramp.

The dishwasher looks so big I don't know how it's going to fit in our little kitchen.

John and Gaylord roll the big white thing through the garage and into the house.

I still can't believe this is happening.

Dad buying a dishwasher. I mean it's like God just stopped the world and turned it upside down and then right side up again, making everything look, like, ninety degrees off or something. I start looking around at everything to make sure it's still there—Dad's black Chevy, our brown house, the apricot tree, Poppy's house, the highway, the potholes in our street, the stop sign at the top of the street, the white fence around the Sierras' front yard, the peach trees next door.

All still there.

And yet my head is spinning so fast I don't trust myself to walk so I just stand there even though everyone else has gone inside, following the dishwasher.

I always thought a dishwasher would be nice but I wish John and Gaylord would turn around and take that thing out of here.

It's like a big square Mom on wheels.

It will sit there in the kitchen and it will remind me, only seven more days.

chapter 38

the dishwasher is totally in the way and we're not even allowed to use it.

We don't want to break it before your mother gets to use it, Dad says.

Like he's convinced that it's definitely going to break, it's just a matter of time.

Dad took the yellow table out of the kitchen where Lisa and I used to have our after-school snacks when I was a kid, and he put the dishwasher where the yellow table was.

Except the dishwasher is bigger than the yellow table and it sticks out all over the place and I've already knocked my hip bone into it twice coming into the kitchen so I have a bruise on top of a bruise.

The new rubber hoses on the new dishwasher smell up the whole kitchen.

The dishwasher sits there for three days, reminding me. For three days it shouts, *She's coming, she's coming, she's coming.*

I try to avoid going in the kitchen. Or I go in with my eyes closed so I don't have to see it.

And then on the fourth day it gets even worse.

I come home from school and there's a strange man in the kitchen with no name sewn over his pocket and he's ripping out the old green tile on the kitchen counter and he already took out the old white sink which wasn't white anymore and it's sitting on the floor in the laundry room.

Mom's been saying for years that she wants Formica counters and a stainless-steel sink in the kitchen but you know what Dad says.

Integrity of the original design.

Dad is in his study correcting papers for his typing class which you wouldn't believe how bad those high school kids type.

I knock even though the study door is open and even though we're not supposed to bother Dad when he's correcting papers.

Dad looks up at me through his big black glasses which make him look like some old librarian lady and which he only wears them to correct papers and he always says he doesn't really need them, it's just easier with them on.

Dad, who's that guy in the kitchen? I say. What's he doing?

As if I don't know.

Dad looks back down at the paper in his hand and says, He's putting in a new counter and sink for your mother.

Like that explains everything.

Here I am, going around the house trying to make sure everything is the same, and here's Dad's ruining everything.

But what about the integrity of the original design? I say.

Dad takes off his glasses and looks at me and there are even *more* lines on his face than ever before but maybe it's only because the light from his desk lamp is lighting up his face all weirdamundo. He puts the papers down on his desk and crosses his legs like a lady which always embarrasses me when he does it in public.

He picks up his pipe off the pipe stand even though it's not lit because Mom won't let him smoke it in the house.

Sometimes things have to change, he says, even though we don't want them to.

I stand there.

I'm waiting for more explanation.

I mean, this does *not* explain anything.

Dad taps out the old tobacco in his pipe into the pipe stand.

I'm still waiting.

He's tapping away and looking at his pipe like it's so interesting.

But what about the integrity of the original design? I say again.

Dad looks at me through his big glasses again, then squints at the empty pipe, like he expects to find gold in there or something.

Sometimes you have to compromise integrity, Dad says to the pipe.

Sometimes there are special circumstances, he says.

The guy in the kitchen drops something on the floor with a big clank and Dad and I both jump and look out the door even though you can't see the kitchen from Dad's study.

I turn back and look at Dad and he looks at me and you couldn't even count how many lines are in his face because there are too many and I stand there and erase them in my mind and try to remember how he used to look, that long time ago when integrity of the original design was the rule which I guess it isn't anymore.

It's like there's no rules left.

Just then I notice that Dad's little sideburns are gray and I try to remember if they were always gray or is this a new thing but I can't remember.

I chew on my bottom lip and look right into Dad's red-lined eyes.

OK? Dad says.

I look up at the ceiling in his study which has those white ceiling tiles with holes all over them just like in my room.

I guess, I say. It comes out kinda sarcastic, but I don't care, I don't even care if I get in trouble for being sassy because worse things are about to happen like my mother is coming home in three days.

Dad looks at me and smiles and puts his empty pipe in his mouth.

All I can think is, he's so dumb he doesn't even know his own pipe is empty.

chapter 39

i can't sleep all Friday night.

I stay in my own bed all night because I know being in Lisa's bed won't help so why bother.

At about two o'clock I can't lie still anymore so I get up. I get a blanket off my bed, the pink one that matches Lisa's blue one from Grandma. I remember when Lisa opened hers, Grandma got all gurgly and said, Oh look, Lisa, it matches your eyes! I wanted to hold my pink one up and go, Oh look, Grandma, *mine* matches *your* eyes!

But I didn't.

I wrap myself up like a pink mummy and lie down at the top of the stairs. I put my chin on top of my two stacked fists.

Lisa is across the hall snoring away, of course. You can't believe snores that big could come out of someone so small, I mean she's almost as loud as Dad and he's like a jet airplane landing right next to your ear.

You can hardly see anything in the living room because there's no street lights on our street, there's only a little light from the lights along the highway.

I look at Mom's empty green chair and I think, tomorrow night, if I'm lying right here at the top of the stairs, maybe she'll be there, reading in her chair.

I swear I can smell her Chanel No. 5 from here.

The green chair is so still, like a dog waiting for someone to come home and feed it.

I see that Dad put the banana coffee table back, next to Mom's chair. Mom uses the banana coffee table to put her books on. She's always reading like a whole stack of books at once. She reads all kinds of stuff, romance novels and history books and funny books like *Cornflakes and Beaujolais* and just regular books like *Emma* and *Little Women*, which she read out loud to Lisa and me, a little every night. Mom would sit in her green chair and Lisa and me would sit on the big stuffed arms of the green chair and Mom would read and her hair would be blue under the lamp and sometimes I couldn't listen because I was thinking about why black hair turns blue in light or else I'd be smelling Mom's Chanel No. 5 and wondering when I'd be old enough to start wearing perfume which I bet the answer was sixteen because sixteen is when you get to start doing everything, according to Mom.

I lie at the top of the stairs and the only thing I can hear is the kitchen clock ticking and the fridge going on and off and sometimes a car going by on the highway with a swish.

It's boring just lying here and I'm not getting sleepy so I tiptoe down the stairs, making no noise at all and skipping the creaky fourth step which Dad *still* hasn't fixed and you'd think he'd want to fix it before Mom gets home but it's too late now. Mom's green chair squeaks when I sit in it, just like it does when Mom sits down, but I don't even care that it squeaks. I know nothing can wake Dad and Lisa, they could sleep through a bomb exploding under their beds.

I lean back in Mom's chair and close my eyes and smell her Chanel No. 5 and I try to get a good picture of her in my mind, a picture of her before she started lying down all the time, a picture of her when she was happy and we were all happy.

I try and try but I can't see it, I just see the sad old tired Mom with the raccoon eyes.

I wrap the blanket tighter around me and I breathe in Mom's smell and suddenly I get this clench in my throat and I don't even know why.

The clench turns into tears that push themselves out of my eyes.

I don't even know why I'm crying.

This cry feels like it's coming from the bottom of something, like it's an old cry, one that's been down there a long time, waiting to come up.

I stuff some pink blanket into my mouth because I feel sobs coming and even though Dad and Lisa probably won't wake up, you never know.

My stomach clenches together with every sob and I bring my knees up to my chest to make it stop but I can't stop.

My throat is tight like someone is wringing it out and I can't stop.

My nose and eyes and mouth are all running and I can't stop.

My body jerks around in those heaves like when you throw up and it makes the chair squeak but I don't even care.

I don't know why I'm crying.

Yes I do.

I'm crying because I don't want my mother to come home tomorrow because whoever comes home tomorrow won't be my real mother and everything will be weirdamundo and awful and I'll want her to go back to the hospital forever because with just Lisa and Dad and me at least I know what's going on, I know what's going to happen next.

With Mom back, every day will be a big don't know.

I just want my real mom back.

chapter 40

Saturday is here.

The day before Easter.

The day Mom is coming home.

Dad went to pick her up.

He said, Do you girls want to go, and I said no and then Lisa said no just to copy me and I don't even know why I said no but anyway.

So here's Lisa and me.

Hanging around the house, waiting for Mom.

It reminds me of one time being over at Maddie Frederick's

house and we waited for her mom to come home with the new baby. Which her mom finally did come home with the new baby but then I had to leave right after that.

But this is different.

This is Lisa and me wandering around the house with nothing to do but wait.

Finally Lisa goes, Do you want to play Barbies?

Which I never play Barbies with her anymore because it's too babyish but I say yes.

I don't know why.

We go up to her room and she gets out the big box of Barbie stuff which some of Dad's high school students all got together and gave Lisa their old Barbies and Barbie clothes.

There are a *lot* of clothes.

Including a wedding dress, two bridesmaid's dresses, a bunch of evening gowns with glitter and fake diamonds and lace and velvet and stuff like that, and a bathing suit and sunglasses and lots of plastic high heels in all colors.

Oh and hats, too. Big round things that go on Barbie's head at a tilt and you tie them under her chin in a big fat bow and she looks like Audrey Hepburn in that movie Mom likes.

Some of the evening dresses are even strapless.

We spread out all the clothes and start the only Barbie game we ever play, which is dividing up all the clothes. I pick one, then Lisa picks one, and on and on.

OK, sometimes we have the Barbies do things like get married or go out to lunch. We don't have any Ken dolls, so the Barbies have to marry my stuffed rabbit named Bunny or Lisa's stuffed dog named Doggie.

I pick the wedding dress first and Lisa picks the black satin strapless evening dress with the fake diamonds down the front.

It's very quiet, you can't hear anything except the house making its usual house noises, ticking and humming, and cars going by on the highway.

I've had the big clench in my stomach all morning. I couldn't eat any breakfast.

I don't even care when Lisa picks my favorite evening dress, the blue strapless chiffon one with the big skirt that goes out to here.

We have lots of little beads we use for earrings. You put a straight pin through the bead and then poke it right into Barbie's plastic head which is empty.

I pick the pink organza with the see-through sleeves.

Lisa picks the tight white dress out of the heavy material like curtains.

You can tell neither of us is in the mood.

The house ticks and hums.

Suddenly Lisa throws down the white dress and looks up at me with these big sad eyes she gets that just go right through you and you want to fix whatever's wrong.

Well, sometimes.

When I'm in the mood.

Ab, she says, do you think Mom will be different?

I look at the pile of Barbie clothes, like I'm trying to figure out what to pick next, but really I'm trying to figure out how not to talk about Mom because I'm really not in the mood and the thought of Mom makes my whole body clench so tight I feel like a human Slinky.

I don't know, I say.

Lisa and I look at each other and just for a sec it's like we're the same age and maybe even the same person and our eyes hold on to each other and those sister things you can't say with words go back and forth between us.

But just for a sec.

Then I throw the white high heels at her.

Here, these go with that dress, I say.

A car turns off the highway and onto our street.

We know that sound. Dad's car.

Lisa and I run to her window and look down and the black car pulls into the driveway.

Lisa's down the stairs and out the door before I even have time to think.

I watch from the window.

And who gets out of the car isn't who I'm expecting.

It's a woman with blond hair. The yellow kind of blond, not like Lisa's white hair.

But the head looks like Mom's head and the yellow-blond hair is cut too short like Mom's hair.

I didn't think my body could clench any tighter, but it just did.

She's wearing a pink plaid suit with a pink blouse and pink shoes.

Mom hates pink.

But she walks just like Mom.

My hands are so tight around the edge of Lisa's windowsill that for a sec I think, if I move, the whole windowsill will come right off the wall.

Lisa runs out there and just about knocks Mom over.

Lisa hugs Mom tight around the waist and Mom bends down and puts her cheek on top of Lisa's head.

I can't hear what they're saying but I hear Lisa's high voice and some other voice which I guess is Mom's but it sounds different, almost like singing.

My whole body clenches even tighter, I must be as thin as a straw by now.

Dad is taking suitcases out of the trunk, Mom's old gray set with the gold locks which she had before she married Dad and inside they smell like that stinky green lotion Mom always puts on her hands.

Dad is looking at the suitcases all *concerned*, like maybe he picked up the wrong ones. His eyebrows are almost covering his eyes.

Mom and Lisa head for the front door, arm in arm.

It's weirdamundo how Lisa just ran down there and decided Mom was Mom, but that's Lisa for you. One minute she's scared and freaked out, and the next minute she's having a party.

I'm so clenched up I don't know if I can even walk.

I force one foot out and then the other. Real slow and I have to think about it otherwise I just freeze up.

Somehow I get to the top of the stairs but it takes like a year.

Lisa and Mom come through the front door and Lisa goes, Mom! You have to see the kitchen! Come on!

I start down the stairs, telling my feet what to do. My hand is gripping the handrail so hard I can feel the iron go right into my finger bones.

I get to the turn in the stairway and that's when I see her and she sees me.

That yellow-haired person in pink which is supposed to be my mother.

I can't take my eyes off that hair which is yellow as mustard.

When Mom and I used to see women who dyed their hair blond, Mom would whisper, Isn't that awful—right out of a bottle.

So all I can think right now is, isn't that awful.

That yellow looks all wrong in this house. It looks awful next to the tan walls, next to the cherry china cabinet, next to the tweedy brown curtains, next to the dark brown piano, next to everything in this entire house, it just doesn't go, not that anything in our house matches anyway, but this Marilyn Monroe hair is just all wrong and I can't look at it anymore but somehow I can't take my eyes off it, it's like it's hypnotizing me.

And that's not to mention all the pink which I won't even go into.

Lisa grabs Mom by the hand and starts pulling her toward the kitchen.

Mom! she says. Come on!

Mom's eyes clamp onto my eyes and she smiles with those big pink lips, smiles all the way to her gold teeth in back.

The gold teeth match the gold hair but so what.

Mom drops Lisa's hand and comes floating toward me like a pink cloud.

Abby, she says in the singing voice.

My whole-body clench gets tighter if that's even possible and I feel like I could break off a piece of the iron handrail with my hand.

I pull a tight horizontal smile across my face, just as I hit the fourth stair which I forgot to skip and it squeaks.

Mom's yellow-blond head tips back and she laughs, a real high laugh like cymbals which hurts my ears.

Hasn't Dad fixed that thing yet? she says.

The squeaky fourth step used to make Mom mad. Any time she heard it, she'd yell, George! When are you gonna fix this step? Someone's gonna get hurt!

I come down the rest of the stairs, my eyes glued to each step so I don't fall. I tell each foot silently, *Down. Down. Down.*

And I'm there.

And she's there.

Right in front of me.

I'm so close I can see her nose hair which is black like her real hair *should* be.

Her arms go around me in a hug and I can't make my arms do anything so they just hang there like puppet arms.

She smells like Grandma which is like roses or lilacs or something flowery.

Which is not what she's supposed to smell like, she is supposed to smell like Chanel No. 5.

Mom pulls me in even tighter and kisses the side of my head and I'm thinking, She's gonna get that horrible pink lipstick all over me.

I can't make any part of my body work so I just stand there.

Oh Abby, it's so good to see you, honey, she says in the singing voice.

How long does this hug have to last, anyway.

Is what I'm thinking.

Finally I back up onto the first stair because that's the only place to back up to. Then I back up a couple more because that yellow hair is freaking me out.

The fake smile is still tight across my face which it's beginning to hurt.

I can't look Mom in the eye, so I look at her pink high heels.

Nice shoes, I say.

I don't mean it, actually they're stupid ugly shoes, but I can't think of anything else to say.

Why thank you, honey, says Mom and she looks so *thankful* that I just want to run upstairs and hide in my closet.

Lisa yells, Mo-om! You gotta go see the kitchen!

I clap my hands over my ears and say, God, Lisa, you don't have to *yell!*

Dad comes in with the suitcases, one in each hand and a small one under his armpit, which I don't know what he was doing out there all this time.

Do you want these in the bedroom . . . Shirley? he says, and it sounds like he forgot Mom's name for a sec.

Yes, that'll be fine, says Mom, only she doesn't look at Dad, she's still looking at me like I'm so interesting.

Mo-om! Lisa yells again and grabs Mom's hand and pulls her toward the kitchen.

Mom finally lets Lisa drag her off to the kitchen and I'm left standing there on the stairs.

I'm like two feet taller this way and it makes me feel like I'm not quite here.

I hear Mom scream in the kitchen, that good kind of scream like you just won a zillion dollars and a car and a boat and a diamond tiara behind door number three.

Oh my! says Mom, almost sounding like Mom.

Then Dad goes in the kitchen and Mom screams, Formica! Oh, George!

So Dad and Lisa and Mom are all screaming and talking and laughing and here I am, standing on the third step, and they can't see me and I can't see them and it's like I'm invisible, which I always wanted to be invisible so I could spy on people and hear what they say about me, but this isn't one of those times. Right now half of me wants to run into the kitchen and half of me wants to run out the front door and never come back.

Although the real truth is, I mean if you asked my deepest-down self, I don't want to be anywhere right now.

So of course I just stand there on the third stair because when I'm real confused I just do nothing.

There is nothing else to do, so I sit down on the stairs.

Squeak.

I'm sitting on the squeaky fourth step.

I'm sitting but I bounce up and down on my butt, making the stair squeak really loud.

Squeak squeak squeak.

I do it harder.

Squeak squeak squeak squeak squeak.

Mom used to be able to hear that squeak from about ten miles away and then she'd yell, *George!*

I bounce some more and listen for the *George!*

But all I hear is three people talking in the kitchen at once which who's even listening if they're all talking at once.

chapter 41

later that afternoon I run over to Poppy's.

I have to get out.

Our house is too weirdamundo.

I mean if you look at it from the outside, it looks normal. Dad is out burning things in his beloved incinerator and Mom is reading in her green chair and Lisa is I don't know.

But it's all wrong.

Like someone sprayed the air with something and it smells all wrong.

I can't be in there.

I go in Poppy's front door and yell, Hey it's me!

In here! Poppy yells from her bedroom.

I go in there and she's playing Jimi Hendrix and lying on her bed painting her fingernails white.

White frost.

I'm not allowed to paint my nails until I'm sixteen, it's a rule.

At least I think it's still a rule.

I mean who knows anymore.

There's probably new rules now that I don't even know about. New rules that Mom thought up while she was in the crazy hospital.

Mental hospital.

So is she back? Poppy says, watching herself paint a fingernail.

Yep, I say. I sit on the bed next to her, watch her paint. She's really good at it, she hardly goes outside the nail at all.

So? she says, looking at me for a sec, then at her nail.

I dunno, I say, jamming my toes into her purple shag carpet. The shag is so long I can bury my toes all the way up so they disappear and I have club feet. At least I think this is what club feet look like.

She dyed her hair, I say.

What color? Poppy says.

Blond, I say. I look at my club feet and wonder what it feels like to have no toes. I mean would you lose your balance and fall forward onto your face or what.

Yeah, my mom did that once, Poppy says, holding her painted hand out to admire her new white nails.

She did? I say. Blond?

I can't believe that black-haired Mrs. Cordesi, coolest mom in the universe, ever dyed her hair yellow.

Yep, blond, she says. It was barfamundo. Wanna see a picture?

Sure, I say. The clench in my stomach unclenches just a little. I mean, if Mrs. Cordesi dyed her hair blond . . . well, I don't know what it means, I just know for some reason my stomach unclenched a little when I heard that.

Poppy runs out of the room and comes back with a big thick photo album.

She flips through it with her unpainted hand, waving her painted hand back and forth slowly to dry the nail polish.

She stops on a page and shows it to me.

Look, she says, pointing to a photo. Here's when she dyed it red.

Red? I say. Sure enough, there's a younger Mrs. Cordesi with curly red hair, a cigarette in her mouth, and a little white dog on her lap.

Oh yeah, she's been every color, says Poppy. She used to dye it all the time but these days she just dyes it black.

She *dyes* it black? I say. That's not her real color?

Heck no, says Poppy, blowing on her nails. I don't even know what her real color is anymore. It's probably all gray.

She giggles and thumbs through more pages of photos.

My stomach unclenches even more.

Mrs. Cordesi dyes her hair.

So it must be OK.

It's not the end of the world if your mother dyes her hair blond.

It doesn't mean she's crazy.

In fact, it might even be a sign that she's normal.

She's OK.

She's all better.

As in, not sick anymore.

My stomach unclenches all the way, which it hasn't unclenched this much in, like, a year.

chapter 42

So mom cooks dinner that night.

Already.

She's cooking dinner already.

With her yellow hair.

She changed out of the pink outfit and now she's in green pedal pushers and a blue elbow sleeve blouse with SHIRLEY stitched across the pocket in white, which I wonder if she's wearing it so she doesn't forget her own name.

She's still wearing the pink lipstick.

And she's wearing shoes. Flat brown shoes I've never seen before. No socks, just shoes.

I wonder if her feet are still white and flaky on the bottoms and hard as steel.

I wonder if they let her go barefoot in the crazy hospital.

There are so many questions.

You go away for a year, there's going to be a lot of questions.

Like, what did you do in there for a whole year.

Like, did you have an operation like Katie Russell's aunt where they cut her brain in half.

Like, did you miss us.

Like, did you miss me.

We're having Swiss steak out of the pressure cooker which we haven't had in about a zillion years and I forgot all about it.

It's one of Dad's favorites.

He's over there eating like he hasn't had a meal in a year.

He scrapes up the last of the gravy and says to Mom, Is there some left out there for seconds?

He's actually smiling.

Kind of.

It's a little tight, like maybe he's out of practice.

Mom with her yellow hair smiles her gold-teeth smile and says, Of course, sweetheart!

In that voice like singing.

She never called Dad sweetheart before.

Dad's still smiling.

But if you ask me, it's not a real smile.

Anyone else? Mom with the yellow hair says, looking at me and Lisa.

I look at my plate. I've hardly eaten anything. Swiss steak is *not* my favorite thing in the world.

I guess Mom forgot that.

Lisa is lining up all her peas in straight lines with her knife.

Mom and her yellow hair just smiles her gold-teeth at the air between me and Lisa.

I'm already sick of that smile which is not Mom's smile.

And I can't get used to that pink lipstick. It makes her look pale and washed out and sick. I mean I never really liked her bright-red lipstick, but at least it was *her*.

Mom grabs Dad's plate and goes into the kitchen and comes back with a heap of Swiss steak. She takes the plate all the way over to Dad and puts it down in front of him and then puts her arm around him and kisses his ear.

There you are, darling, she says in the songy voice.

She never used to call Dad darling.

She never used to kiss Dad on the ear.

Or put her arm around him that way, at least not at dinner.

I mean people are trying to eat here.

And that voice.

Dad's ears are red on both sides.

I can't sit here anymore.

My stomach is clenching.

Can I please be excused? I say, looking at Dad.

Me too, can I be excused, too? says Lisa.

She always has to copy me.

Dad looks at me and then Lisa and then me again and he gets that look on his face like someone stabbed him in the back of his head and it's giving him a real headache and he says, No you may not be excused. This is the first night your mother is home, and we're going to have dinner as a family.

Mom with the yellow hair smiles at no one in particular, just the air in the dining room which by the way seems to be getting very thin because every time I breathe it's like I didn't take in any oxygen.

I roll my eyes at Dad and I do not look at Mom with the yellow hair and pink lipstick who is smiling at air.

I push my plate away and cross my arms and slouch down in my chair, as far down as I can go and not fall off, and I put the most bored expression I can think of on my face.

Lisa goes back to lining up her peas.

Mom with the yellow hair takes a bite of salad and crunches on it really loud.

Dad cuts his Swiss steak and his knife screams across his plate.

Dinner lasts for eleven thousand days and nights.

chapter 43

it's sunday morning, Easter, and I wake up early.

The first thing I think is, it's Easter and I wonder if Mom with the yellow hair remembered to put the Easter baskets by the front door.

I mean for Lisa.

I'm too old for Easter baskets.

I sit up and listen to the house, see if anyone's awake, but I don't hear anything.

I get out of bed and tiptoe to the top of the stairs and look down.

There's nothing by the front door.

Damn her.

I mean I know she just got home and everything but geez, I mean this is a major holiday.

I go down the stairs on quiet bare feet, skip the squeaky fourth step, and make no noise going through the living room.

The Easter baskets are stored in the hall closet on the top shelf.

I figure I can get them down, scrounge up some candy or cookies or something, and put them by the door before anyone else gets up.

I hear a noise coming from the kitchen, a little thunk like someone putting a cup down on the kitchen counter.

I freeze and listen.

Then I hear strange little tinkly noises, like metal hitting metal, also from the kitchen.

Real slow and silent, I get across the dining room.

I'm flat against the wall, right next to the kitchen doorway. There used to be swinging doors into the kitchen just like a saloon but Dad took them down a long time ago because Mom said they were going to whack some kid's head one of these days.

More tinkly noises, almost like little bells.

I get half an eye around the corner.

It's Mom.

Mom with the yellow hair.

She's sitting on the kitchen stool next to the new yellow Formica counter.

She's in her faded red robe and some new red slippers I haven't seen before, bright red velvet with feathery stuff all the way around.

She has the Easter baskets out, two of them, sitting on the counter.

Next to the baskets is one of her jewelry boxes, the old wood one with the carved Hawaiian flower on the top and green velvet inside.

She picks up a gold bracelet from the jewelry box. It's a skinny gold chain with a little pearl on it but I think it's fake. She's had it since forever.

She drops it into one of the Easter baskets.

She picks up a long silver necklace with a teardrop of shiny black obsidian that an old boyfriend made for her back in high school.

It goes into the other basket.

Her yellow hair looks darker than it did yesterday, and her lips with no lipstick are full of crooked lines, just like Grandma's lips.

There's something wrong with the way she's picking up the jewelry and dropping it in the baskets. The way she moves, it's not Mom, it's like a robot, like she's not even thinking about what she's doing, her arm just moves back and forth, back and forth.

Her eyes stare at the baskets like she's been hypnotized or something.

A cough comes up in my throat and I try to hold it in but I can't, and out it comes.

Her head snaps around like a cat seeing something move in the bushes.

I step into the doorway.

She stares at me with her yellow hair and her blank, hypnotized eyes.

I stare back. I'm not breathing. I don't know what to say.

She points to the Easter baskets.

No candy, she says in a flat voice like she's reading a grocery list out loud.

I didn't have any candy, she says.

Her face and voice are so cold I get goosebumps from my heels to the top of my head.

I back out of there and run upstairs.

I get under my covers and make myself into a tight ball and put my hands tight over my ears, trying to squeeze out her voice and her face and her eyes and her robot arms.

I tell myself good things.

Like, at least she's home.

At least she's not dead.

And her black hair is just under the yellow hair and maybe it'll grow back in.

chapter 44

t's monday morning. A school day.

The first thing, I wake up and I forget that Mom is back home. I wake up and I'm waiting for Dad to yell up the stairs for us to get up.

Then I remember about the yellow hair and the pink lipstick and I lie there and wonder who's going to wake us up.

I wait and seven-fifteen comes and goes and nobody yells up the stairs or comes up or anything.

Lisa's room is all quiet so I go down the hall to her doorway and hiss, Lisa! Get up!

She doesn't even move.

I go in her room and shake her teeny little shoulder through the blue blanket from Grandma and go, Hey! Get up! School!

She slaps at my hand.

Get out, she mumbles without even opening her eyes.

I go to the top of the stairs and listen downstairs.

There's someone in the kitchen running water in the sink.

Oh crap, if it's Mom it means we have to eat eggs for breakfast.

I hate eggs.

And I don't want to go down there and see that yellow hair.

I go back to my room and get my shortest miniskirt out of the closet, the avocado green corduroy with the very large wale, which wale is how fat the velvety stripes are in the corduroy which you would know if you had to take dumb old Home Ec from Mrs. Rosen.

I get out my shirt with the lowest scoop neck, which is the yellow poorboy with the choker collar, not that it shows my boobs or anything because I have nothing to show anyway except a bunch of moles.

Mom used to say I was the moliest kid she ever saw.

I get out the one pair of high-heeled shoes I own, which Dad bought me a few months ago, which I had to cry to get. They're dark brown leather with a big buckle across and three-inch heels.

This is everything I'm not supposed to wear.

I put turquoise eye shadow on my eyelids.

I am *really* not supposed to wear eye makeup, that's a total rule, no makeup till you're sixteen.

Or at least it used to be the rule.

I look at my face in the mirror. If I keep my eyes open real wide, you can't see the turquoise eye shadow.

I put my biggest gold hoops in my ears which my hoops are pretty big but not as big as Poppy's which are so big they touch her shoulders.

I stand in front of my mirror and I'm not even shaking.

Well, maybe a little.

I put on my bead necklace which Poppy made for me.

There's no rule about bead necklaces.

Look in the mirror one more time.

My heart's beating a little fast but so what.

I'm not afraid.

What can Mom do to me, just send me upstairs to change right now, young lady, that's all.

And wash that makeup off your face, young lady.

No makeup till you're sixteen.

Young lady.

I take a deep breath and walk out of my room and down the stairs.

I hear Mom and Dad talking, Mom in the kitchen and Dad in the dining room, and just for a sec it's like old times, with Mom's and Dad's voices and the smell of coffee and the sound of boiling water for the eggs and Mom's bare feet slapping on the linoleum.

Except I don't hear any slapping feet, I hear slippers scooting across the linoleum.

And Dad's voice is too high.

And Mom's voice is that weirdamundo song.

I get to the dining room and Dad is sitting in his chair reading the paper.

Hey Dad, I say.

Hey Ab, he says from behind the paper.

The table looks so different.

There are yellow napkins in the napkin holder.

The glass salt and pepper shakers are full.

There's a plate, knife, fork, spoon, and napkin at every place.

There's even a sprig of purple lilac in a glass vase.

And right in the center is Mom's funny little angel with the missing wing.

It's been a long time since our table looked like this at breakfast.

Just for a sec everything heavy lifts off of me and there's almost like a giggle in my stomach.

But just for a sec, then it all comes back, heavy in my head and heavy on my shoulders.

I get into my chair fast, right before Mom comes out of the kitchen.

With her yellow hair.

Every time I see that hair I jump a mile inside. It's like seeing a rattlesnake which we had one come up on our patio once and Dad hit it on the head with a shovel and killed it. It flopped over on its back to die and you could see its white stomach and Dad scooped it up with the shovel and put it in the outside garbage can and which I refused to take out the garbage for a month because I was afraid the snake didn't really die and it was just waiting for me in the garbage can, ready to bite me on the wrist.

I'm in my chair before Mom can see my miniskirt.

She gives me the gold-teeth smile and says, Good morning, honey!

Oh god, that voice. It gives me shivers inside.

I look at Mom with my eyes open real wide to hide the turquoise eye shadow.

Stretch a rubber smile across my face.

Morning, I mumble.

Mom puts a little bowl with a soft-boiled egg in front of me.

Just the smell makes my stomach turn over.

One thing I definitely did *not* miss was eggs every morning for breakfast.

Eggs which are *protein*.

Young lady.

I'm waiting for Mom's eyes to take in my low-cut shirt and my big hoop earrings and my pierced ears and my turquoise eye shadow.

But her eyes say nothing, they're like two mirrors, all you can see in them is your reflection of yourself back at yourself.

Where's Lisa? Mom says.

I look at my egg and say, Bed.

Dad closes his paper and yells, Lisa! You're late! I'm counting to three! One, two . . .

I'm up! yells Lisa.

Once upon a time, there was no yelling at our house.

It was a rule.

Once upon a time, Mom would have taken one look at my low-cut shirt and sent me back upstairs to change.

Young lady.

Once upon a time, wide-open eyes hiding turquoise eye shadow wouldn't get past her.

Once upon a time, scooting fast under the dining room table to hide a miniskirt, that wouldn't get past her, either.

Mom with the yellow hair walks over and pours more coffee for Dad. Her slippers slide across the weirdamundo green rug in the dining room which looks like it should have been a hammock instead of a rug.

There you are, honeybunch, Mom says to Dad, and gives him a quick one-arm hug.

Well thanks . . . dear, Dad says, and turns his head to kiss her but he's too slow, she's already gone.

Dad sees me watching and gives me this weirdomundo laugh, like he's nervous or something.

Lisa finally comes downstairs, looking like she left part of herself upstairs in bed. Her eyes are all squinty and her hair is all over the place.

I look around the table at the four of us.

I swear, everyone in this family is a space alien.

Except me, I mean.

Finally it's time to go and I stand up and head to the front door in full view of Mom with the yellow hair and she can see what I'm wearing and I even blink right in her face and she can't miss the turquoise eye shadow.

But nothing.

Just, Bye honey, have a good day.

Bye honey, have a good day.

God, that voice.

I just want to kill it.

I carry it in my head all the way to school like I'm dragging a log behind me.

I don't talk the whole way to school and Poppy doesn't even ask what's wrong.

She knows.

She can read my mind better than anybody except sometimes Lisa.

chapter 45

finally the end of April comes which means finally my fourteenth birthday comes and Mom says I can have some friends over on Saturday night for dinner and cake and presents and all that, and I say I only want to invite Poppy because she's my best friend and I don't really have any other friends. OK, I do have other friends, just no one as close as Poppy, just girls I see at school and maybe hang out with at lunch or walk to classes with but that's it. No one who knows all my secrets and for sure no one who gets that my mom is the way she is. Plus it's so who-knows with Mom these days, you never know when she's gonna do something weirdamundo. I mean she hasn't done anything really weirdamundo lately, but it's like I don't trust it, I keep waiting for her to do something.

So Saturday night Poppy comes over and has dinner with us and we have steak and twice-baked potatoes and red Jell-O with pineapple in it and canned spinach which is all my favorite things although I could care less about steak but what else do you have with twice-baked potatoes with American cheese on top and besides steak is Dad's favorite. It's raining so Mom cooked the steak in the broiler and now the whole house smells like steak.

We're all eating dinner and so far Mom hasn't done anything weirdamundo although I'm kinda holding my breath. I mean mostly I don't care if she does something weirdamundo in front of Poppy, but I kinda do. But so far all she's done is just smiled that gold-teeth smile too much and called everyone at the table sweetheart and honey about thirty-nine times including Poppy but that's not so bad.

Mom brings out the cake which she made which is angel food, my favorite, with blue icing, which I specifically said I wanted *blue* icing and I specifically said *it's my favorite color* and there it was, light blue icing all over the big tall cake and written in squiggly white icing is HAPPY 14TH ABBY and then some little blobs that are maybe flowers, who knows. Mom isn't the best cake decorator in the world but oh well, at least it's blue.

Mom lights the fourteen candles on top and everyone sings "Happy Birthday" but of course Poppy and Lisa sing *You live in a zoo* instead of the real words and we all laugh and then I close my eyes and make a wish.

Which there are so many things I want to wish for but I have to decide on one so I wish for my real Mom to come back even though I'm pretty sure she's gone forever but you never know and anyway isn't that what wishes are *for*, is to wish for things that are so hard to come true.

I blow out all fourteen candles at once and just for a sec I look at Mom to see if my wish came true yet, but she gives me the gold-teeth smile and says, *Good for you, sweetie pie!* in that drippy voice I hate so I knew it hadn't come true, at least not yet.

We all eat cake and then finally it's time to open presents, which there's a stack of them over on the toaster cart, including a pretty big one that says TO ABBY LOVE MOM.

I open Poppy's present first, and it's three pairs of beaded earrings and a poster of Cat Stevens, which I *love* him. Poppy has all his albums which that's all I ever want to listen to at her house and if I could buy only *one* album it would be *Teaser and the Firecat* but I'm not allowed to buy records of anyone you ever heard of since the only kind of music allowed in our house is classical which how boring is that.

I open Lisa's present next and it's a stuffed cat with orange fur and green eyes.

Lisa says, You can name it anything you want!

Which I wanted to say *Well duh* but I didn't. I just smiled and said, Thanks, Leese, maybe I'll name it Lisa.

She goes, Really? with her eyes all open wide and I go, *No*, not really.

Then I go, Maybe I'll name it Cat Stevens, and Poppy and Lisa and Dad and me all laugh and Mom goes, Who's that?

I just roll my eyes at her and unroll my new Cat Stevens poster in her direction and she goes, Oh, that rock and roll singer.

Rock and roll singer.

She kills me.

I mean at least Dad has *heard* of Cat Stevens, I mean he does teach at the high school so he's not totally out of it.

I open the present from Grandma next which is stationery, which is what she sends me every year. This year it's purple and pink balloons which is pretty dumb but the only person I ever write to is her anyway.

Then I open the small boxes from Mom and Dad, which is pink underwear (yuckamundo), a little gold bird pin which I'll never wear because nobody wears pins except old ladies like Grandma, some red-and-white striped socks which who wears red and white stripes, and a black velvet choker with nothing on it but which I could add something like a hand-painted bead and then I would actually wear it so that was actually a pretty cool gift.

Then the big box.

Actually it's not that big, maybe one foot all the way around.

It says *To Abby Love Mom.*

Not *Mom and Dad*, which is kinda weirdamundo.

Some little voice inside me says, Watch out, but I push it right down.

Nothing is going to ruin this day.

I'm hoping it's a hair dryer. Or maybe a beach towel, the real kind of beach towel that's bigger than a bath towel and has something groovy on it like a sailboat or a peace sign or Ziggy. Every time I go to the beach with Poppy and her mom I have to take one of our old bath towels which is so embarrassing.

Or maybe it's a phone for my room.

OK, there's like *no* chance it's a phone, but I can dream can't I.

There's also no chance it's a stereo, or any records I'd want to listen to.

And there's no chance it's white go-go boots or a leather fringe jacket.

You know, things I'd actually want.

That little voice comes back and says, Don't get your hopes up, it might be something weirdamundo.

Which I push it right down again.

I rip off the aqua tissue paper. Mom always wraps things in tissue paper, I guess because it's the cheapest, but half the time you can see right through the tissue and know what it is already.

But not this time.

It's a brown box, no words or anything on it.

I tear off the tape and open it up.

It's a pillow.

It's a shiny lime-green pillow with black fringe.

Homemade, you can tell.

I pull it out and there's words embroidered on it in red.

ABBY LOVES MOM.

I turn it over and the other side has nothing on it.

That little voice says, See? Told you so.

I tell it to shut up.

There's this sharp thing in the pit of my stomach.

I tell it to go away but it stays there, flipping over and over like it's grinding a hole in the bottom of my stomach.

Poppy says in her polite voice, Oh, that's nice, Mrs. Goodman, did you make it?

Lisa goes, That green is pukey.

Sometimes you just have to love Lisa. For just a sec I wish the pillow said *ABBY LOVES LISA*. I mean at least that's true. Sometimes.

Dad says, Wooooow, with his eyebrows way up which is his way of saying How weirdamundo is that.

I put on a fast polite smile, that horizontal kind that hurts your face, and I look at Mom, and she's smiling back even farther than her gold teeth, she's smiling so wide you can see that dangly thing in her throat, it's just right there. Her eyes are all lit up like it's Christmas and she says, Do you like it, sugar?

I say, Yeah, it's nice, and my voice sounds like I just threw up.

Then I see what else is wrong which it didn't hit me at first.

It says *ABBY LOVES MOM*.

Not *MOM LOVES ABBY*.

ABBY LOVES MOM.

That sharp thing in my stomach turns faster and faster, I can feel the hole getting bigger.

I put the pillow back in the box and say, Thanks Mom, without looking at her. Then I look around the table and say, Wow what a birthday.

It's all I can think of to say.

Lisa pulls the pillow out of the box and runs her hands over the red words.

You made this, Mom? she says, her face all squinched up like she's holding a road-kill squirrel or something.

I sure did, darling, and maybe you'll get one for your birthday! says Mom.

No thanks, says Lisa, and tosses it into the box.

You just have to love Lisa.

I choke down the rest of my cake and think about where in my room I can lose that pillow.

chapter 46

this is when I start stealing from Mom.

I mean, this is when the evil daughter starts stealing.

The first time, it just sort of happens. My hand sort of accidentally slips into Mom's purse when she's out in the driveway talking to Mrs. Sierra.

My hand goes in and comes out with three one-dollar bills.

Three dollars can buy a lot of beads at Tasso Bead Shop.

Three dollars can buy a lot of Slushees after school.

Three dollars can buy pink fishnet stockings or Bonne Bell lip gloss or *'Teen* magazine or a mood ring.

I put the three dollars in my pocket and run upstairs before Mom gets back inside.

Mom with her yellow hair, out there with Mrs. Sierra, acting like everything is normal.

That yellow hair is not normal.

I sit on my bed, looking at the three bills in my hand.

This is not only a rule, it's a commandment. Thou shalt not steal.

The ten commandments, now there's ten rules that mean something, no matter how sick your mother gets.

I look at that broken commandment in my hand.

The more I look at it the faster my heart beats.

Two voices are talking to me.

The angel with the missing wing is saying, Go put it back.

The evil daughter is saying, It's yours, you deserve it. It's for all the times Mom wasn't here last year, every holiday, every birthday, every report card, every piano lesson, every Girl Scout meeting, every first day and last day of school.

And every day after school.

And every Saturday and Sunday.

It's a lot of days.

The angel with the missing wing says, It's not Mom's fault that she got sick and had to go away.

The evil daughter says, Yes it was too her fault, she should have been stronger. Other mothers have the same lives as Mom and they don't get sick.

I put the three dollars in my purse which used to be Monica Ger-litz's purse but I traded her for my turquoise ring, which later I regretted and I tried to trade her back but she wouldn't trade me so I don't talk to her anymore.

I put the bills in the purse and snap it shut and the evil daughter says, That's right, it's your money.

It's just the start.

I start stealing from Mom's purse every week and she never notices.

Every time she picks up her purse I hold my breath, waiting for her to stop and do that thing where you start counting your money and your brow gets all wrinkled up because you were *sure* you had three more dollars than what's in your hand.

I take different amounts every week. Sometimes only a dollar, sometimes as high as five dollars.

Mom never asks where I got the new pink fishnet stockings.

She never asks where I got all the *'Teen* magazines that are piling up beside my bed. At first I hid them under my bed but then I got lazy and left them on the floor.

I even save up for seven weeks and buy myself a new turquoise ring to replace the one that Monica Gerlitz won't give back.

Lisa sees it one night at dinner and goes, Where'd you get the new ring?

I kick her under the table and give her the big-eyed look which means *shut up* and she kicks me back and sticks her tongue out at me.

What ring? Mom says.

Did you get a new ring? Dad says.

No, I say, showing my hand with the new ring to Dad, then Mom, then Dad again.

The new ring is almost exactly like the one from Janet, a long oval of turquoise set in silver. But the turquoise isn't quite as big and the color is greener.

Leave it to old Lisa to notice the difference.

It's just my same old turquoise ring that Janet brought me from Mexico, I say.

Janet is my cousin on Dad's side. She's five years older than me and I don't really like her because she's a snob, which the only reason she brought me that turquoise ring from Mexico was because her mom made her, and which is why I traded Monica the ring for the purse in the first place.

Mom takes my hand and looks at my ring and her hand is icy cold which gives me a shiver and I look at her yellow hair which is turning dark at the roots and I hope she lets it grow out and then cuts off all that yellow.

Oh, I guess that is the old one, says Mom.

I give Lisa a victory smile.

after a while stealing from Mom's purse isn't fun anymore. It's too easy.

So I start stealing from stores.

I don't even know why, because now I have all this extra money from Mom's purse and I can buy anything I want.

The first time is at Tasso Bead Shop. I'm there with Poppy and while she's looking at the hand-painted beads I bend way over a box of tiny silver beads and pick up a bunch in my fingers and put them in my hand and close my fist.

I stand up and move down a row to where the clear beads are and I'm looking at them like I'm really interested in clear beads but which really I'm keeping my fist connected to my chest and I'm trying to look out the corner of my eye at the long-haired guy at the counter who's maybe the owner but he's not even looking my way.

I slide down another row and look at dark blue beads and then I stroll over in Poppy's direction, all casual and cool.

I put my fist in my jeans pocket and open my hand.

Feel the tiny beads roll off my hand.

Flick my fingers around to get them all off.

This is maybe twenty-five-cents' worth of beads. No big deal.

Poppy buys some gold wires and a few hand-painted beads and we leave.

I hold my breath as we go out the door and into the sunlight. I've got my ears cocked back, waiting for someone to yell, Hey! That girl stole some beads!

I hear this in my head like a hundred zillion times but I keep walking.

I don't tell Poppy.

I have *really* broken the commandment this time.

But the thing is, I don't feel bad or guilty, I feel great. As I'm walking away, this surge of energy goes through me like I just got electrocuted or something.

I feel like I own the world.

I feel like I could do anything.

I feel like if someone shot me right now, the bullet would bounce off.

The angel with the missing wing starts saying something but I refuse to listen.

They're just beads.

All week I keep saying, *They're just beads.*

All week I won't listen to the angel with the missing wing even though she keeps trying to tell me things.

. . .

the next week I steal a denim miniskirt from JCPenney.

I put it on under my skirt which I'm already wearing which is longer and I walk out of JCPenney and I get that surge of energy again.

I can't hear the angel with the missing wing anymore.

Even when I sit there at dinner and I look at her sitting there in the middle of the table, she doesn't say anything.

I wear the new stolen skirt on Monday morning and Mom doesn't even notice it.

The mom with the yellow hair, I mean, she doesn't notice.

I come downstairs and she's sitting at the breakfast table and I walk right at her, real slow, See this skirt, I stole it, what are you gonna do about it.

But all I get is the gold-teeth smile and the songy voice.

Good morning, honey! she says.

I stop right in the doorway to the dining room and pretend to check the zipper on the side of my new stolen skirt, like I forgot to pull it up or something.

Mom with the yellow hair drinks her orange juice.

I fiddle with the blue button at the top of the zipper.

Lisa turns around and looks at me but I already showed the skirt to her and told her it was an old skirt of Poppy's that she didn't want anymore.

Mom smiles at Dad and says, More coffee, sweetheart?

Yuckamundo, that *sweetheart* crap again. I just want to gag. I mean gagamundo. Hey, that's a new one.

Well sure, says Dad, and holds his cup up, smiling at Mom.

Oh my god, now *Dad's* smile is going all the way back to *his* gold teeth.

I sit in my chair and look at Lisa.

We look at each other a long time, at least long for Lisa and me.

The angel with the missing wing just sits there, silent.

chapter 47

poppy notices the stolen skirt in a sec.

We meet in the middle of the street to walk to school and Poppy says, Where'd you get the new skirt?

Poppy's wearing a hat which she made out of old jeans which has this floppy brim all the way around and a fake daisy in the front.

Poppy can make anything. I mean you could give her a bunch of sugar cubes and four Band-Aids and she'd make something cool.

JCPenney's, I say.

I say it like it's nothing, no big deal, just a new skirt.

Except Poppy knows how often I get new clothes from JCPenney's which is never.

Poppy gets all quiet and I know she knows.

Where'd you get the money? she says in code voice. Code voice means what you're saying is not really what you're saying.

Really she's saying, I don't believe you.

I earned it from doing chores, I say in code voice.

Really I'm saying, I don't care if you believe me or not.

I look down at my shoes and watch them walk, black and tan

suede with square cut-outs on the sides and they lace up like tennis shoes with these fat black laces.

I can feel Poppy looking at me and my cheeks start to get all hot but I don't look at her, I keep looking at my shoes like they're so interesting.

You stole it, she says, not in code voice.

I don't say anything.

You did, didn't you, Poppy says. You stole that skirt from JCPenney's.

Her voice jabs at me like I stole the skirt from her.

I look straight ahead and I start dragging my heels and making scuffing noises on the sidewalk for no reason. Poppy's white go-go boots click on the sidewalk next to my scuffing.

Out of the corner of my eye I see her fling her hair once on each side.

So what if I did, I say in code voice, and I fling my hair, too, even though it doesn't fling, it just bounces.

Really I'm saying, Shut up, you don't have a crazy mom with yellow hair so just shut up.

We get to school and we're walking down south hall. We have different first periods so I just mumble Bye without looking at her and I go into room three which is History.

It bugs me all during History that I lied to Poppy which Poppy and I never lie to each other.

chapter 48

So i finally get caught.

Of course.

It happens at The Girlfriend, which is this tiny little clothes shop over by the bead shop. It's run by this snooty old lady named Mrs. Suchliss who wears these huge green glasses on a chain of green beads. The glasses are square and look like something Elton John would wear.

We call her Old Lady Suckless behind her back.

I don't even know why I try to steal from there. Old Lady Suckless watches every move you make with her little weasel eyes behind her big green glasses.

Old Lady Suckless is about nine hundred years old and you can tell her silver pile of hair is a wig.

It's a pirate blouse, the one I steal.

I mean try to steal.

It's all white with a big lace collar around the neck and a big fat lace thing in front like a huge man's tie and long sleeves with about seven inches of lace cuffs which fall over your hands.

I mean, what a dumb blouse to try and steal, all that lace going everywhere.

I'm in the dressing room for like an hour, trying to tuck all that lace under my sweatshirt.

Old Lady Suckless keeps checking on me.

All you all right in there, dear? she says in her scratchy old voice.

I'm fine, I say. My voice is about twenty-two octaves too high.

It's the lace collar/tie thing I'm having the most trouble with. Finally I unbutton the blouse down the back and let the front of it droop around my bra which makes me look really stacked but oh well.

I look at myself in the mirror. Nah, you can't tell.

I open the door of the dressing room and Old Lady Suckless is standing right there and in half a sec I know I've made a *big* mistake.

I forgot to take something else in there with me, something else like another blouse or a skirt or a pair of pants.

Because behind me in the dressing room right now is nothing but an empty hanger.

My heart skips about nine beats.

Old Lady Suckless smiles at me and her teeth are all outlined in gold and you can see the cracks in the thick makeup she's wearing all over her face which ends at the bottom of her jaw and her neck is all red and wrinkled.

Did it fit, dear? she says, looking behind me at the empty dressing room with the stupid one hanger hanging there stupidly empty.

What? I stupidly say, while my mind is going a zillion miles an hour trying to think of how to get out of this and my feet are starting to get all clammy in my red go-go boots which I stole from Gearhart's last week.

The blouse, honey, did it fit? she says, and her painted-on eyebrows, which by the way are painted on crooked, which I mean doesn't she own a *mirror*?, her eyebrows go up on her forehead and into her fake silver hair.

What blouse? I say, trying to sound all innocent.

I'm going to pretend there's no blouse.

This is not brilliant but it's all I can think of.

Her crooked eyebrows go down in one huge wrinkle over her glasses and her old-lady-pink mouth cracks into a frown.

She steps into the dressing room and grabs the hanger, holds it out in the air toward me.

The white blouse, she says, the one with all the lace. You took it in here to try it on.

Her voice is all high and scratchy and mean and her whole face goes in this giant frown and her head is shaking and her wig starts to wobble.

And suddenly I think, maybe that wig will save me.

Old Lady Suckless is not very big. She's shorter than me and super skinny. I could knock her down, easy.

I look down at my hand and there's a teeny piece of lace making its way out from under my sweatshirt sleeve.

Time to act.

I grab the hanger out of her hand and whip it through the air, catching her wig on the hook end.

I jerk it down hard and there it is, a pouffy mass of silver hair on the floor.

There's a scream which is not mine.

I don't think, I just run.

I'm out the door and down Hickman Avenue and I run against the light across to Blackwell Avenue and keep going, faster and faster, my throat too tight I can't breathe and my heart too big for my chest and pounding like a bass drum and I keep running and I think I hear sirens blasting and people chasing me and screaming things like *Stop, thief!* but I can't stop and the wind is a slosh in my ears and I keep running and I run down to the intersection of Highway 9 and down the skinny path past the Georgian House and Our Lady of Fatima, past the Mosses' house, past the Kerns' house with the baby blue geraniums, get to my street and run down the hill.

And stop.

And listen.

All I can hear is my own hard breathing and my heartbeat in my ears.

I'm so out of breath I have to bend over.

The stolen white lace is everywhere, over my hands, around my neck, down my chest.

All of this is really stupid.

Because I haven't really escaped.

Old Lady Suckless knows who I am, knows my parents, knows where I live, goes to Mom's D.A.R. meetings, lives two streets over.

I'm not free.

I tuck in all the lace and walk into the house, trying to look and breathe normally.

The house smells like chicken cacciatore, which we haven't had in like forever. Just for a sec, that smell makes me feel like I'm about eight.

I start to go upstairs but Mom hears me.

Is that you, Abby? she yells from the kitchen.

Yeah, I yell.

All this yelling. No wonder the angel with the missing wing gave up trying to talk.

Come in here and tell me about your day, Mom yells.

Come in here and tell me about your day. Mom never used to say that.

Mom used to say, Good day at school? And that was it. You could answer anything, it didn't matter because she was usually doing nineteen zillion things at once in the kitchen and the laundry room and was too busy for details.

You'd think you'd want your mom to say, *Come in here and tell me about your day* but I don't. I want to hear, *Good day at school?* and have no one care about the answer.

Just a sec, I yell back and charge upstairs because if I don't get this blouse off I'm going to pee my pants or throw up or both.

She yells something back but I can't hear what it is.

I'm just waiting for the phone to ring.

And then for Mom to answer it and get a look on her face which I don't want to see.

And then for Mom and Dad to come up to my room and shut the door with just the three of us in my room which means I'm in big trouble.

Only it doesn't happen that way.

What happens is we're all sitting at dinner and I can't eat because I feel like I'm going to throw up any sec so I just make little piles of white rice and canned spinach and chicken cacciatore and play a fascinating game of trading places—I make the chicken and the spinach trade places, then the rice and spinach, then the rice and chicken, and my stomach has a bowling ball in it and my head hurts worse than the time I fell out of the willow tree and cracked my head on a rock and needed eighteen stitches and still have a scar on my forehead in the shape of a seagull.

I'm waiting for the phone to ring.

I know it's going to ring.

It's already ringing in my head.

For once Mom notices something. She points her fork at my plate.

Abby, you're not eating, she says. Do you feel OK, honey?

I am *really* tired of all this honeying, which Mom never did before, all this honey dear sweetheart darling crap.

I glue on a smile, look at Mom's yellow hair with the black roots.

I'm fine, I say. Guess I had too many Oreos over at Poppy's.

Which used to be a big rule, no eating before dinner or you'll ruin your appetite, OK, you can have a piece of cheese if you're that hungry.

I'm thinking, please please *please* punish me for eating Oreos before dinner. Ground me, send me to bed without dinner, make me do chores with no pay, I'll clean all three bathrooms for the rest of my life, *please.*

Mom and her yellow hair just frowns and says, Well maybe your father will eat it.

I don't even have time to react to *that* weirdamundo statement because the phone rings and both my knees jerk up and hit under the table and everything on the table jumps and the silverware and plates all clank together and sound like a train wreck.

Mom presses a yellow napkin to her mouth and gets up.

I am completely frozen and Lisa is looking at me with a smirk because she knows what's going on because she can read my mind.

I look down at my plate and my ears are roaring and I look at the angel with the missing wing and I silently ask her for help but she just kneels there praying toward Mom's plate.

Hello? Mom says. Yes?

And then comes this long string of *um-hm* and *oh dear* and *I see* and *oh yes* and *no I didn't* and *yes we will.*

And *thank you.*

And *I'm so sorry about this.*

And *yes they do, I don't know what gets into them.*

And *um-hm, um-hm, OK, bye-bye.*

Oh god.

That bowling ball in my stomach weighs twelve hundred pounds.

You'd think I'd be relieved that finally the phone rang and finally it's happening but I'm not, I'm petrified.

No one has ever done anything this bad in our family. Not even close.

I don't even know what the punishment could possibly be.

I close my eyes and pray, God if you're there if you get me out of this I swear I'll never steal again or break any other commandments and I'll go to church every Sunday and pray at night and give all my old toys away to needy kids and read my Bible if I can find it and not wear makeup or short skirts except maybe to dances when I'm sixteen and I'll take the garbage out without being asked and rake all the leaves in both yards not just the easy ones in the front and do the dishes every night until I leave for college and try not to hate my mother with her yellow hair and I'll be nice to Lisa and never swear again and practice the piano every day without Mom yelling at me about it and please oh please God get me out of this, I'll change, I'll be a new person, I swear, you won't even recognize me.

Mom clears her throat with her mouth open and comes back to the table and I just look at my plate and then I take a forkful of chicken and put it in my mouth and even though I want to vomit I make myself chew it and swallow it because maybe if I eat Mom's dinner the punishment won't be so bad.

Dad says, Who was that? through a mouthful of rice even though the rule is, I mean *was*, no talking with your mouth full.

Mom clears her throat with her mouth open again and I know she's looking at me, I mean it's a small table and I can see the whole table out of the corner of my eye so looking at my plate doesn't really do anything.

That was something that Abby and I will discuss after dinner, Mom says. And clears her throat with her mouth open again.

Oh god.

The only good thing is the throat clearing because that's what

Mom used to do before she got sick, it was the signal that boy are you in trouble.

It's a really good sound because I haven't heard it in *so* long.

I replay it a zillion times in my head and it makes me feel better.

A little.

Dad looks over at me and Lisa is tapping her fork on her plate just to be a little creepamundo and the whole stupid dumb world is looking at me and I take another bite of chicken and force myself to chew and swallow even though both my throat and stomach are telling me, get that chicken *out* of here!

Is Abby in trouble? Lisa says, all dripping with sweetness.

I kick her a good one under the table.

Ow! she yells. Mom, Abby kicked me!

I kick her again. I mean, I have nothing to lose.

Ow! Mom, she did it again! Lisa yells.

I look at Lisa and stick out my tongue at her.

I'm breaking every rule I can think of.

Oh, if only I could make myself burp real loud like Poppy can.

Abby, Dad says in his one-more-and-you're-in-trouble voice that's so sharp it hurts your ears. I know he's staring at me but I don't care.

Leave your sister alone and eat your dinner, Mom says.

She sounds mad.

It's a beautiful sound.

I shut my eyes and hear it over and over.

I take two more bites of chicken and swallow hard.

It's all I can manage. I feel it coming back up.

May I be excused? I say to my plate.

I figure I might as well wait in my room for my execution. At least in my room I can hold on to Bunny and have a good cry and think about how unfair my whole life is.

Mom looks at Dad and Dad nods and Mom says, Yes but you're not leaving this house.

Ah, that voice. Mean, angry, wonderful music.

so I'm lying on my bed holding Bunny real tight and I'm crying and the tears are going into my ears and my stomach is gurgling and not in a good way and I know I'm going to be up all night with diarrhea or throwing up or both.

I'm waiting for two sets of steps on the stairs, one heavy, one light.

I'm waiting for the murmur of two voices coming up the stairs, one high and one low, the discussion, What Are We Going To Do With Her.

I don't know what happened, she used to be such a nice girl.

This is taking forever.

I know they're doing this on purpose, making me soak here in my own tears and guilt.

They know this is worse than the punishment, the waiting for the punishment.

Almost as bad as waiting for that phone to ring.

Finally, there are the steps.

Except there's only one set of steps, only the quick light steps that are Mom's.

She knocks and comes in.

Her yellow hair looks darker, almost brown in this light.

She closes the door and leans against it.

I sit up on my bed, holding Bunny tight against my stomach.

Do you want to tell me what happened with Mrs. Suchliss today? Mom says.

Her face has that waiting look. Waiting to see if I'll tell the truth or not.

I've already decided to tell the truth, mostly because I'm so tired of everything.

I'm so tired and I don't care what happens to me anymore. I don't care if I never leave this room again which that will probably be my punishment, grounded until I'm forty-three. I'll have gray hair and lines all over my face and I'll still be lying on this bed with that dorkamundo pink blanket from Grandma, clutching Bunny and waiting for my life to start.

I look at Mom and she's still waiting. She puts her hand on one cheek and tips her head sideways like Dad always does when he's waiting.

There's a funny scar on her wrist which I haven't noticed before, a long skinny triangle going all the way across. It's bright pink and sorta looks like a birthday party hat on its side.

What do you mean? I say, and I don't even know why I say it. It's not like I need more time. It's not like I'm going to invent a story or anything.

Her pink lips go into a straight line.

The Old Mom line.

I mean what happened down at Mrs. Suchliss's shop today, she says.

No song in *that* voice.

My eyes are going all around my room, like I'm buying time to make up a lie.

Then I finally meet her eyes.

I stole a blouse, I say, my voice all flat and hard like I don't care which I don't.

It's over there in my closet, I say, pointing to my closet which is pretty stupid because she knows where my closet is.

I don't break that eye-line between us.

She crosses her arms across her chest but she doesn't break the eye-line either.

I can't see the pink scar anymore.

Her other hand goes up and massages the back of her neck.

There's a pink scar on that wrist, too.

Suddenly I know what those pink scars are.

Both my hands grip Bunny real hard and my heart does about forty somersaults.

Suddenly I know why we couldn't visit Mom for almost a whole year.

Mom closes her eyes and tilts her head back and lets out something between a breath and a sigh.

Oh Abby, she says.

Her voice is so heavy I don't know how it got out of her mouth.

Wait, this is not how this is supposed to go.

Mom is supposed to be yelling right now even though there is no yelling in this house young lady.

She looks at my ceiling.

Why would you do something like that? she says. Her voice sounds so tired, like she can hardly force the air out.

All I can think of is those pink scars.

In my mind I see the blood running down her arms, onto the white sheets of her bed at the crazy hospital, nurses running, men in white pinning her down, there's screaming, there's blood everywhere.

Why would you do something like that?

I look down at Bunny.

I don't know, I say real soft.

This would be a good time to cry and beg forgiveness, but I'm all cried out. My throat isn't even tight.

I haven't told your father, Mom says. Her heavy voice hits the floor like wet cement.

Why not? I say, lying back on my back. Not that I really care. I don't care who knows anymore, not even Lisa who probably already knows because she can read my mind and also right now she is probably outside my door with a glass to her ear hearing everything.

I taught her how to do that.

I look at Mom's yellow hair with the black roots. Some of the hairs are gray at the roots, not black.

Poppy says your pubic hair turns gray when you get old. I don't know how she knows these things.

Mom comes over and sits on the bed next to me.

I can see her bra through her blouse and I remember how I used to look at that bra and be so jealous because I wanted a bra so bad and then I finally got one and now it's no big deal but when I think of all those times when I wanted one, well, it just seems like a very long time ago and we've all lived about fifty-nine lives since then.

Mom puts her hand on my knee and squeezes it.

Which this is not a Mom thing to do and it makes my leg go cold from the knee down.

She looks at me and I look at her.

I didn't tell your father, Mom says softly, because I want us to start over.

She's still holding my knee.

I move that leg and cross it over my other leg, getting it out of her hand.

I want you and me to start over, she says, and she's looking at me real intense, like she's trying to say stuff with her eyes, too, only I don't know what it is.

What do you mean? I say. For some reason, this comes out all sarcastic even though I wasn't thinking sarcastic thoughts. It's like my mouth has a mind of its own sometimes.

I mean I think we got off on the wrong foot, says Mom, when I came back from Meridian.

Meridian? I say, all sarcastic. *That's* what you're going to call it? *That's* what you call twenty-seven Seconals?

I didn't know I was going to say that.

It just came out.

And it came out all mean and angry.

Mom looks at me and slowly, slowly the corners of her mouth slide down and her cheeks slide down and the bottoms of her green eyes slide down and everything on her face slides down until it's such a huge sad thing I can't even look at it.

Except I do.

I look at her and she looks at me with her slipping-down face and we sit there for seven hundred years and look at each other without moving or breathing.

The only thing in the air is *twenty-seven Seconals.*

It bounces all over the room, off the walls, off the ceiling, off the floor.

Twenty-seven Seconals.

It multiplies every time it bounces, pretty soon there are ten thousand voices yelling, twenty-seven Seconals! twenty-seven Seconals! twenty-seven Seconals!

I don't know if Mom can hear it but I can. It's so loud I can almost see it.

Finally Mom gets up, oh so slowly, like she's a hundred and two, and walks, oh so slowly, to the door.

She doesn't look at me.

She opens the door just wide enough for her body and squeezes through it.

She snaps the door shut so slowly that I have to wait a zillion years for the click.

Bunny is looking at me and the three dolls with pink kimonos which Grandma brought back from Japan (which of course Lisa got blue ones) are looking at me and the eight palm trees lining the highway are looking at me and the big oak tree is looking at me and they're all chanting: *bad, bad, bad, bad, bad girl.*

chapter 49

t he end of the pirate blouse story is that the next day Dad took me down to The Girlfriend and made me return the pirate blouse to Old Lady Suckless in person and apologize right there in front of him. All the old fart said through her tight pink lips was, I hope you've learned your lesson, young lady.

And then she says, And you come from such a nice family, Abby.

Which I guess Old Lady Suckless hasn't been hanging around *our* house much lately.

Then Dad says, Go wait in the car, Abby. In this voice like nails.

I'm sure he wanted to explain to Old Lady Suckless about what a devil child I've turned into and then apologize up and down a zillion more times and probably try to pay her for the blouse even though she was getting it back.

Which she'll probably take the money, that old bitch.

The other end of the pirate blouse story is that I stopped stealing because it just wasn't fun anymore.

chapter 50

t's summer and it's so hot that everyone's talking about how hot it is and that's all they ever talk about.

I'm over at Poppy's, swimming in her pool and working on my tan. Of course Poppy is already super dark, she has a tan all year round, probably because her mom is Greek or Lebanese or whatever she is. In the summer Poppy gets almost black which with her long blond hair makes her look like the total California girl. I tan pretty easily, but I can never get as dark as Poppy.

We're drinking iced tea and reading our books under the white-hot sun. It's so hot you have to go in the pool like every five minutes to cool off.

I'm reading *Jaws* but I can only read it when I'm at Poppy's because my mom would never let it in the house. Poppy's reading *Rosemary's Baby* which is some scary book about this woman who has a demon baby, which Poppy always reads the coolest stuff.

Mrs. Cordesi is inside having iced tea with Mrs. Sierra. They had been out here, but they said it was too hot for them so they went inside. I can hear their voices a little through the window screen, but they're mostly talking about the hot weather so I just tune them out because this great white shark is killing everyone and it's a lot more interesting.

It's so hot there's not even any bugs around, even the twenty-four-hour bugs. Everything is bright and white and super still, like the whole world has just been zapped by electric shock or something.

Poppy turns over onto her stomach and puts her book down and closes her eyes.

Which I decide that looks pretty good because I'm so sleepy under this hot sun, so I put down my book and close my eyes, too.

I don't even care that sweat is running down my face, down my sides, down my chest, between my fingers.

The voices of Mrs. Cordesi and Mrs. Sierra are low murmurs, like a fan going.

I'm not even listening.

I'm almost asleep.

Except then I hear the word Shirley.

And there's only one Shirley in our neighborhood which is Mom.

I keep my eyes closed but my ears go wide open.

I just don't understand it, Mrs. Sierra says. She's got a nice husband, two lovely girls, a nice house, her husband has a good job, why would she throw it all away?

I don't know, but the same thing happened to my sister-in-law, Mrs. Cordesi says. And they put her on so many happy pills she doesn't know which end is up.

Mrs. Sierra goes tch-tch-tch.

Well you can sure tell they have Shirley on those things, Mrs. Sierra says.

Mm-hm, says Mrs. Cordesi. You sure can.

There's a long silence. The ice in their glasses clinks like maybe they're sipping.

My heart is beating so fast I just know I'm going to have a heart attack.

I can't breathe and the sun is hitting my head like a sledgehammer and I'm getting all dizzy.

Happy pills.

I hear it in my head, in Mrs. Cordesi's voice.

Happy pills, happy pills.

I hold my breath and I wait to hear more.

I don't want to hear more but I can't move and I can't stop listening.

A chair scrapes across the floor and Mrs. Cordesi says, More iced tea?

Sure, says Mrs. Sierra.

I'm still frozen and listening.

There's sweat all over my body, I'm wet and greasy and my skin is baking to red under the hot sun, I can feel it.

They start talking about someone else, someone named Sybil which I don't know any Sybils.

I listen some more, just to make sure they're done talking about Mom.

I open my eyes and look at my arms, which are red and glistening. I'm completely covered with sweat all over and my hair feels like it's on fire.

I can't stand it anymore.

I get up and jump in the pool.

I sink to the bottom.

The cold water feels so good.

I can't hear anything down here.

If I could just stay down here.

I wave my hands around to make myself stay on the bottom.

Happy pills.

I don't even know what happy pills are but which you could tell from their voices it's not good.

In my mind I see Mom's gold-teeth smile.

A smile that's too happy.

And all the darling-sweetheart-honey-pie crap.

Too happy.

And that songy voice.

Too happy.

I lie flat on my back on the bottom of the pool and pinch my nose shut.

I look up and see the sun up there, trying to pierce the water, but it can't get me, not down here.

Down here there is only me and the aqua-blue water and my bubbles going up.

I tell myself to think about something else, anything but happy pills.

But all I can hear is Mrs. Cordesi's voice. *They put her on so many happy pills she doesn't know which end is up.*

Doesn't know which end is up.

Doesn't know which end is up.

I can't hold my breath any longer, I have to go up.

I let my body go and it floats to the top.

My face breaks the water and I let out air and gulp in more.

What were you doing? Poppy says, squinting over at me from her chair. You were down there forever, I was starting to wonder.

It's coldest at the bottom, I say. It felt good.

I smile a weak smile at her.

I'm going down again, I say. Too hot up here.

Back at the bottom I start wondering about the color of those happy pills.

The Seconals were red, what would happy pills look like? Blue? Green? I try to think of a happy color. Yellow?

Happy pills.

I didn't know you could take pills to make you happy.

But the thing is, when I think about Mom, I don't think of happy. I don't know what she is, but it's not happy.

She's, like, too happy. Like her train passed the happy station and kept going.

Now I've thought about the word *happy* too many times and it starts to sound funny, like it's not a real word, like I made it up.

I sit on the bottom of the pool with my legs crossed Indian-style and my hands pushing the water up so I can stay at the bottom.

I've got a little clench in my stomach, the kind of clench that maybe you can ignore for a while but eventually you have to pay attention to it.

The little clench is I thought we were all done with pills and now there's more pills.

And what happens if she takes too many happy pills. We don't have any Seconal anymore, except the two I left in the bottle, which are still there because I keep checking.

Mom brought a lot of new bottles home from the hospital with her.

Which I wonder what the happy pills are really called and if I want to go look for them what do I look for.

And what do I do when I find them.

I've held my breath all I can and I have to go up again for air.

Just as I'm coming up, Poppy dives in right next to me and we both pop up at the same time.

Just our heads are above the water and Poppy says, Didja see that one?

No, I said. See what?

My dive, she said. It was a perfect swan.

Poppy has been working on her swan dive since forever.

Nope, I say.

I turn to climb up the ladder and Poppy says, What's wrong?

I swear she has ESP.

I turn to her and smile the best real smile I can come up with and go, Nothing, nothing's wrong.

Poppy dives underwater and I get out.

It's still so hot you can't even stand on the cement or it burns your feet so I run to my chair and lie down and let the sun beat down on my stomach which maybe it'll burn out that little clench.

I try to read but I can't concentrate.

No white shark is as scary as happy pills.

chapter 51

Of course i have to go look for the happy pills.

I wait till Mom goes grocery shopping on Saturday and Dad is outside burning something in his beloved incinerator and Lisa is, I don't know, over at Annie's or something.

I go into Mom and Dad's bathroom and open the medicine cabinet.

You have never seen so many bottles of pills. Brown bottles with white caps, all from Terry's Pharmacy over on Sixteenth.

All with Shirley Goodman's name on them.

I look at all the names of the pills, see if anything sounds like happy pills.

I mean what would you call a happy pill. Not that pill names ever sound like what they're for. Seconal doesn't sound like sleep. Neosporin doesn't sound like a skinned knee. Calamine doesn't sound itchy.

There's so many bottles with so many different names. I'll never find them.

A little panicky moth starts flying around in my head.

And anyway what if I did find them.

What would I do with them.

I didn't have a plan. I just wanted to see what they looked like.

Maybe I'd hide them, like for a day or something. Just to see what she's like with no happy pills.

I open the drawers next to the sink and paw through all the bottles there.

Nothing that sounds like happy pills.

What did you think you would find, I ask myself.

I close the drawers and the medicine cabinet and look at myself in the mirror.

My face and chest and neck are all red from too much sun.

I'm as red as a Seconal.

My hair is starting to bleach out from the sun, going from dark brown to light brown, never blond. Last summer I tried putting lemon juice on it to bleach it even more but it didn't work.

So what if she's on happy pills, I say to the mirror.

At least it's better than melting people's galoshes.

chapter 52

it has finally cooled off even though it's August which is usually when it's the hottest, so everyone is *still* talking about the weather like there's nothing more interesting going on in the world.

Not that I keep up on the news or anything but I mean there *is* a war going on in Vietnam.

Not that you'd know it by walking around this neighborhood.

Every night Dad waters the lawn by standing there with the hose and he talks over the fence to Mr. Sierra about the weather and which Mr. Sierra also waters his lawn by standing there with the hose and haven't they ever heard of sprinklers.

Cooler today, Dad says.

Unusual for August, Mr. Sierra says.

Supposed to get warmer tomorrow, Dad says.

Hope not, Mr. Sierra says.

I mean it's the same conversation every night and it makes you want to scream.

Anyway it's a lazy Saturday afternoon and Dad and Lisa went over to San Jose for a car wash and a haircut so it's just Mom and me alone.

We're reading on the couch which you'd think oh boy, just like old times, but Mom keeps picking her nose and playing with her hair and tapping her feet to no music I can hear and flipping around in her book like she's not reading it in order and she's driving me crazy.

Finally I say, Do you want some coffee?

Thinking maybe coffee would calm her down.

She gives me the gold-teeth smile and says, That would be lovely, dear.

So I go in the kitchen and start making the coffee but I can still hear her in there squirming around and making all these little noises in her throat, like she's talking back to her book in some weirdo-mundo language.

I decide that when I go back in, I'm sitting in the green chair and I don't care what she thinks. I mean she makes the whole couch move when she squirms around.

And she used to call *me* squirmy.

Pretty soon coffee smells fill up the house and Mom calls out, Smells good out there, sugar!

I get two coffee cups down from the cupboard.

I don't know why. I don't drink coffee, although I love the smell.

I figure I can put sugar and milk in it like Grandma does.

I pour the two coffees and add sugar and milk to mine.

I sip it.

It's actually pretty good.

I carry both cups out, real careful and slow.

Mom looks up and her eyebrows go down.

I don't need two cups, sweetie, she says. One will do.

I set hers down on the banana coffee table and take mine over to the green chair.

One's for me, I say, looking into my coffee like it's suddenly so interesting.

Mom puts her book on the banana table and swings her legs down. I know she's looking at me but I refuse to look at her so I just stir my coffee and watch the spoon go around.

Since when did you start drinking coffee? she says.

I still don't look at her, I just blow on my coffee and watch the steam go up.

Like, a year ago, I say, all sarcastic. I don't even mean to be sarcastic, it just comes out that way.

You're too young to drink coffee, she says. It'll stunt your growth.

That's just a myth, I say. We learned it in Health.

I'm totally making this up but I feel like I'm on a roll because she has not said what I thought she'd say which is Take that coffee right out to the kitchen young lady and pour it down the sink, no fourteen-year-old is going to drink coffee in this house.

Mom sips her coffee, still giving me the Mom Eye, I can feel it.

All that silence just hangs there in the air with the coffee steam.

I'm waiting.

I'm watching my coffee and waiting.

I blow on it and sip.

I sneak a little look at her and she's staring into her own coffee like it's so interesting.

This is not going how I planned it.

I don't know what to say so I just sit there.

I can't believe this silence.

I mean Mom and I are the two big talkers around this house, usually Dad and Lisa can't get a word in edgewise, which what the heck is *edgewise*, anyway.

Mom puts her cup down and I think, OK, here we go.

She scoots back on the couch and swings her legs up.

Picks up her book and starts reading.

This is too weirdamundo.

I sip my coffee really loud, just to remind her.

Hey, we were in the middle of something here. We were having a conversation.

Her foot taps against her other foot. She's wearing socks which I just noticed for the first time. Red socks.

She starts flipping backwards in her book, opens to a page and starts reading where she already should have read.

One of her hands goes up and starts combing through her hair, which her hair is now half black and half blond and if you don't think that's weirdamundo, look again.

My heart is beating all funny and light and uneven, like a stone skipping across a lake.

Maybe it's just the coffee.

I set down my cup and pick up my book. I can't concentrate to read anything, but I have to at least pretend.

Mom's fingers are tapping against her chin.

It's weird because it makes no noise.

chapter 53

this is when Hector Martinez comes into my life only I don't know it at the time. I mean I know he's there but I don't know what all's going to happen which is a lot.

It all starts with the T-shirts for our glee club which this year I'm in the ninth grade glee club which is boys and girls, not just girls, even though there's still more girls than boys. Anyway, Hector Martinez is in it but I don't even notice him till later.

We decide we're all going to get T-shirts for glee club, and Mr. Goldberg makes me in charge of ordering them and collecting the money and all that which I don't really want to do it but you can't argue with Mr. Goldberg because he's old and he was in a concentration camp and he even has the number tattooed on his arm and everything and when you look at that number you just can't argue with him. I mean I don't know anything about concentration camps but my uncle Rex was one of the army guys that went into those camps when the war was over and he says you never saw humans look like that and he had to go over to the ditch and throw up when he saw them.

It takes forever to decide on what color of shirts to get and how big to make the glee club logo which is this stupid logo that the glee club has had since forever, I mean since before I was even born, and you can tell it's ancient because it has a picture of a boy and a girl and they're smiling these huge dorkamundo smiles and the girl's hair is in pigtails and I'm sorry but teenagers just don't look like that anymore but Mr. Goldberg won't let us change it.

We finally vote on blue T-shirts.

I take all the orders and then six weeks later the big boxes of shirts arrive and this is when Hector Martinez comes in.

Mr. Goldberg keeps me and Hector Martinez after glee club one day and says the shirts are in and would we please go down to the office to get them.

I never really noticed Hector Martinez before.

I look at him for the first real time when we're walking down South Hall and he's actually pretty cute. He has really curly black hair and real dark skin and eyes that are so black you can't see the pupils and he's about six inches taller than me and he's real muscular all over, you can tell because his white T-shirt is real tight and so are his jeans.

He doesn't look at me as we walk in silence down the hall but then I can't stand it so I say, How do you like glee club this year?

Which I know is totally dorkamundo but I couldn't think of anything clever at the moment.

He looks at me kinda sideways and smiles this huge white smile that's about eighty miles long and something happens to my heart which it starts beating super fast and then takes this nose-dive right to my feet and then starts floating back up.

Which is so weirdamundo. I mean I don't even know Hector Martinez.

My whole body is beating with my heartbeat and it's so loud and hard I think he must be able to see it.

It's all right, I guess, Hector Martinez says.

I smile back and our eyes do this *zoing!* thing when they meet and this is when everything really starts happening.

We get to the end of South Hall and we're supposed to turn down the last hall to go to the office but instead Hector Martinez grabs my arm, not hard but not soft either, and we start walking the other way, down West Hall.

I don't say anything, I just follow him.

My mind is thinking so many thoughts they keep crashing into each other and nothing in my head makes sense right now.

Where his hand is on my arm, it's a ring of fire.

He walks me to the end of the science building and then behind it.

It's deserted and we're hidden on three sides by buildings.

And then it *really* happens.

Hector Martinez pulls on my arm until I'm up real close to him and he bends down a little and kisses me right on the lips.

I don't know what to do so I just stand there and let him kiss me.

He smells so good, like a boy is supposed to smell, not that I know what that is, but when you smell it you know it, and it's good. I close my eyes and breathe in his smell.

All inside me is fire alarms and bells and fireworks and I swear my blood is exploding.

The more I breathe in Hector Martinez's smell, the more fireworks go off and I never, never, never want this to end.

I never really got what kissing was all about but now I get it.

Totally.

Oh my god.

Hector Martinez stops kissing me and I open my eyes and we look at each other.

I don't know what to say.

But I think I should say something.

I smile and go, Wow.

Which is pretty dumb but it's all I could think of.

Hector Martinez smiles at me, his big white smile all the way out to there.

And just when I think something big has started, in fact possibly the biggest thing ever in my whole life so far, it's over.

Hector Martinez grabs my arm again and pulls me back down the hall.

Back toward the office.

It's over.

The best moment of my entire life just started and now it's over already.

I could have stood there the rest of my life kissing Hector Martinez.

Everything in my body is still going Wow, Wow, Wow, a zillion wows going in all directions like fireflies inside me, even though we don't have fireflies in California but I've seen them at Grandma's in Ohio.

My arm is still on fire where his hand is.

I wish he would hold my hand.

I want to reach up and grab his hand in mine but I can't move anything on my body except my legs and feet which are going by themselves and just following Hector Martinez.

Hector Martinez, Hector Martinez, Hector Martinez, Hector Martinez.

It's all I can think.

We get to the office and he lets go of me and goes in the office door and I follow and he asks Miss Greenaway for the glee club T-shirts and I just watch him and I think my mouth might be hanging wide open and my tongue must be on the floor but I can't do a thing about it because my brain has turned to water.

I watch Hector Martinez's muscles move in his tight white T-shirt and I am breathing all jerky and weird like the way you breathe when you're crying hard.

His saliva is still all over my lips, drying up.

I lick my lips and I can taste him.

It's a good taste. Boy taste, like boy smell.

Miss Greenaway puts a box in my arms and I can't believe I don't drop it because my arms have turned to water, too.

I follow Hector Martinez with his box back out the door.

This must be a dream.

No way did I just kiss Hector Martinez behind the science building.

I mean I've never kissed anyone before and I didn't even know I liked Hector Martinez.

I follow him down the hall and watch the back of his head and all I want to do is throw my box down and put my hand on the back of his dark neck, just to feel his skin on my skin again.

We get to the music room and everything is all floaty and foggy like a dream, Mr. Goldberg is there but I don't hear what he's saying, and someone takes the box from my arms and there are voices in the background but everything is very far away.

Then Hector Martinez picks up his books off the piano and waves at me and smiles.

And leaves.

Goes out the door and disappears.

Before I have time to say, I don't know, something, anything, even something dumb.

He's gone.

I'm standing there like a dork next to the piano, watching the empty door.

My face hardens into cement.

Then my whole body.

I can't move.

Mr. Goldberg says something to me and he goes out the door, too.

I am alone.

With Hector Martinez's kiss on my lips.

And all that wow turned to cement in my veins.

I tell myself to move.

Get out of here.

Go.

Now.

I pick up my books and my legs somehow move forward like zombie legs and I go out the door, too.

There's no one around, the halls are deserted because it's after school.

This little gray fog gathers around me as I walk to my locker and get my books and my purse.

Poppy's not around, she doesn't wait for me on glee club days.

I close my locker but I don't start walking home.

Instead I look everywhere for Hector Martinez.

I check all the halls, the cafeteria, the basketball courts, the tennis courts, the baseball field, even the auditorium.

Yeah, right, like he's gonna be in the auditorium.

There's no one around.

It's just me and my little gray fog.

Me and my fog walk down East Hall and out past the office, cross behind the office building and down the grass path that leads to the orchard.

It's a sunny day and warm even though it's fall.

But the sun doesn't burn off my little gray fog that's still around me.

I lick my lips.

I'm sure I've licked off all of Hector Martinez's saliva by now but I can't stop licking.

I put my fingers on my lips and feel all the way around, touching where Hector Martinez's lips were on my lips just twenty minutes ago. Or was it ten. Or was it fifty.

Or did I make it all up.

I feel my lips again with my fingers and they feel puffy, like someone was there.

My fingers are cool on my hot lips.

Over and over I replay it in my mind.

I still can't believe it.

Hector Martinez kissed me.

Kissed *me*.

Out of like four hundred girls at our school.

I'm totally, *totally* in love.

With Hector Martinez.

chapter 54

i get home that same day and I lie on my bed with my head ringing and my ears roaring and my heart running a marathon.

Zinging through my head are all kinds of questions. Did it really happen? Did Hector Martinez really kiss me? Are you sure?

It really happened.

I can feel on my arm where his hand was and it's still warm.

My lips still feel puffy and soft, like they're full of liquid.

that night at dinner I don't say anything and I don't look at anyone, I just eat my dinner, I eat everything on my plate.

Well, it's something I actually like—chicken 'n' cornflakes.

No one notices that I'm so quiet.

Mom says, How was school today, honey? And I have to look at her to see if she's talking to me or Lisa or Dad.

It's me.

Fine, I say to my yellow hominy.

She keeps smiling at me with her gold-teeth smile, I can see it out the corner of my eye.

She nods about eighty times, like I just filled her in on every minute of my day.

How about you, Lisa? she says.

I can still feel Hector's kiss even though there's cornflakes on my lips.

I can't believe everyone else can't see it.

This isn't me sitting here anymore.

Not Abby Goodman.

She's been replaced.

We have a new girl now.

Abby Martinez.

She's dark and dangerous.

She'll do anything.

chapter 55

right after dinner I run over to Poppy's.

She'll never believe this.

That someone kissed me.

Poppy has kissed a guy before, she kissed Kevin Stark at the Sadie Hawkins dance last year which I didn't go to because I was too chicken to ask anybody.

It's me! I yell as I come through their door.

Poppy is playing Janis Joplin at full volume, so I'm sure she doesn't hear me.

Hey! I yell even louder, as I'm going down the hall to her room.

Hey yourself! she yells back.

My heart is still going like a steam train that's late.

Poppy's lying on her floor doing homework. I turn down the music and flop onto her bed.

Guess what? I say. I'm trying to sound cool and calm but I have a feeling I sound more like a jumpy puppy.

What? she says without looking up.

You'll never guess what happened to me today, I say. I want to draw this out, make her guess, make it into a puzzle.

Make it last forever.

Because the second-best thing about being kissed is telling your best friend about it.

Of course the first-best thing is the kiss itself.

OK, what? she says, sticking a pencil in her mouth and chewing on the eraser.

She's not even looking at me, she's reading her dumb math problems.

Something big, I say. Something *very* big. The biggest.

It's all I can do to keep from giggling. There is giggle juice going through my veins.

Finally, she looks up at me.

What? she says. Tell me!

Nope, you have to guess, I say. I roll onto my stomach to keep the giggles from coming up.

Um, you're getting a swimming pool, she says.

Nope, I say. Bigger.

Bigger than a swimming pool? she says.

Well not in *dimensions*, I say. Bigger, like more important.

The waiting is killing me. I have to grab onto Poppy's bedpost with both hands to keep from exploding.

I dunno, just tell me, she says. She giggles because she sees my face and something big is written all over it.

I kissed somebody, I say.

No way! she almost screams.

She's up on her knees, her eyes popping out all over.

Yep, I say, all casual, like this happens to me every day, this has happened a zillion times before.

Who? she says. Her voice is a scream and a giggle.

I sit up and cross my legs Indian-style.

Hector Martinez, I say. His name even feels good on my tongue. I realize it's the first time I've ever said his name out loud. When I hear it, it sounds like it's part of me, something of me I just shared with Poppy.

The Mexican guy? she says, her eyebrows all bunched up into some kind of opinion.

Yes, the Mexican guy, I say. What's wrong with that?

Poppy looks at me with her eyebrows still bunched up, then she tilts her head, like I'm a kitten in a pet store and she's thinking about buying me.

Nothing, I guess, she says, and shrugs her shoulders. I barely even know who he is. Wait, how do you even know him?

He's in glee club, I say.

So how did it happen? she says. She puts her pencil in her math book and closes it, then lies on her back with her feet up on the bed. Her toenails are painted a real dark red, even darker than blood.

So I tell her.

I tell her the whole story from beginning to end. And just telling it makes my heart go fast again and makes that place on my arm turn to fire and makes my lips grow huge and hot.

Hector Martinez.

I'll never love anyone else but Hector Martinez.

I'm going to marry him and have nineteen children and live up in the hills with a view and a swimming pool and a big dog named Fritz.

chapter 56

i can't sleep all night.

I watch the cars go by on the highway, and then it's so late that there are no cars.

I know I won't sleep tonight.

I look at the stars.

I think about Hector Martinez with his dark curly hair and his wide white smile that goes the whole way across the country.

And what will happen tomorrow.

I'll see him in third period math.

He sits in the back of the room, in the very back corner, and I sit more in the middle.

God, I wish I sat in the back.

I'll sit there in math and wonder if he's watching me.

What to wear.

What do I have that looks good from the back.

I touch my lips in the dark and for the first time I wonder if I kissed him back. Maybe I should have been doing more, maybe there's something the girl is supposed to do that I don't know about. And what if I didn't do it and that's it—I had my chance and now he'll move on to some other girl, maybe Tina Caswell or Karen Boyce, one of those girls that knows how to kiss a guy.

Oh god.

My life is suddenly happening too fast.

I wasn't ready for this.

But I wouldn't trade it for a whole truckload of miniskirts and go-go boots.

chapter 57

i can hardly breathe all through first period and second period. I keep looking for Hector Martinez in the halls, but his locker is in a different hall from mine.

Finally third period comes and my hands are so slick I can hardly hold on to my books and my heart is beating away in my throat and I can't swallow.

A jumble of students goes into the room and I go with them, looking everywhere for Hector Martinez, but trying not to look like I'm looking for him.

There he is.

In his seat in the back, laughing with Steve Sampson.

He's not even looking this way.

My feet feel like bricks.

I don't know how I get into my seat but I do.

I wish I had eyes in the back of my head.

My left ear is open as wide as it will go, listening for his voice.

I think I hear him but I'm not sure.

Oh god, maybe I *did* make it all up.

I put one finger on my lips, just for a sec.

His kiss is still there, I can feel it, I didn't make it up.

Oh god, I hope he didn't see me do that.

Miss Thorpe is up there talking about geometry.

I can't hear anything she says but my eyes are on her like I can't wait to hear her next word.

Oh if she only knew.

I wish I had eyes in back of my head.

My heart is pounding like some wild thing. One more pound and it's going to leap right out of me.

Third period lasts forever and then it's over.

My insides turn to water when the bell rings.

I stand up and I don't look over in the direction of Hector Martinez.

I am such a lily-white chicken.

I ask myself, How's he gonna know you like him if you ignore him?

I keep licking my lips even though I can't taste him anymore.

It's when I'm bending down to get my books from under my chair that it happens.

I see a pair of jeans and I smell that smell in the swish as he goes by.

Hey Abby, he says.

It's so quiet I almost don't hear it.

And then he's gone.

And maybe I just made it up.

Except I see his back go out the door.

My arms go so weak I almost drop my books.

Everything inside me sings.

chapter 58

So that's how Hector and me got started.

And then we kept going.

Not by anything I did because I am the biggest, whitest, stupidest, chickenest person from here to the sun.

Hector Martinez did everything.

I just followed along.

I kept wondering how he knew what to do, because I'm pretty sure he never had a girlfriend before. I mean, it's not that big a school, everyone knows who's with who.

Like now, everyone knows I'm with Hector and he's with me.

hector starts walking home with me and Poppy because he lives in the same direction. Only he turns left in the middle of the orchard so he can get to his street which is Bonnie Brae Avenue. How I know is I looked it up in the phone book and then I made Poppy walk over there with me this one time and we saw his house but we had to walk by real fast because I didn't want him to know I was there, checking out his house.

It was a white house with black trim, very modern, with a little pond in the front and lots of flowers. Not like our dumb old brown house with faded red trim, which whoever heard of that.

Every day the three of us walk home from school together and when we get to the middle of the orchard where Hector has to turn left, Hector and I stop so we can make out, and Poppy walks on home by herself.

Poppy is totally cool with this.

I checked.

She said, If it was the other way around, wouldn't I be cool with it.

I said, Duh, of course.

Sometimes Hector and me make out in the orchard for a really long time and then I get home real late and Mom says, Where have you been?

I have a different lie every time.

I stayed after school to help Mr. Goldberg.

I stayed after school to help with the school float.

I stayed after school to do some homework.

To get help on math.

To finish my art project.

To tutor a seventh grader.

Oh, I have a zillion of 'em.

And Mom believes every one.

The weirdamundo part is, some little bitty teeny weeny eensy part of me wants Mom to not believe me.

It's like I want to be found out, caught in the lie.

I have no idea why.

chapter 59

hector and i are now definitely boyfriend and girlfriend.

Everyone at school knows.

But our parents don't know.

It's just this thing that didn't happen. Telling our parents, that is.
I never go to his house and he never comes to mine.

We don't see each other on weekends.

Sometimes me and Poppy go to the orchard on weekends and hang out, just to see if Hector might show up. But he never does.

It makes the weekends really, really long.

I write long love notes to Hector on the weekends, but I never give them to him because they're too sappy, all full of this I-love-you junk that would probably make Hector throw up.

Everything is going pretty fine until one day.

When Mom finds out about Hector.

She finds one of those love notes which I stupidly left in the pocket of my jeans and she takes it out when she's doing the wash and she *reads* it, which I mean how rude is that.

She comes upstairs and I don't know what's going on, I'm just up there reading on my bed and in she comes with that gold-teeth smile.

Honey, she says, and her voice is this sugary goo-goo crap. Is there something you want to tell me about a boy in your class?

She's standing in the doorway with that sick smile and I just want to slap her.

A *boy* in my class. How dorkamundo.

No, I say. I look at her for one second and then go back to my book.

Not even a boy named . . . *Hector*? she says with an even sicker smile and her eyebrows go up all the way.

She pulls the love note out of her pocket and dangles it in front of me, swishing it back and forth.

Just for a sec I get this weirdamundo flash in my head and it's like I'm looking at Lisa standing there instead of Mom, because it's like something Lisa would do, dangling that letter in front of me, teasing me with it.

Gimme that! I yell, and grab the note out of her hand.

Mom sits down on the bed.

Honey, I don't mind if you're seeing a boy at school, she says, I'd just like to meet him. Why don't you invite him over for dinner some night?

This is totally the opposite of what the old Mom would have said.

The old Mom would have said, No boyfriends till you're sixteen, you're too young, blah blah blah blah blah, big lecture.

All this niceness is totally throwing me off.

She sits there, smiling with her gold teeth and gold hair which is now half black and half yellow, waiting for me to say something.

I'm looking at my book, pretending to read.

I don't know, I say to the book. Let me think about it.

Do you want me to call his mother and arrange it? she says, getting up.

NO! I scream. God, Mother, I'm not *eight*!

I flip over onto my back and put the book over my face.

This conversation is over.

. . .

i'm so confused now.

Whether to invite Hector Martinez over for dinner or not.

Part of me wants to and part of me doesn't.

I don't even know the *why* of the part that doesn't.

I mean, what's the big deal?

I go back and forth.

I don't tell Hector at first, because I want to think it through.

I mean, Hector meeting my dorkamundo family. Hector meeting my crazy mother. I just don't know.

Although she's been pretty good lately.

I mean except for the gold-teeth smile and the sweetie-honey-darling crap and that goo-goo voice and that half-and-half hair. And except for being a total zombie and not noticing anything unless you jam it right in her face.

Other than that, she's fine.

Although you never know.

finally i just say Oh what the hell and figure maybe this way I can see Hector on weekends and maybe even after school and not just in the orchard.

So he comes over on Tuesday night.

For dinner.

It turns out this is the worst decision I ever made in my entire life.

It happens as soon as I open the front door and Hector Martinez walks in.

I see it on Mom's face right away.

How her smile droops down at the corners as soon as she sees him.

It's not an obvious droop, but I can see it.

She looks like she's still smiling, but I can tell.

She doesn't like him.

I look over at Dad and I can't tell anything by looking at his face. He's smiling at Hector but I can't tell if it's a real smile or not.

Dad shakes Hector's hand, man to man, and says, Hi, Hector, nice to meet you.

Dad's voice sounds pretty normal but sometimes it's hard to tell with him.

But Mom.

Mom is all changed.

She closes her lips when she smiles at Hector and you can't see her gold teeth.

Which you'd think would be a good thing but what you get with closed lips is an even yuckier smile than the gold-teeth smile.

And she talks to him in that high, polite voice which she always uses with my other grandma, Grandma Goodman, which is Dad's mom, and which my mom and her hate each other like poison and which it's a good thing Grandma Goodman lives in Pennsylvania because then she and Mom only have to see each other once a year when Grandma comes to visit.

As soon as I hear the Grandma Goodman voice I get a chill and my lungs go flat.

Oh god.

I *knew* this was a bad idea.

And Hector is being so nice and charming and cute and Mom even lets us sit next to each other at dinner and we hold hands under the table and curl our feet around each other.

Mom is totally creeping me out with her little act.

I don't get why she doesn't like him.

And she doesn't just not like him, she *hates* him.

You can tell.

She might not be the old Mom, but you can tell.

I mean her voice is practically a strangle as she asks him about his family.

What does your father do? she strangles out in the Grandma Goodman voice.

He's a city engineer, Hector says, smiling at Mom and taking more mashed potatoes.

That's nice, says Mom, nodding. But you can tell she think it's about as nice as rotten cabbage.

It goes on like that. The whole rest of the night and I can't wait to get Hector out the door and on his way home.

Even though I love that I can smell him all through dinner.

chapter 60

mom waits all of about six seconds to lower the boom.

I kiss Hector good night quickly in the shadows on the front porch so no one can see us, then I come back inside.

I know immediately something's wrong because Mom and Dad are both standing in the living room with totally serious hound dog faces and when I come in they stop talking in mid-sentence.

My heart beats as fast as a baby sparrow.

Mom's hands are on her hips and her mouth is in a straight line.

Dad's arms are folded across his chest and his face is a blank page.

Abby, you're not to see that boy anymore, Mom says.

It almost sounds like the old Mom and for just a sec my heart lifts up in my chest.

But just for a sec.

What? I say, all high and sarcastic but I don't even care. I shove my hands in my front pockets, and I look at Mom, then Dad, then Mom again.

I said you're not to see him anymore, Mom says, her eyes looking hard into mine.

It's the old Mom eyes but I can't even be happy about it.

Why *not*? I say. My voice is loud and screechy but I don't care.

Because you're too young to have a boyfriend, that's why not, she says.

Which makes, like, no sense to me, because why did she have me invite him over for dinner in the first place if I was too young to have a boyfriend?

I look over at Dad with my mouth wide open because I can't believe this is happening and why is he just standing there doing nothing.

But . . . he's not my boyfriend, I say to Dad, which is a lie, but it's all I can think of to say. I'm trying to calm my voice down so I sound reasonable. Talking to Dad, adult to adult.

Forget Mom, she has no idea what she's saying, she's just crazy.

Dad just shakes his head.

Whatever *that* means.

Mom crosses her arms across her chest.

I look at the two of them, standing there with their arms crossed like two big tanks.

The two of them against me.

How did this happen? Just a few hours ago it was the old way,

Dad and Lisa and me on one side, and Mom by herself on the crazy side.

But here they are, together.

And me on the crazy side.

You're to come *right home* after school, Mom says. It's almost the old Mom voice but I can't even care.

My mouth is still hanging open, waiting for words to come.

None are coming.

I hate it that they caught me off guard like this.

I haven't had time to think.

But I know one thing for sure.

I am *not* going to stop seeing Hector Martinez.

I'm going to marry him and have nineteen children and a dog named Fritz.

I cross my arms across my chest and I make my eyes real skinny and I step back and look at both of them at once, into both their eyes.

I'm *not* going to stop seeing him, I say real slow and real low.

Then I sprint upstairs and slam my door.

Which is three broken rules at once but who's even counting.

chapter 61

i **think i've** won but I know I haven't really.

Because now I'm so nervous about being watched and being punished that I can't even make myself stay very long in the orchard with Hector.

I mean we make out for like five minutes and then I get too nervous and I have to go.

Some rebel I am.

I can't even stand up to a crazy woman.

so this one day Hector and me are sitting in the old rotted-out tool shed in the orchard which no one uses anymore and it's raining and we're making out and I finally say, I gotta go.

Hector holds me really tight and says, Don't.

I kiss him a long kiss and then I say, I have to or I'll get in trouble.

Mom has been watching me like some army general, looking at the clock the second I walk in the house.

I'm not speaking to her these days. Which I'm making a point by not speaking to her but I'm not really sure what the point is but it feels good not to speak to her. I also try not to look at her.

Just a few more minutes, Hector says, kissing me.

I could stay here forever.

In my mind I play out the movie, what would happen if I didn't go home.

Or if I got home really, really late.

I'd be grounded for sure.

I'd be picked up by Dad every day after school.

Mom would phone the school office and put all the teachers on the alert that I am not to be seen with Hector Martinez.

I'd be a prisoner at my own school.

You don't get it, I say to Hector. My mother is crazy, she'll do anything.

Then I get the best idea I've ever had.

Wait a minute, I say. I know what we can do!

I put my hands on either side of my head to keep my brain from exploding with this wonderful idea.

We can sneak out at night! I say.

Sneak out? he says, like he doesn't get it.

Yeah, we can sneak out of our houses at night and meet! I say. We don't live that far apart, it's perfect! Oh my god, I can't believe I didn't think of this before!

Everything inside me is bursting open and flowing.

Hector gets it and his eyes get real big.

Oh! Sneak *out*! he says. Oh my god, Ab, that's a great idea!

We could try it tonight, I say. Let me think . . . my mom goes to bed pretty late . . . but I can set my alarm in case I fall asleep, although I'm sure I won't. She usually goes to bed around eleven thirty . . . so we could meet at midnight.

OK, he says. And we can meet at the Montalvo gate, that's halfway in between.

Perfect, I say.

I can hardly breathe, this is *such* a good idea. I don't know why I didn't think of it sooner.

chapter 62

i'm lying in bed listening to Mom read downstairs.

You wouldn't think you could listen to a person read but you can. They turn pages. They clear their throats. They change positions and make the chair squeak.

And I'm watching the clock.

Eleven fifteen.

I'm wide awake.

I'm more awake than I've ever been, even during the day.

I already have my clothes on, under the covers. I changed into my PJs, said good night to Mom and Dad, went up to my room, and changed into my clothes again.

I am *so* tricky.

I could be a spy.

I go through it a zillion times in my head. How I'm going to tiptoe downstairs, skipping the squeaky fourth step, tiptoe across the living room, open the front door without making any noise, then run down the street in the shadows and across the highway and into Hector's arms.

Not making a peep.

I have to go out the front door because it's the only door that doesn't squeak.

I pay attention to these things.

You know what squeaks and what doesn't when you're up late a lot.

I never knew not sleeping could turn out to be such a good thing.

Mom's chair squeaks really loud, like she's getting up.

Eleven twenty-five.

There go her footsteps, out to the kitchen, probably putting her coffee cup in the sink—yep, there's the clink—then down the hall to her and Dad's bedroom. And the door shuts.

And I'm free.

Dang, I shoulda said eleven thirty to Hector, or eleven forty-five.

My alarm is set for eleven fifty-five.

But I won't need it.

I'm so wide awake I'm not even blinking.

I hear the toilet flush in the back of the house and I know that's the last sound of the night.

Now the house will be silent except for the hall clock ticking and the fridge humming on and off.

A car goes by on the highway.

The big hand on my clock moves one tick.

Eleven forty.

It'll only take me five minutes to walk to the Montalvo gate which by the way Montalvo is where all the rich people live and there's this huge stone gate at the entrance and which Yehudi Menuhin used to live there which he's this famous violinist from Hungary or China or something and Dad's always playing his records.

And which by the way Hector doesn't live in Montalvo and neither do I.

Eleven forty-one.

I wonder if my clock is slow so I get up and check my watch on the dresser.

Nope. Still eleven forty-one.

I could walk to Montalvo now but then I'd have to stand there in the cold, I mean it *is* November.

Unless Hector is already there.

He could be there right now!

I turn off my alarm clock, spring out of bed, grab my shoes and jacket, tiptoe past Lisa's room where she's snoring away and I don't really have to tiptoe, then go super slow and quiet down the stairs, skipping the creaky fourth step.

Stop at the bottom and listen.

Nothing.

Tiptoe to the front door and turn the lock sooooooo slowly, then wait and listen, then turn the door handle.

I'm not making a sound.

I'm good at this.

It's like I've been in training my whole sleepless life for this moment.

And I'm out the door.

Oh my god it's so cold.

You might think it doesn't get cold in California but boy does it.

I look up and down the street, just to make sure some neighbor isn't up and walking around for some reason.

It's silent.

And dark.

There's no street lights on our street, but there's street lights lining the highway, right next to the eight palm trees, so I can see just fine.

I run, staying in the shadows.

The cold air slices through my throat and lungs but I don't care.

Each of my footsteps is a beat: Hec-tor, Hec-tor, Hec-tor, Hec-tor.

At the top of my street I look down the highway, down to where the Montalvo gate is.

I don't see anybody.

My heart freezes.

What if he doesn't come?

What if he forgot or fell asleep?

Oh, I'll just *die*.

I run down toward the gate.

My running footsteps sound loud but I don't care. There's no one around, even the highway is deserted.

There's such a blast of excitement inside me, it's a good thing I'm running, otherwise I'd explode.

I jog up to the gate and look around.

Someone comes out of the shadows.

My heart stops. What if it's not him? What if it's a burglar?

But I don't have time to answer because there he is.

chapter 63

We sneak out every night now.

Hector and me.

We meet at the Montalvo gates, then go over to the orchard and sit in the old tool shed.

All we do is make out and talk.

I'm so happy and alive, the second I see him. It's like I'm asleep all day, and then at night I snap awake.

I mean we still see each other at school, but it's not quite the same.

For one thing, I'm paranoid.

I'm afraid someone will see us and report it to my parents.

So I'm real careful at school and I try not to make out with Hector *too* much at school.

But it's hard.

I told Poppy I'm sneaking out at night to see Hector and she was so impressed. Sometimes I feel like I suddenly got older than her.

I feel like I'm eighteen or maybe twenty.

chapter 64

i found out something about sleep.

Which is, after a while a lack of sleep catches up with you.

For the first few weeks I was fine, and then I started to get tired.

I started falling asleep in class.

In French last week, Madame had to jiggle my shoulder to wake me up.

Which that scared me and I told Hector we could only sneak out every *other* night.

Which that worked for a while but then it didn't.

I have raccoony bags under my eyes just like Mom and I have, like, no energy anymore.

Mom has started looking at me funny, especially at breakfast.

I still get the Good morning, honey! dripping-goo greeting and the gold-teeth smile, but then I get this other look, like she's peering down a rabbit hole, only the rabbit hole is my face.

Her eyes squeeze down like she's looking for something.

I usually try to force a smile and say Good morning! all cheery and happy.

Then I turn away from her and talk to Dad or Lisa or something.

One morning I'm sitting there eating my egg and suddenly my right hand goes numb and I can't grab my fork and it goes falling to the floor.

I bend down fast to pick it up.

When my head comes back up, there's the Spanish Inquisition waiting for me.

She gives me that rabbit-hole look.

I'm hoping there isn't guilt all over my face.

I massage my numb hand under the table and look at my plate.

My fingers still won't work right so I start eating with my left hand, hoping the Spanish Inquisition won't notice.

But she does.

Is something wrong with your hand, darling? says the dripping-goo voice.

Her face is all knotted up into *concern*.

I dunno, I say to my egg. Which is the perfect *wrong* answer for the Spanish Inquisition.

I shake out my right hand under the table and bend my fingers. The feeling is coming back.

Let me see, sweetie, says the Spanish Inquisition, holding out her hand.

She sounds all caring and loving, but I don't believe it. It's a trap.

I roll my eyes at her.

It's *fine*, I say. I just got a twitch, that's all. Probably from practicing piano so hard yesterday.

I flex my fingers in her face to make my point. Then I force my right hand to pick up my fork, which fortunately it works OK now.

Everyone goes back to their eggs and boy was *that* close.

I'll have to be more careful.

Although I don't know how you avoid numb hands.

Maybe I should start eating with my left hand.

Or, better yet, trade back and forth, throw everyone off.

But here's the thing I found out.

Which is, not sleeping will *always* catch up with you.

If it's not numb hands it's something else.

Like, say, irritability.

Which when I was at home, I was mad at the whole goddamn world.

Not that this was anything different from before, except I was madder.

Like Lisa comes in one morning and asks real nice if she can borrow my silver cross necklace from Grandma and I yell, No! Why do you always have to borrow my stuff?!

Which I always let her borrow it before because I don't even like it.

Lisa's eyes get real big and she backs out of my room and says, real snotty, I *don't* always borrow your stuff and you don't have to be such a creepamundo about it.

Get out! I yell, even though she's already out, and I slam the door.

And then I realize that maybe I might have overreacted just a little and what the hell was I thinking?

So I pick up the silver cross and take it into Lisa's room and throw it on her dresser and go, Here, you can have the stupid thing, I don't even like it.

I try to say it nicely but it comes out all sarcastic.

And I think, What is *wrong* with me?

chapter 65

the other thing about sneaking out is if you do it long enough and get away with it, you start to get lazy. You forget to be extra-extra careful.

You take it down a notch.

And then you get caught.

I am *so* dumb.

One thing I always made sure to do before I left at night was to leave my window open a crack, just in case Mom or Dad got up for some reason and locked the front door while I was out.

And sure enough, one night I come back and turn the front door handle and it won't turn.

Locked.

A little sparrow of panic flies through me but then I remember my open window and I calm down.

I blow out a long breath through my lips and tell myself I'm fine. My window is open.

Except, it's on the second floor.

Not a huge deal, I can get the ladder.

Except then I'll have to sneak all the way downstairs again and go put the ladder away.

Why didn't I just leave a downstairs window open?

I am *so* dumb.

I get out the ladder, trying not to make a sound, although I do bump it a couple times getting it out.

After each bump I freeze and listen.

But I don't hear any footsteps, I don't see Dad's flashlight jumping around in the windows.

I set the ladder under my window and climb up.

Pop out the screen.

Wait a minute.

There's a problem.

I have the crank kind of windows. There's a little handle on the inside you have to crank to get the window open.

I only left the window open about two inches and I can't reach the crank, the opening isn't wide enough for my arm. There was plenty of room to pop out the screen because all you have to do is breathe on that screen and it'll fall out.

But the window.

Oh god.

This is not good.

I have to reach that crank.

I take off my sweater and roll up my shirt sleeve to make my arm as skinny as possible. The cold air clamps down on me but I tell myself to ignore it, it will all be over soon.

My heart is beating so loud the whole neighborhood could hear it if they were awake.

I'm freezing cold but I'm sweating.

My throat clenches together into the start of a sob.

Don't cry now, I tell myself. Save it for later.

I reach my skinny bare arm through the two-inch crack. The window wiggles, stretching open a little more, and maybe I'm bending the metal frame but I don't care.

I can barely brush the crank with my fingertips.

Just a little bit more.

I flatten my back into the house and make my arm stretch even more.

My fingers are stretched as far as they'll go but I make them stretch more.

Just a little more, I'm almost there.

I reach just a little more.

Crack!

The window breaks.

It sounds like a gunshot.

My heart stops.

And then I go into the most fast-forward double-time movie you ever saw.

I'm not even thinking, my body is moving on its own, fast as lightning.

I crank open the broken window and hop in my room.

Bring the screen inside and throw it on the floor.

Rip off my clothes and throw them in the bottom of my closet just as Lisa comes in.

Oh god, if it was loud enough to wake up Lisa . . .

Pull my nightgown over my head so fast a button pops off.

What are you doing? she yawns, her eyes barely open.

Don't tell Mom and Dad! Don't tell Mom and Dad! I hiss. I'll tell you everything later but swear you won't tell!

OK, OK, she says and yawns again.

There are footsteps coming up the stairs.

Dad's footsteps.

I'm breathing so fast my head is going all swimmy.

I shut my closet door.

Oh god oh god oh god oh god oh god oh god oh god oh god.

I'm swearing and praying at the same time.

Dad comes in.

What the hell? he says, going over to the window. What happened?

He doesn't even look mad or sound mad or anything.

I can't believe it.

I start to cry.

The w-window w-wouldn't c-close and I was c-c-cold, I blub-ber. The c-c-crank w-wouldn't w-work so I just p-pulled on the w-window a little b-bit and it b-broke.

Wow, that was a pretty good lie.

I'm sobbing like a two-year-old and it's not even fake. I don't know why I'm crying but I'm letting it happen. It's a good thing to add to this little scene.

Mom comes in.

Oh my Lord! she says, looking at the window. What happened? Are you all right, honey?

She smoothes my hair back from my face, checking for cuts, then runs her hands down my arms and looks at my hands.

Are you hurt anywhere? she says.

She doesn't sound mad, either.

Oh my god.

I just got away with murder.

I'm crying like a baby and my parents are falling for the biggest lie I ever told.

Oh my god.

I didn't even know I was this good.

I told Mom what I just told Dad, still blubbering like an idiot but I'm not going to stop because it seems to be working quite well.

Oh honey, Mom says, and puts her arm around me and squeezes.

Then she starts picking up the big pieces of glass that are lying on the carpet, and she sends Lisa downstairs for the vacuum cleaner.

Dad is busily turning the crank one way, then the other, like he's trying to figure it out. Of course, the crank is working just fine. Broken window opens, broken window closes. He sticks his head out into the open space where the window was and I hold my breath.

The ladder is right down there.

If he looks hard enough into the shadow of the oak tree, he'll see it.

Oh my god.

I can't breathe.

My knees become unglued and suddenly I have to sit down on my bed.

Dad pulls his head back in, shaking it.

Hmph, he says, like he's stumped. His eyebrows are pulled down over his eyes.

Oh thank god, he didn't see the ladder.

I'm just glad you didn't get hurt, Mom says. She picks some glass off the bedspread.

Dad shakes his head and continues to turn the crank around and around, watching the metal frame move forward and backward.

Lisa comes in with the vacuum cleaner.

I'm shaking all over and still crying. I look at my fingers and it's like there's twenty of them, that's how bad they're shaking.

My heart is beating so hard it's giving me a headache.

Oh god.

If I ever get through this.

I can't stop crying and Mom comes over and puts her arm around me, rubbing up and down on my arm.

It's OK, honey, no one's hurt and it's not your fault, she says. She rubs my back.

It's OK, sweetie, she says.

Oh, if only she knew how *not* OK it is.

I'm standing on the edge of a cliff and I am this close to falling off.

I wipe my nose with my hand and my fingers are pure ice.

If I ever get out of this.

The broken window scared me enough to stop sneaking out at night, but only for a few weeks.

Then we started up again.

Now I leave the kitchen window open so I don't need a ladder to get in if I ever get locked out again.

And I leave my window open all the way.

chapter 66

nothing perfect can go on forever, it's like a rule.

For instance, like me and Hector.

It's too perfect.

We sneak out at night and we don't get caught, we walk home through the orchard and we don't get caught, we kiss at school and we don't get caught.

Something has to break.

And it does, one day in East Hall.

Hector and me are walking arm in arm down East Hall, down near the office end.

It's a gorgeous spring day and everything smells like violets and lilacs and for some reason, right at the second before everything breaks, I think, I'm the happiest, luckiest girl alive, even if my mother is crazy.

Which she's been really good lately and I'm starting to think, maybe, just maybe, all the bad stuff is behind us.

This is what I get for thinking too many good thoughts at once.

Because just as Hector leans over to kiss me in East Hall, I see this figure, the outline of a person which I know really well but I can't figure out who it is. It's one of those out-of-place moments, where someone is in the wrong place so you don't recognize them, like seeing your minister at the dentist or something.

It's my mother.

It takes me several seconds to believe it.

My brain rejects what I've just seen and I keep kissing Hector but then I see the figure walking toward us, really fast.

I'd know that stride anywhere, no one else walks like her, especially when she's mad.

And that hair. The half-yellow, half-black hair. No one else has that.

I pull away from Hector and he turns and sees her.

Oh shit, he says.

Oh god, I say.

Mom's whole face is pulled down into so much anger it's practically dripping off her chin. And you have never seen a human being walk like that. Her feet are pounding so hard I don't know why the cement isn't cracking around her.

Hector and I just stand there, our shoulders touching.

He grabs my hand and squeezes. Like that's going to help.

You know those times when you know you can't get out of something, and it's just hopeless to even try?

This is one of those times.

My heart is all the way up in my brain, pulsing away, and I'm just waiting for it to blow open my skull.

In fact, I'm kinda hoping that's what will happen.

Because with the steam engine of Mom coming toward us, well, you just wish *anything* would happen that would keep her from getting to us.

But of course nothing happens.

We stand there and we watch her getting closer and closer.

And madder and madder.

She's wearing a pink elbow-sleeve blouse and white pedal pushers and red Keds with no socks.

You know how your brain does weird things when a big crisis starts happening?

Here's what my brain was thinking: She looks just like a pretty spring day.

Except for her winter-storm face.

She finally gets to us, puffing hard because she's not in shape to be walking that fast.

Her eyebrows are pulled into a V so deep you could fall into it.

She doesn't say anything.

Hector and I just stand there, dumb and mute and frozen.

Mom grabs my upper arm so tight that her fingernails dig deep into my skin and I can't see but I'm sure they've broken the skin and I'm bleeding in five places.

She pulls so hard that my arm almost rips out of my shoulder.

My hand rips out of Hector's hand.

She starts dragging me back toward the office.

I look at Hector and he has this look on his face like he just got hit by a car.

He gets smaller and smaller and pretty soon he's only an inch high.

My feet slip around on the cement because Mom is walking too fast for me to keep up. Her fingernails are still deep in my arm and my arm is starting to go numb and just for a sec I wonder if you really *can* rip someone's arm right off their body just by pulling really hard.

You'd think footsteps in red Keds would be quiet, but every step she takes echoes all the way down the hall.

I start to pull backward, away from her, not caring if my arm rips off my body.

But she's too strong for me.

And her fingernails have gone all the way through my skin, through my muscle, right to my bone.

If I could scream I would, but my voice is lost somewhere deep inside me.

Classes have just let out and people are walking down the hall, staring at us.

This is the shortest hallway in the school but I feel like she's been dragging me for a zillion years.

It's one of those dreams you keep trying to wake up from but every time you wake up you're still in the dream and the dream just keeps going on and on and on.

You just wake up into another dream.

And another, and another.

And just like in a dream, I see and hear all kinds of weird things.

Like Sherry Judd turning the lock on her locker and then she snaps open the lock and it sounds like a bomb going off. Then she opens the locker and the green metal door hits another locker door and it sounds like thunder.

Terry Salinger smiles at me even though I am being dragged through the hall by my psycho mother and Terry's braces are so huge and shiny that they blind me and I have to close my eyes.

For some reason I look up at the ceiling of the hallway and the creamy yellow paint is peeling, and underneath is a dark orange. The peels of paint look so heavy and sharp that I pray none of them fall on me because they would slice right through me like razors.

The daffodils lining the walk up to the office look so perky and bright and yellow and not part of this dream, like maybe they're part of someone else's dream which is happening right next door to my dream.

There it is, right over there, the good dream someone *else* is having.

Right next to my nightmare.

Mrs. Chako passes us, smiling her big hot-pink smile and nodding her head hi at me and Mom, which makes the red bun on top of her head wiggle.

I close my eyes and I try to convince myself this is all a bad dream.

chapter 67

Pacing.
      That is what my mother is doing in the dining room and which she never paces so this is still a strange weird nightmare.

Dad paces, but never Mom.

I am sitting at the dining room table and Mom is pacing back and forth in front of the fridge and which the fridge is in the dining room at our house which I already know is weird so just shut up.

I have my hands around something. My fingers are telling my brain what it is but my brain isn't working so I can't tell what it is. I look at it, and I still can't tell what it is.

Mom has one hand on her forehead and one hand on her hip.

She keeps looking at the ceiling and mumbling to herself.

This should be scaring me but I am frozen and I don't care about anything right now.

I'm not here.

I'm in the orchard with Hector.

It's a warm, sunny day and the sour grass is in bloom and you can smell the mustard flowers.

Hector's fingers are running through my hair and we are laughing.

I'm lying in the sour grass and Hector bends over me and kisses me and I can taste him.

An explosion wakes me up.

The house is shaking.

My mother has just hit the wall with her fist.

This should scare me. My mother does not beat on walls with her fists.

But I'm not scared at all.

I am frozen and I don't care about anything.

She rubs her eyes with both hands.

Oh my god, Abby, she says, in this voice like a moan.

It's a voice I haven't heard before. It's like a ghost voice, and it hits me hard, dead center in my chest.

I should be scared.

I'm not.

We've already covered why.

I look up into her eyes real slow, keeping my eyelids halfway down like Lauren Bacall in that movie Mom likes. I tilt my head to one side and cross my arms. I blink real slow, like I might go to sleep any moment.

Let her kill me, I don't care.

I'm not going to say anything.

There's nothing to say.

And besides, I've lost my voice.

I can't even clear my throat.

I used to be afraid of death.

But this is so easy.

I never knew you could die without caring, that you could just drift off, like a leaf in the creek.

Let yourself be carried.

Mom stops pacing and pulls out the dining room chair across from me, scraping it hard on the green-rope rug that should be a hammock not a rug.

She slaps both hands down on the table, which makes another huge explosion.

I look at her through my half-closed eyes.

If I keep my eyes half closed like this, my eyelashes are like this lace curtain between me and her.

She sits.

She puts a hand on each side of her face and her face slowly drops down, with all its weight, with all that anger, settling into her hands and her elbows resting on the table.

Her hands slide up on her face, drawing the skin on her chin and cheeks paper-tight.

How she'd look with a face lift.

Pretty darn good.

Her fingers dig in next to her eyes, giving herself Japanese eyes.

She looks at me.

Her face is as blank as mine feels.

Our green eyes are locked.

I could sit here forever.

I have never left my life before and it's a strange feeling.

I'm not floating, I'm not flying. I'm just not here.

It's just my bones and my skin and my organs, sitting here, and my brain which is now only a tape recorder, seeing and hearing and recording.

There's not an emotion anywhere near me.

I can stare at her like this for as long as she wants.

She blinks.

Her pink lips open.

I give up, she says. I don't know what to do with you anymore, Abby.

Her voice is low and hollow, empty as fog.

I continue to stare at her.

I am completely empty.

We sit there like that for sixty-six days.

Finally she takes in this huge, slow breath and then lets it out like it's her last breath on earth. She gets up, real slow, and pushes the chair in under the table.

She stands there a moment, looking at me, both her hands on the chair.

I look at her through my lace-curtain eyelashes.

She turns and walks slowly down the hall to her room. She closes the door so slow that I sit there and wait and wait and wait for the click, which it finally comes after two eons.

It takes me a while to realize I'm alone.

I go upstairs and lay on my bed and watch my clock.

It's only four thirty, but I'm waiting for midnight, when I can see Hector again.

chapter 68

dad comes up at six to call me and Lisa for dinner. I hear him in Lisa's room, telling her it's dinnertime and we're having TV dinners because Mom doesn't feel well.

Then his heavy footsteps across the hall and a knock on my door.

Come in, I say.

My voice sounds so dead.

Dad comes in and closes the door.

Which means he knows.

Mom has told him everything.

He pulls the chair out from my desk and sits on it.

It's a stupid chair, white with pink flowers all over it, from Grandma.

Dad looks so silly sitting in it.

He crosses his legs.

Even sillier.

He looks at me with those lines all over his face and red lines in his eyes and his gray-streaked straight hair which he always greases back and all together he looks like an old crumpled-up piece of paper.

He takes in a deep breath.

Now I'm in for it.

I don't even care.

I'm still lying down and I'm looking at Dad through my curtain of eyelashes.

I put both hands behind my head so I look even more casual.

Because I don't care.

Your mother is very upset with you, Dad says, very quiet and even and slow, just like he walks and writes and does everything.

I raise my eyebrows and look at him.

I don't care.

He can do whatever he wants.

Nothing is going to stop me from seeing Hector. They can put guards in my bedroom all night long and I'll figure a way to sneak out.

But just between you and me, Dad says, I don't think she's really upset at you or your boyfriend.

I have to blink a few times to take this in. This isn't going how I thought it was going to go. I was ready to hear *grounded for life* and *can't see him* and *off limits* and *never again.*

When will I learn not to be surprised by anything that happens in this house.

There are other . . . things . . . happening, he says. Things you don't need to worry about.

His crumpled-up face looks so pinched up with worry I just want to hug him.

But I won't.

I have other things on my mind.

Like Hector.

So can I still see Hector? I say.

Dad nods.

Sure, he says. He seems like a nice kid.

He is nice, I say. He's the nicest person I've ever met.

Well . . . that's good, Dad says, nodding. You hold on to that.

You hold on to that.

What the heck does that mean?

Dad gets up and catches his own face looking at himself in the mirror.

He goes over to the mirror and takes his white handkerchief out of his back pocket.

What did you get on your mirror? he says, and starts rubbing the mirror with the handkerchief.

I dunno, I say. I think it's just dust.

He wipes off the whole mirror till it's perfect, then folds up the handkerchief into a neat white square and puts it back in his pocket.

He opens the door and goes out, then sticks his head back in.

I almost forgot—dinnertime, he says.

OK, I say. I'll be down.

The door closes.

Dads.

I'll never figure them out.

They're like space aliens.

chapter 69

i'm standing at the Montalvo gate, waiting for Hector.

I'm early.

I left at eleven thirty because Mom went to bed early and because I couldn't breathe in that house anymore.

It's freezing out here, even though it's supposed to be spring.

I have my coat on and a sweater underneath and jeans and I'm still freezing.

It can get so fucking cold in California.

I walk from one side of the big stone gate to the other, trying to get warm, my hands tucked under my armpits and my coat collar all the way up.

Hector finally comes and we walk to the orchard, to the tool shed.

He holds me as close as he can, trying to warm me up.

He hasn't asked me anything about anything yet. He's like Poppy that way, he knows when to shut up.

I still can't get warm. I'm shaking so hard it's starting to hurt.

Hector rubs me all over, rubs my arms and legs and back, trying to warm me up.

My teeth are chattering in Morse code.

Hector says, You should take off all your clothes.

What? I say. I look at him like he's as psycho as my mother.

No no no, he says. It's the only way to get you warm, we have to get our bodies together, so you can use my body heat to get warm.

He starts taking off his shirt.

I'm too cold to care either way.

I don't want to move.

Come on, he says.

He helps me get my jacket and sweater and jeans off, I'm down to my underwear. I can't even see the outline of my body, it's all blurry, that's how bad I'm shaking.

He puts his coat down on the floor of the shed and I lie down on it.

My body is snow white. My fingers have turned gray.

Hector lies on top of me in his underwear and then piles all our clothes on top and around us, making a sleeping bag of our clothes.

His arms go all the way around me.

I can't stop shaking.

I look into his black eyes and he looks into mine and we just lie there, looking so deep into each other, so beyond where our eyes are. You can see so much stuff in a person's eyes, if you know where to look. Stuff like what they're thinking, what they're dreaming, who they are, who they want to be, how they see the world and if they see it like you do.

In Hector's eyes right now all I see is worry.

We lie there kissing and I start to warm up.

When I am finally all warm is when he asks me.

He says, Do you want to go all the way.

I say, Yes.

chapter 70

the next day is Saturday and first thing I run over to Poppy's to tell her.

Everything.

From my mom charging down the hall to making love with Hector and everything in between.

Sometimes Poppy sees things that other people don't.

Like when I tell her about Mom charging down the hall at Hector and me, Poppy says, What was your mom doing at school, anyway?

Which I never even thought of before.

What *was* she doing there?

I dunno, I say. Someone must of called her and told her about Hector and me.

No way, says Poppy. Who would do that?

We're sitting on the floor of Poppy's room eating Oreos and drinking Coke.

Everything I'm not supposed to have.

Which is not even a rule anymore.

I don't think there *are* any rules anymore.

I don't know who would do it, I say, it could be anyone—Mr. Simpson, Miss Walker, Mr. Grimes—could be any of the teachers, or anyone from the office.

Poppy sucks on her Coke and shakes her head.

No way, she says. They have better things to do.

OK, if no one told, then what was she doing there? I say, popping a whole Oreo into my mouth.

Another rule.

You're supposed to take ladylike bites. Young lady.

I think she drove over to the school just to spy on you, and she just got lucky and saw you, Poppy says.

Really? I say.

Really, she says.

I don't say anything else. It's something to think about later, when I'm lying in bed waiting for midnight.

I tell Poppy about the rest of the day, about Mom hitting the wall with her fist and telling me she was giving up on me and how I got so cold and went to meet Hector and then I get to the big part.

So we took off all our clothes, I say, flipping an Oreo into the air. I try to catch it in my mouth, but it bounces off my front teeth.

You mean . . . everything? Poppy says. She stares at me and her brown eyes are as big as two states.

Yep, everything, I say. I take a swig of Coke and look at the red can, like it's so interesting.

This is the fun part.

The telling-your-best-friend part.

Yeah, so? she says. Then what? Did you see it?

Oh yeah, I saw it, I say.

I'm pretty sure she means *penis*. Did I see his penis.

Yeah, then what? she says. How far'd you go?

I look at her with my eyebrows all the way up and my eyes half closed.

Very Lauren Bacall.

What do *you* think? I say.

No way! she says. Her eyes get even bigger than two states, they're as big as France.

I just look at her and give her this little Mona Lisa half smile.

I'm getting that old-age feeling again, like I'm suddenly about ten years older than Poppy.

You went all the way? she whispers.

I don't know why she's whispering. Her mom is at the grocery store.

All the way, I say.

Funny how it sounds so simple, like it's not a big deal, when you say it that way. Just three words. *All the way.*

All the way where? Or on the way to what?

Oh my god, Poppy says.

She has this look on her face like she's seeing me for the first time, or like maybe she sees that old-age thing, too. Maybe my face really *does* look ten years older.

Wow, she says. So how was it?

I twist apart an Oreo and scrape out the white center with my front teeth.

I dunno, I say. Fun, I guess.

You just can't explain it to someone who hasn't done it. There's no words for it.

Wow, she says again. That is like . . . wow.

She nods real slow with her eyes big as France, looking at me like I just turned into someone famous, like maybe Janis Joplin.

Which maybe in a way I have.

chapter 71

mom **is lying** down again.

It's all my fault and I don't even care.

Every day after school again, she is lying down.

I cook dinner almost every night.

Dad looks worried all the time.

Lisa talks to herself a lot.

Something has happened inside me, something has broken.

I don't know if it's my soul or my will or what.

It snapped the minute I saw Mom in East Hall that day.

I carry the broken thing around inside me. I can feel it. Some days it's turned the wrong way and it cuts me like broken glass.

Everything in our house is so quiet.

I don't talk to Mom and she doesn't talk to anyone.

Lisa doesn't talk to me because I'll just get mad at her.

I can't help it, it just happens.

Mom and Dad go to the doctor a lot together.

Poppy says it's probably not the doctor, it's probably a shrink.

Every Thursday they go, at four o'clock.

They come home and everything's the same as it was yesterday, which is the same as it was the day before that.

Mom is like this sheet walking around. Her skin is all white and her face is flat and she sort of floats from room to room.

I'm afraid to lift up the sheet.

Afraid there's nothing under there.

There's something else walking around our house, too.

The thing nobody talks about.

Which is that we are all afraid that Mom is going to try it again.

I think about it all the time.

I come home from school every day and I don't want to open the front door and walk inside.

Some days I make Poppy come home with me, just in case.

So far, Mom has only been lying down.

On her bed.

Alive.

chapter 72

I am tired of having to sneak out at night to see Hector.

I mean I'm almost fifteen now and I'm tired of sneaking around like I'm eight.

So one day Hector and me are walking through the orchard and I say, You wanna come home with me? You can stay for dinner.

I haven't asked anyone if this is OK.

I don't have to.

Nobody cares anymore.

Hector smiles his big white smile and goes, Sure. But I'll have to call my mom from your house.

He's so easy that way. He just takes whatever comes walking through the orchard at him.

Like that first day he kissed me.

He told me later he didn't plan it, he just thought of it and did it, right then.

He said he'd been checking me out for a long time but he was too chicken to just come up to me and start talking.

I told him that kiss was still the best moment in my whole life. I still get goose bumps when I think about it.

So we walk all the way to my house and I'm not even nervous or anything. I know Mom will be lying down and I know even if I drag Hector all the way into her bedroom, which I won't, she won't care.

We get in the house and Mom's door is shut just like it is every day now.

Just for a sec I get that little *ping* in my stomach which is the thing that makes me not want to go into Mom's room and check on her.

But I still do every day. I'm always the first one home now because Lisa is now in this special program for "gifted" kids so she gets out later than me.

Gifted. That kills me. Who woulda thought dumb old Lisa was smarter than everybody. Lisa with her mind like a sieve.

I look at Hector and he smiles at me and I swear the whole room gets warmer and I say, Let me go check on my mom, I'll be right back.

Hector knows all about my mom. I've told him everything.

He says, Should I go with you? And he looks so cute and *concerned* that I just have to kiss him.

Nah, I say. Wait here, I'll just be a sec.

I open Mom's door a peep and say quietly, I'm home!

It's our daily ritual.

She turns her head on her pillow and waves a weak wave.

How was your day? she says.

I brought Hector home with me, we're just gonna have a snack in the kitchen, I say.

OK, she says, and closes her eyes.

I close her door and let out my breath which I didn't even know I was holding it.

chapter 73

hector comes over for dinner all the time now and one night we're about to start eating when Mom comes out of her room.

Which she hardly ever eats with us anymore.

Dad usually takes her some rice or something into her room after we've all eaten.

She comes in and she's actually dressed, which is another thing she doesn't do much anymore.

Her hair is all long and straggly now because she hasn't gotten it cut in like forever and she has tried to brush it into something, but it's standing straight up and which she looks just like the bride of Frankenstein with all that gray in her black hair.

She's wearing stuff that totally doesn't match, green-and-blue zigzag pedal pushers and a red-and-white polka-dot blouse.

Her eyes have gotten so raccoony it's like looking into two caves.

Hector leaps up to get another chair, because he's sitting in hers. He's kinda taken over her spot.

You'd think by now I would've forced Lisa to trade places with me so I could look out the window again, but I kinda got used to this spot. Also I can see Mom's door from here, not that there's anything to see, because it's always shut.

Mom sits in her regular chair and Hector drags in an old kitchen chair from the back porch and I scoot over so he can sit next to me.

Hi, Mrs. Goodman, Hector says, smiling his big white smile at her.

Mom blinks at him several times without saying anything, looking like a total zombie, which makes Dad clear his throat to fill up the silence.

Well hello there, she finally says to Hector and pats him on the arm too many times. Her voice is like when Mrs. Carmichael gets drunk, I can't explain it, but it's like she's a little too friendly. This one time I was over at the Carmichaels' and Mrs. Carmichael was drunk and she put her arm around me and kissed me right on the mouth and said in this sloshy voice, Yer a good kid, Abbilly, I wishew were my daughter. Which totally freaked me out and I got out of there dirt fast.

Mom straightens herself up real tall in her chair and daintily places her hands flat on the table.

What are we having? she says in the drunk voice.

Stir fry, Dad says, picking up the big platter of stir fry and passing it to Lisa.

Abby made it, he says.

Abby made it, Mom says, almost like to herself, like she was checking with her brain to see if she knew anyone named Abby.

I just noticed that I've been gripping Hector's leg since he sat down next to me. I make myself relax my hand and his hand comes down and closes over mine.

I look around the table and everyone has stopped eating and is watching Mom put like a tablespoon of stir fry onto her plate.

I notice her pink fingernail polish is all chipped and for some reason it makes me get this big fat lump in my throat.

I want to get out Dad's razor and shave her whole head. She'd look better bald than with that rat's nest she has now.

I want to crawl under the table. I'm so embarrassed that Hector is seeing this.

For the first time, I see my mother through someone else's eyes.

Oh my god.

I don't know who she is anymore.

Could you pass the rice, please, Harold? Mom says to Hector and gives him something which she probably thinks is a smile but isn't.

It's *Hector*, Mom, I say, like I'm talking to a two-year-old.

I look into Mom's eyes and there's nothing there, she doesn't even see me.

I want to say, And I'm *Abby*, remember? Your daughter?

Hector passes Mom the rice but she's looking out the window and doesn't notice that it's there. Hector clears his throat to get her attention, but she just looks out the window and the rice is sitting there in the middle of the air, in Hector's dark brown hand, and we're all staring at Mom and the rice and I can't stand it so I finally grab it from him and set it back down on the table.

Mom just looks out the window and doesn't eat.

Dad clears his throat about nineteen times, then finally gets up and turns on the TV.

Even the sound of the TV doesn't break Mom's trance.

Look at the hydrangea, isn't it lovely, Mom says.

Her voice should give me the shivers but I don't care anymore. I'm not surprised by anything about Mom anymore, not how she looks, not how she sounds, not what she does . . . nothing. It's like I have this metal shield all around me that protects me from her and her surprises.

I look to where she's looking but I can't tell what she's looking at but it doesn't matter.

We don't have a hydrangea, Mom, I say. My voice sounds bored, like I have to explain this to her every day.

Hector eats his stir fry and doesn't look at me, but his foot and ankle are wrapped around my foot and ankle, and every so often his foot rubs on my shin real gentle and slow, like how you pet a rabbit.

chapter 74

the worst of the worst of the possible worst thing in the whole possible world of possible worst things happens.

Which is I think I might be pregnant.

My period was supposed to be here seven days ago and it still hasn't come.

I haven't told Hector yet but he knows something is bothering me because he keeps asking what's wrong and I keep saying nothing.

Or sometimes I say, Oh just my mom, you know.

And then he hugs me and says, Well you still have me.

Which is so sweet.

I have to tell myself a zillion times a day, You don't know if you're pregnant or not, you're just late.

Except I'm never late, my period is like Big Ben, which isn't Big Ben that clock in London that never loses time. Or is it Greenwich. Or Greenland. I can't remember.

The thing is, I don't know how to find out if I'm pregnant except by going to the doctor and you can bet I'm not going to old Dr. Rawson and look in his old withered blue eyes which they've been looking at me since I was born and say, Oh by the way, while I'm here, would you mind giving me a pregnancy test?

Not to mention he'd call my parents in a heartbeat.

This is when my head starts spinning too fast that I have to hold on to my locker or desk or something and I start breathing too fast and pretty soon things go in and out of focus and I have to tell myself to get a grip.

You're not pregnant.

Probably just a false alarm.

Oh Jesus god.

This is the worst yet.

I thought having a crazy sick mother was all I was going to get. I mean, isn't that enough? Why do I get two things? I mean most people just have one thing. I mean Poppy doesn't have a dad, that's her thing, and Hector has dark skin that some people make stupid comments about, that's his thing, and Mrs. Billawalla lost her husband and Annie Billawalla lost her dad, and Grandma has to live in Ohio, and Mrs. Sierra's son Jimmy is over in Vietnam getting shot, and Janie Morris has to walk with a limp because her foot didn't grow right, and I mean why do I get *two* things is what I want to know.

Which makes me think maybe I'm *not* pregnant. Because who has two things, nobody.

The eighth day and the ninth day pass and still no visit from Aunt Flo.

I run to the bathroom between every class to check.

I have never wanted my period so bad except maybe before I started which I wanted to start so bad.

I don't even care if I get horrible cramps for the rest of my life, I'd take horrible cramps instead of pregnant any day.

Do you hear that, God.

That's right, I'll take the cramps.

I'll take cramps, I'll take heavy flow, I'll take a period that lasts forty-nine weeks, I'll take red stains that show on my jeans, I'll take the stink times a hundred, I'll take mood swings, I'll take irritability and crying jags and uncontrollable outbursts, I'll take it all.

Just don't make me pregnant.

On the tenth day I tell Hector.

We're walking through the orchard with Poppy and Poppy leaves us at the turnoff in the path and goes on ahead and something happens when I watch her walking away, I get this ache inside me that makes me want to run after her and tap her on the shoulder, and when she turns around we'll both be ten again and we'll go climb as high as we can in the old apple tree and watch the creek go by and talk about ten-year-old things like which of us likes Donny Osmond more, and how come Herbie Shriver always follows Poppy around the playground like a lost puppy.

I stand there holding Hector's hand and watching Poppy and I get a big watery tear in each eye and I don't want to blink because Hector will know something's wrong. I keep my face turned away from him and I watch the blurry white figure of Poppy get smaller and smaller and I feel like I'm watching my whole childhood walk away from me.

I always want to be older than I am and now here it's happening to me and I want to take it back.

Make me ten again.

Or even thirteen.

Hector puts his arms around me and I bury my face in his chest and I can't help it, I start sobbing all over the place like a little kid.

Hector pulls me into him real tight and keeps saying, It's OK, Ab, it's OK.

I'm crying so hard I can hardly breathe, my throat has swelled shut and my mouth is forced wide open into big baby sobs. I put my mouth on Hector's chest and I can't help it, I start to wail, only the wails are muffled in his shirt.

We stand there in the orchard among the just-blooming apricot and plum trees, which if I took the time to smell them would smell like heaven, and a little April breeze whips past us, sending warm air up my miniskirt.

It's a good thing no one ever walks through this orchard except us.

Hector strokes my hair with his big brown hand and for a sec I wait for him to offer me his handkerchief and then I remember it's Dad who always has the handkerchief, not Hector.

I fumble around in my purse for a Kleenex and finally pull up an old blue one that's in a ball.

My breaths are still coming in sobs but it's the end-of-crying kind of sobs, when your body is trying to calm itself down, and if you just clear out your mind and stop thinking about what made you cry, you can pull yourself together.

Sometimes.

Hector tilts my face up and says, Are you going to tell me what's wrong now?

His eyes are so clear and so dark at the same time. Even though Hector has real black eyes, you can still look in there and see everything about him. I love people who you can look in their eyes and there they are.

Not like some mothers I know which you look in their eyes and nothing.

Now I have the hiccups so I have to hold my breath for one

minute. I give Hector the wait-a-minute finger and watch the second hand on my watch.

Hector rubs up and down on my back. My hiccups finally stop.

Oh god, I say, and I almost start crying again.

I close my eyes and put my hand over my nose and mouth and tell myself to pull your fucking self together you big dorkamundo.

I take a deep breath.

I look up at Hector.

I think I might be pregnant, I say.

Then I start crying again.

Hector's eyes go so big it scares me. And it's not the good kind of big.

Oh shit, he says. Are you sure?

He stuffs his hands in his front jeans pockets and starts pacing back and forth.

I'm trying to blow my nose in the tatters of the blue Kleenex. Then I wipe under my eyes because I'm sure my mascara is all over the place and I look even more raccoony than my mother.

No, I'm not sure, I say through sniffles.

I'm just late, by ten days, I say. I blow my nose in the blue Kleenex wad.

Yeah? he says like he's all relieved. Ten days? That's all?

He says it with his thick Mexican accent which only comes out real strong when he's upset about something.

Which by the way I love his accent.

I tilt my head sideways and give him the half-closed-eyes look I give my mother when she says something stupid which used to be all the time but now she never says anything, either stupid or smart.

Ten days is a lot, I say, my voice all flat.

Right now I'd give anything for a cigarette. I don't even smoke but somehow a cigarette sounds really good right now.

Hector puts both hands on top of his head and goes, Ay-yi-yi-yi.

Oh Jesus, Abby, he says.

Well, I say, we don't know for sure yet. I shrug my shoulders.

Suddenly I'm so calm.

Hector pounds the heel of his shoe into the grass, hitting it over and over again and making a big dent.

Oh Christ, he says, and he lets out a long whistle.

chapter 75

i keep looking at myself naked in the mirror, to see if any part of me looks pregnant.

It's been two weeks since my period didn't show up.

Every morning I run my hand over my flat stomach to see if there's even the slightest bulge there.

Some mornings I think there is one.

It took Hector three days to get over his shock and start acting like a normal person again. He went around with this sad hound dog look on his face and I was sure everyone was going to guess what was wrong. I wouldn't let him come over to the house unless he promised to look cheerful and happy.

I finally told Poppy and her jaw practically fell off her body.

Pregnant? she said. As in, *baby?*

I said I didn't know what other kind of pregnant there was.

Are you sure? she said.

Which I wish people would quit asking me that.

I told her it had been two weeks and she whistled just like Hector did.

Which I wish people would stop whistling.

Wow, what are you gonna do? Poppy said.

I shook my head and picked at a hangnail.

I wish I knew, I said.

So far, I've told two people and they haven't been any help at all.

Somehow I feel like this is only happening to me.

I guess I thought Hector would do something magical, would make it go away, like he can make other stuff go away, like all my bad feelings about my mom.

But every morning I wake up and it's still there.

Every morning I wake up and I put my hand on my stomach and I close my eyes and I tell my stupid body to please please *please* start bleeding today.

I've given up on God.

So now I pray to my body.

Which hasn't helped either.

I am feeling more and more alone here.

Hector hugs me and tells me he loves me and tells me everything is going to be OK.

But he doesn't make it go away.

And anyway, how does *he* know everything is going to be OK.

That age thing is happening to me again. I feel like I'm about twenty-three and I'm leaving everyone behind me: Hector, Poppy, everyone in the ninth grade.

Ninth grade sounds so silly when you're having a baby.

Not that I'm having one.

. . .

what i think about all day now is what are my options.

I can barely listen in class because all I can think about is what to do, what to do. I figure if I think about it long enough, eventually I'll hit on the answer.

I'm trying to think of every possible option.

Including knitting needles. Not that I'd ever do that, but it's on the list of options.

I also heard that riding a motorcycle on railroad tracks works.

I wish you could just drink something.

Or take a pill.

chapter 76

What's furthest from my mind now is Mom.

I don't even notice her anymore, that's how far away my mind is from everything in my real life.

I come home from school and sometimes I forget all about her until dinnertime.

She wants us to call her for dinner now.

She says she needs to force herself to get up and get dressed for some reason and that dinner is a good reason.

Which all I can think is, why isn't your two kids or your husband a good enough reason.

I mean, dinner. What kind of stupid reason is that.

But I don't even bother worrying about it anymore.

She drags herself to her chair at the dinner table and either Dad or I make dinner and we all sit down and eat to the noise of the TV.

Sometimes Hector is there but it doesn't change anything when he is.

I don't even see him as separate from our family anymore, he's like a brother that was always there.

chapter 77

i **keep myself** in this foggy daze so I don't have to think or feel or remember anything.

It's much easier this way.

I pretend I am a normal ninth grader with two nice parents, a nice boyfriend, a nice best friend, and an OK sister.

The Mother-Daughter Tea is coming up and I'm pretending that I'm going to take my mom.

My last period was six weeks ago but I don't think about that.

Hector and Poppy know not to bring up the subject.

It's a big game of Let's Pretend which if I don't play it I'll go crazy.

Sometimes in the middle of the night when I can't sleep, that's when it's hardest to play it.

In the middle of the night there's just you and the black sky and the four walls of your room and the truth.

Some nights I have to get up and stare out my window at the eight palm trees. Some nights I have to count the palm trees over and over, to keep the truth from coming into my room.

One, two, three, four, five, six, seven, eight.

And again.

Some nights I curl up in a ball under my covers and put my

hands over my ears and sing to myself. I sing Christmas carols because they're the only songs I know all the words to.

I sing "Winter Wonderland."

And "White Christmas."

And "It's Beginning to Look a Lot Like Christmas."

I stay away from the religious ones, the ones about baby Jesus.

chapter 78

the eighth week goes by since my last period but I don't let myself count the weeks anymore.

chapter 79

a strange thing wakes me up one morning.

The smell of bacon.

Which we don't have bacon for breakfast anymore.

We have cold cereal every morning because Mom doesn't get up to fix breakfast anymore.

I listen downstairs and I hear feet in the kitchen, busy feet.

More smells: coffee, toast, frying eggs.

It can't be.

I fly into my clothes and run downstairs.

There's the back of a faded red bathrobe in the kitchen.

And bare white feet.   .

She turns and sees me.

Hi honey, she says and yawns.

She looks like crap but she *is* in the kitchen on a school morning, cooking breakfast. Her hair is standing straight up and her bathrobe is open, showing her dirty old pink nightgown with the lace coming off in the front and half the buttons missing. I mean if she bends over, her boobs will come swinging right out of it.

But she *is* in the kitchen cooking breakfast.

I mean just the fact that she is standing up is a miracle.

Can I help? I ask.

I can't even believe that came out of my mouth. I mean the last time I said that to my mother I was probably like eight.

Well, it's nice to know that sometimes my mouth can surprise me with something *good*.

You can set the table, she says, and pulls open the silverware drawer, which is weird because it's not like I've forgotten where the silverware is.

Or maybe *she* wasn't sure where it was anymore and was giving herself a little test.

Bingo, she aced it.

I'm setting the table and Dad comes out and sits down with the paper.

Mom's making breakfast, I whisper. I raise my eyebrows and give him the big eyes.

I see that, he says, and nods. Then he smiles at me.

I was hoping for more information here.

I was hoping for some sort of proclamation, like, Oh, didn't we tell you? It's all over. Your mother's not sick anymore.

Or even, Yes, isn't it great? We finally got her on the right medication.

I wait, looking at Dad, but he starts reading the paper.

I swear you could die of secrecy, living in this house.

Mom comes in and serves up the bacon and eggs and tells Dad to yell up to Lisa.

Lisa! Dad yells. I'm counting to three! One, two . . .

OK! yells Lisa.

It's a comforting ritual.

Lisa gives me the big eyes when she sees Mom is up and sitting at the table.

I mouth to Lisa, *She made breakfast,* and point to my plate.

Lisa looks down at her plate and studies it, like she's making sure it's real food. She pokes her fork into her egg yolk and it runs in a yellow river all the way to her bacon. Which I have one thing to say about mixing bacon and egg yolk and that is, *grossamundo.*

Mom passes the toast around. She looks kinda pale and out of it, like she's not quite here, but she *is* sitting here at the breakfast table with us like somebody's real mom. Dad asks for more coffee and she smiles at him and passes the coffeepot, but it's a small, stretched-out smile and she looks tired right afterward.

But hey, at least she's *up.*

Nobody says much, but I don't care. We're here, together, all four of us.

Almost like a real family.

chapter 80

i walk around in the baby haze until one day at Poppy's.

It's just Poppy and me at her house after school and we're in her room playing her new Santana album because Hector had to go home and help his Mom move a bunch of stuff for their garage sale which is this weekend.

We're both lying on Poppy's purple bed.

Poppy says, My mom wants to go to Miami and visit my grandma at Christmas.

Christmas, I say. That's months and months away.

Well you know my mom, Poppy says. She likes to have something to look forward to.

Poppy says, Mom says I can bring a friend, but . . .

She looks over at me and sucks in her lips.

But what? I say, knowing that of course she would ask me, I mean I am her best friend.

But . . . you'll be having a baby, she says real slow, looking at my stomach which was still flat as a door.

I mean, won't you? she says.

Something in my stomach which is definitely *not* a baby starts rolling around, something huge and heavy like a bowling ball.

I look at Poppy and she's just staring at me, all serious and not blinking and her face completely still.

The bowling ball in my stomach starts to roll faster, side to side like a pendulum.

My heart beats a thousand times on each roll.

Oh god.

Oh god I can't breathe oh god.

I roll over on my side, staring back at Poppy.

There's something wild and loose inside me.

Something screaming and wild and loose and terrible.

My whole body tenses itself into a knot, trying to catch and hold the terrible loose thing.

I pull my knees up to my chest and wrap my arms around my legs.

Suddenly I am very, very cold.

I put my forehead on my knees.

Poppy, I whisper. Am I really going to have a baby?

You are if you don't do something about it, she says softly.

She puts her hand on top of my head.

Oh god, I whisper.

I start rocking myself, with Poppy's hand on my head.

Poppy, I say, I can't have a baby.

I know, she says.

What am I gonna do? I say. My voice is starting to crack but I don't want to cry because if I start crying I'm going to fall apart completely and all the little pieces that I've been keeping together for so long will fly apart and that will be the end, I will crack up just like my mother and they will never put me back together again.

I don't know, says Poppy. She sounds so worried, almost like it's her having the baby instead of me.

What do you want to do? she says.

The wild thing inside me is going crazy.

I can't let it out. If I let it out, it's all over.

The wild thing is a scream that's louder than the whole world put together.

It's so loud inside me but if it gets out, it will shake the whole planet. Everyone will hear it, from here to Mozambique to China to one of those countries in South America which we had to learn the capital of and I can't remember the name of it right now.

The scream is right under my skin. If you cut me right now, you'd hear it.

I don't know, I say. I'm shaking and cold and I can't stop rocking.

Poppy puts her arm all the way around me and touches her head to my head.

I can't have a baby, I say. I can't.

chapter 81

O f course it happens on a day when Hector doesn't come home with me. He has to help his sister move so he turns left in the orchard and me and Poppy walk the rest of the way together.

Poppy says, Are you and Hector gonna get married?

Just out of the blue like that with no warning.

I stop and just about drop my books.

Are you crazy? I say.

Poppy shrugs and starts walking again.

I just wondered, she says. Some people do, you know.

This is her way of talking about the baby without talking about it.

This is her way of saying, What the hell are you going to do, Abby?

Yeah, well, not me, I say. My voice sounds so firm and strong and loud, like I know what I'm talking about.

Which I don't.

I'm still playing Let's Pretend.

Let's pretend there is no baby.

Let's pretend my mother is fine.

Let's pretend I'm a normal fifteen-year-old girl with nothing more on her mind than miniskirts and Bobby Sherman.

Which by the way I hate Bobby Sherman.

Poppy and I cross the creek and start up the hill to our street.

I just got the new Who album, Poppy says. Wanna come over and listen to it?

Nah, I say. Not today.

I don't even know why I say no. I have nothing better to do. What I'll do instead, I know, is lie on my bed and stare at the ceiling and count the holes in the ceiling tile and wait for Hector to call.

This is my life now.

But it doesn't matter because I'm not in it anymore.

The only way I stay sane is by counting. I count everything. The palm trees, the holes in my ceiling, the number of bumps on my bedspread, the number of stripes on my curtains. I count whatever I can see from my bed.

In school I count people.

Four girls with black hair, nine girls with blond hair, seven boys with brown hair.

Ten girls in miniskirts.

Fourteen girls with heels that aren't perfectly flat.

Eight of those leather hair pieces with the sticks going through them.

It's the only thing I can concentrate on.

The only class I listen in is math.

. . .

i say good-bye to Poppy and walk up our cement walk. The sun is hitting my bare arms hard and hot, even though it's only May. Every flower in our front yard is blooming, blue ceonothus and red bottle-brush and yellow forsythia and all those other flowers I don't know the names of.

I stand in the front yard and breathe it all in.

For just a sec I feel like I'm six again.

Oh, to be six again.

I get to our icky pink front door and the sun is beating right on it. The brass doorknob is almost too hot to touch.

I open the door and walk in and yell, I'm home!

No one answers.

Lately Mom has been up doing something when I come home. Reading or knitting or crocheting or repotting her African violets or cleaning the fish tank with the zillions of guppies. It's like her hands have to be busy every second.

The house is so quiet I swear there's an echo.

Mom? I yell.

I don't know why I call out for her. We are just like strangers now, polite and courteous and nothing else, two residents of the same hotel.

For no reason I put my hand on my belly which is still flat and walk down the hall to Mom and Dad's room.

The door is shut.

I put my ear flat on the door and listen.

Nothing.

I knock and call out softly, Mom, are you in there?

No answer.

There's this tiny voice in my head talking to me. Like a mosquito and you want it to shut up and go away.

It says, Don't open that door.

I put my hand on the handle and turn it.

Open it just an inch and peek inside with one eye.

What I see makes me stop breathing.

Flaky white feet.

Sticking out on the rug.

Where they shouldn't be.

I open the door so slow, watching those feet which don't move.

Mom? I say, only I know I don't need to say anything, it won't do any good.

I take a step in, so I can see more.

Even though I already know what's there.

There she is on the green shag, just like that movie that used to go in my head, over and over.

In her white pedal pushers and navy elbow-sleeve blouse.

She got dressed today.

Her hair is pinned up neatly.

My feet find their own way.

I stare.

Maybe my mouth is open.

Maybe I'm shaking all over.

Maybe I'm very, very cold.

Maybe my breathing is fast and shallow, or maybe I'm not breathing at all.

Maybe I put my hand on the bed railing to hold myself up.

Maybe I suddenly bend over because of the pain that rips through me like a chainsaw, cutting me in half.

Maybe my hands clutch the top of my skirt, grab at the skin around my waist.

Stop it.

Stop.

Maybe my knees fold and hit the floor, hard, but I don't even notice.

Maybe I start getting those dry heaves like you're throwing up but nothing comes.

Maybe blood starts to pour out between my legs.

I am on my knees.

My body forcing itself to pray.

There beside her.

My arms wrapped around my belly and I'm bending over into the heaves and this is some kind of prayer, a prayer forced on me by God.

The blood leaks through my skirt.

Creeps down my legs.

Her body is so white and so still.

Her face looks like a smile even though she isn't smiling with her lips. Her red lips are closed like she's sleeping.

I can't think of what that is, that expression on her face.

I've never seen it before.

Happy, maybe.

Or peaceful.

Resting in that delicious Sunday-afternoon way with the sun on you and no homework to do.

A cramp hits me so hard I can't breathe. I fall on my side on the floor and pull my knees into my chest.

I have never felt a cramp like this before.

I squeeze my eyes shut and start counting.

Hector taught me how to count in Spanish.

Uno, dos, tres, cuatro, cinco, seis.

I have to stop and take short hard breaths that hurt.

A flash of a thought goes through my head.

Isn't this what you asked for.

Cramps instead of a baby.

I grind my teeth together as another wave of pain hits me.

The pain goes all the way through me, all the way from my toes, up my legs, up my back, out the top of my head.

I make myself breathe even though I don't want to.

Then it stops for a moment, just half a second.

Just enough time that I can open my eyes and see her again.

Her fingernails painted freshly red.

She even has on earrings, the little pearls Dad gave her.

And her silver watch that she's had since forever.

I start counting the moles on her arms.

Mom and me have the most moles of anyone you ever saw.

Hector says if my moles would just grow together I'd look Mexican like him.

He likes to take his Bic pen and connect my moles.

One, two, three, four, five moles near her wrist.

Six, seven eight, up around her elbow.

Nine, ten, eleven, twelve, *YEOW!!*

Another cramp starts and I have to shut my eyes and hold my breath.

Nothing, *nothing* is like this pain.

Another thought flash: I'm getting blood all over my mother's green shag carpet. The green shag she wanted so bad and fought and fought with Dad and finally won.

It will stain.

Blood stains everything, you can't get it out.

They will carry her away and me away and all that will be left is a big blood spot.

Something to mark this day.

The day we both died.

I reach out and put my hand on her arm, grip it tight as the wave of pain eats through me.

Oh Jesus God, I pray.

Jesus God, take away this pain and I'll . . .

I can't think of anything to give Him in return.

He's already taken my mother.

I have nothing else to give. There's nothing else in my life I care about.

Her arm is neither warm nor cold. My fingers dig in hard as another wave comes, and another.

When the pain stops for a second, I lift my fingers off and see the white finger-marks I've left in her arm.

They stay there, those white marks.

Another wave comes and I grip Mom's arm again.

I squeeze my eyes shut, hard, harder, and pretty soon the blackness spreads across my eyes, across my head, across my chest, the blackness encloses me completely and tells me I can go to sleep, it will take care of me, I don't have to wake up anymore.

chapter 82

the day of the funeral is stupidly sunny.

Hector is there, and Poppy. They sit with me up front, in the second pew, Lisa on one side of me and Hector on the other side and Poppy next to Hector. Dad and Grandma are in the first pew, right in front of us.

Everyone is crying except me.

I'm done crying.

I was done days ago.

I hold Lisa's hand and squeeze it, again and again, and pass her Kleenexes which somehow I remembered to stuff a bunch of fresh ones into my purse.

I don't know where Dad's white handkerchief is.

Grandma keeps dabbing at her eyes with a little lacy handkerchief with red and blue embroidery. I wonder if Mom embroidered it for her.

The funeral goes on forever, two or three days, I think.

All I remember is singing.

Mom's old choir singing. They stand in the upper balcony of the church, in the back, and sing, and so many times I hear her voice. A high soprano which when she hits that one special note you know it's her.

I don't dare turn around and look.

Because I don't know which is scarier—that she's up there, or that she's not.

And anyway I don't care which it is.

We all sit there for two or three days while the choir sings a hundred thousand songs.

The wooden pew is very hard.

Everyone cries except me, even Poppy and Hector are crying.

I feel like ashes inside.

we're all standing outside the church afterwards, in the stupid sunny sunlight. There's a great huddle of people around Dad, everyone touching him on the arm, or patting his shoulder, everything will be OK, pat pat pat.

I look at Dad's face and I swear it looks relieved.

Or maybe I just made that up.

And anyway who knows why he's relieved—that the funeral is over, or that she's gone, or what.

Lisa comes out holding Grandma's hand. She and Grandma stand by Dad and people huddle around them, too.

I'm in my own little huddle of me and Hector and Poppy. Then Mrs. Cordesi comes out and huddles in our little huddle so then there's four in my huddle.

And about a hundred in Dad's.

For a sec I wonder if a person can keep going, can get along, in just a four-person huddle.

Mrs. Cordesi puts her arm around me and says, You did good, kid.

I don't know what she means by that, but I don't even care. I know that however Mrs. Cordesi says anything, she always means, You're a good kid and pretty cool, too.

Mrs. Cordesi says, You all want to ride with me?

Meaning my little huddle of four.

Four which includes me and Mrs. Cordesi. And Hector and Poppy.

Hector says, Sure, thanks. He and Poppy head for Mrs. Cordesi's green station wagon across the street and I'm not sure what to do.

I mean am I supposed to hang around with Dad and Lisa and Grandma, or is it OK for me to leave?

I look over at Dad and he's talking to some tall old guy I don't know. The tall old guy has his hand on Dad's shoulder, gripping it with a Vulcan death grip.

Well, maybe not that hard but anyway.

Hector says, Come on, Ab.

I catch Lisa's eye, over there by Dad.

We hold eyes for a sec. Or longer. She's still holding on to Grandma's hand.

I point to myself, then to Mrs. Cordesi's car.

I'm going with them, I mouth to Lisa.

Her eyes go wide and her mouth opens and says something, I can't tell what. Then she says something to Grandma, who's talking to some lady with orange hair, and rips her hand out of Grandma's hand which Grandma barely notices.

Lisa comes running across the street toward me, her white hair flying behind her.

Can I come with you guys? she says.

For once I didn't even mind that she has to always copy me.

Sure, I say.

I get in next to Hector in the back seat and Lisa gets in next to me.

Just for a sec I put my head on Lisa's bony little shoulder.

I'm kind of kidding, kind of not.

OK, mostly not.

What I mostly am is tired and worn out and fresh out of emotions.

At least in my huddle of four, now five, I don't have to have any emotions. I mean you stand around with Dad and Grandma and I'm sure you're expected to cry or at least look sad.

The thing is, I don't feel all that sad.

Maybe that relief I saw on Dad's face was really my own. Looking through my relieved eyes into Dad's whatever eyes.

And I wish someone would write a book on how you're supposed to be at funerals because I don't know how I'm supposed to be.

And from now on, starting tomorrow, and then the next day and the next, I don't know how I'm supposed to be.

I mean are you supposed to be sad all the time, all droopy-faced and dragging your feet and blank eyes and Oh me, or what.

I just don't know.

What I feel inside is nothing.

But how do you show nothing on the outside.

There's no one I can ask in this car.

I bet even Mrs. Cordesi wouldn't have an answer for that one.

We drive away from the church and down the street full of eucalyptus trees. Hector rolls down his window and Lisa of course copies him and I can smell the eucalyptus.

And I think, I bet from now on when I smell eucalyptus, I'll think of Mom.

Mom, Mom, Mom. I can say her name over and over and nothing happens.

There must be something wrong with me.

chapter 83

it's our first night with no casserole from a neighbor.

I made chicken 'n' cornflakes.

I didn't even know how to make it, I just did it.

Here we are at the table.

Dad, Lisa, and me.

A huddle of three.

The TV is off.

I'm sitting in Mom's place.

I can see Mom and Dad's bedroom door from here and it's open.

Dad remembered to put a napkin at everyone's place.

We are all crunching on our chicken 'n' cornflakes.

It's the only noise.

Crunching mouths and forks hitting plates.

The thing is, this isn't a sad scene.

Someone might walk in here and think it's a sad scene but it isn't.

It's just three people having dinner.

A quiet dinner.

Lisa goes for her milk and almost knocks it over somehow.

Dad says, Watch it, honey!

The way he always used to.

Like half joking and half not.

Lisa rolls her eyes at him.

Everything is so normal.

Just three people having dinner.

Except for that empty place.

Which no one is ever going to fill.

I look over at the empty place, where I used to sit. If Mom walked in right now, I guess she'd have to sit there.

This is my place now. Where Mom used to sit.

There is only one difference.

Mom's little wooden angel.

It's pointing at the empty place now, instead of at Mom's old place, where I am.

I don't know who turned it.

I look at it and suddenly I see something that I've never seen before.

I blink a few times to make sure I'm really seeing it.

Yep, there it is.

No question.

Sneaking out from under its little angel dress, just barely, you have to look close to see it, are—two bare feet.

I can't believe I've never seen those feet before.

Two tears spring into my eyes for no reason.

But that's all.

Just two tears. They don't even fall out of my eyes so no one knows about them except me.

No crying jag, no tight-throat sobbing, just two tears.

I can handle two tears.

chapter 84

i am far from being sixteen but I feel more like forty.

I know things no fifteen-year-old should know.

Things I can't tell Hector or Poppy or anyone.

Things maybe only Mrs. Cordesi would really get.

Things like, a faded red bathrobe can hide a lot.

Things like, even if all you do is lie on your bed, counting ceiling holes, things around you will keep moving, stuff will happen. Even if you do nothing, your life will change.

Things like, you can't save someone who doesn't want to be saved.

This is what I know at fifteen and it makes me really wonder about forty.

Because I mean what else is there to know.